SECRETS OF THE DEAD

When Chris Simmers was jailed for the bloody, brutal and sordid murder of his mother, the neighbours wondered why he hadn't done it years before! Her raucous, vulgar voice and prying ways had obviously brought Chris to breaking point. But did he do it? After 12 years, Chris is released and returns to the scene of the crime to discover the truth. There is a nagging blank in his memory of those drunken hours when the fatality occurred. A series of 'accidents' persuade Chris that someone is out to kill him. But why, and for what?

SECRETS OF THE DEAD

SECRETS OF THE DEAD

by
Barbara Whitehead

Magna Large Print Books
Long Preston, North Yorkshire,
England.

British Library Cataloguing in Publication Data.

Whitehead, Barbara
  Secrets of the dead.

  A catalogue record for this book is
  available from the British Library

  ISBN 0-7505-1176-1

First published in Great Britain by Constable and Company
Limited, 1996

Published in Large Print 1998 by arrangement with Constable
and Company Limited

Magna Large Print is an imprint of
Library Magna Books Ltd.
Printed and bound in Great Britain by
T.J. International Ltd., Cornwall, PL28 8RW.

For Roger, John and Alan

1

When Chris Simmers murdered his mother the neighbours wondered why he hadn't done it years before. The row of terrace houses was a short one, and they had all had the benefit of her raucous, vulgar voice, her shouted conversations, her opinions and her prying ways. They had had enough of it—couldn't call their lives their own—and poor downtrodden Chris had obviously reached breaking point, had lashed out and put an end to it once and for all.

It took a while for them to see the other side of things. By the time Chris came to trial they had begun to forget about Mrs Simmers's nuisance value and realised what a horrible deed had taken place in their midst. He must have another side to him, a side they had never seen. You couldn't condone it, not really, whatever the provocation.

The murder had been bloody, brutal and sordid.

The judge condemned Simmers to life imprisonment. The house was shut up. The trees opposite grew new leaves, then dropped them, again and again. People changed jobs and moved house, died, married, were born.

It was twelve years later.

Chris Simmers had walked from York railway station. It wasn't far. He turned into the road and stopped, feeling in his pocket for tobacco and papers, expertly rolling a thin cigarette, then lighting it. He stood near the corner, smoking with a curiously wary, alert look about him. He was of medium height, dark-haired, slim, thirty-four years old. In the terrace stretching away on his left, every house door was closed, and the road ahead was empty. On his right a green bank clothed in trees rose up to the city walls. The parapet walkway had, as usual, a few tourists passing slowly along. None of them looked down into the quiet road. Where the battlemented wall was lower they stopped to peer down outside, where another green bank sloped away, smothered in daffodils in bloom.

The whole of the Vale of York was verdant in the late spring. York itself, which had once been tightly encircled by its walls, had long since spread out beyond them; but its historic core was what tourists had come to see, with the defences which now constituted one of the charms of the place, and the daffodils which at this time of year encircled the city in a ring of gold.

Chris's home was in Bishophill, a suburb which sloped from the southern crest of the medieval walls downward to the river in the north. As a child it had seemed to him that the walls rose against his sky as if they were the end of the world. Outside, the void.

He seemed calm, although he was full of volcanic emotions. You don't express feelings like that. You hide them and show the world a face that tells it you don't care, feel nothing, nothing at all. He had spent over a third of his life behind bars. Had that changed him? It had.

Childhood memories surged, of playing with the neighbours' children, rolling down the grassy bank between the trees which were there for climbing, playing tag round the gateposts, spying on the tourists from upper windows, learning to ride a bicycle on the pavement. Through the years he had walked back every day to his home, first from school, then college, then from his work at the bank. To this peaceful domestic untroubled road. He looked at it and knew that it too had changed.

It had been gentrified, that was what it was. He remembered the old residents and knew they would not be living behind lavishly lined and draped curtains, or neatly matching tubs of flowers. If he went on standing here much longer someone would notice him. They would come out to ask if he was lost, if they could direct him to anywhere. You didn't ignore happenings in a road like this. You controlled them, kept menace at bay, politely shooed off strange layabouts. He nipped out his cigarette and put the stub away in a tin in his pocket. He walked along the row of houses lightly, silently, a wild animal from the forest.

One of the houses stood out from the rest like a bad tooth. Where they were clean, it was dirty. Where their windows shone, its windows were grey blanks surrounded by peeling paint. Variegated ivy planted in some bygone time of hopefulness rioted over the steps and tried to climb the door. The buddleia in the front garden was now a small tree, cluttered by dead flowers from previous years.

Chris pushed open the low gate, which gave a metallic scream, stood on the ivy-covered path to the front door, and felt in his pocket for the key. Heavy, large, made of iron, and rusty, it looked a fit companion for a jailbird and for the huge old lock. It turned reluctantly, stiffly, the guards creaking backwards. The door shuddered as he pushed against it, opening half-inch by half-inch. He found himself glancing round as though he was doing something forbidden, then climbed inside over the strands of ivy, his feet kicking at them as he went, yet without impatience or anger at their clinging untidiness.

The road was as quiet and untroubled as if he had not arrived.

The Probation Office was round the corner on Priory Street, a big old terrace house on a wide road that was still impressive, with its two places of worship built to last for ever, the Baptist Church and the Wesley Chapel. The road was now given up to good causes. The Priory Street Centre was the heart of the community with classes and café. The terrace of stately houses included headquarters for the disabled.

Two hours after Chris arrived home, his probation officer, Steve Watson, noticed that it was moving towards lunch time. He had been feeling restless. At last he got up and went to the door, spied round it, then said to a colleague, 'Do you reckon the boss is in?'

'He was out earlier.'

'Came in about half an hour ago,' said another colleague. 'Hurry up if you want to see him. He's meeting his wife at lunch time to choose a new carpet.'

Steve tapped on the supervisor's door, then went in.

13

John Brook, preoccupied, glanced up at him. 'Yes, Steve?'

'My new parolee—the lifer—came out today.'

John looked at the calendar. 'So he did.'

'You remember I had my last interview with him when he came to York on his pre-release.'

'I remember your Part C report. He wants to go back to his old home.'

'That's right. I tried to persuade him not to. I put all the arguments, how difficult it would be, the prejudice he would meet, everything. He persisted.'

'Was he difficult? Obstinate?'

'Calm, quiet, polite, but kept saying it was his home.'

'Is it his? Literally?'

'Apparently he owns the house. It has been shut up since he went inside. I walked past the other day. It'll take a hell of a lot of work to get it anything like right.'

'Well, time's something he has got, I expect. He isn't likely to get a job.'

'I thought I'd go round and see him this afternoon.'

'Good idea. You haven't had many murderers, have you?'

'I dealt with a couple when I was in Selby area, and as you know I have one other on my list at present.'

'The thing to guard against is him being a danger to the public. A violent murder, wasn't it?'

'Very.'

'Never let him forget that he's only out on licence and it will be revoked if he puts a foot out of place.'

'Well, yes.'

John Brook got up, reached for his raincoat with the remark that it looked a bit doubtful, didn't it, and he might be late back, but he'd see Steve during the afternoon, then followed him out on to the landing and set off down the stairs. Steve Watson felt reassured by the conversation. He had not needed advice, only the sensation of sharing his slight apprehension with someone. Usually he was so full of self-confidence he never had to think about it, but Chris Simmers unsettled him and he wished he knew what it was about the man. They'd met a number of times in the prison and once over here on Simmers's pre-release weekend, and he'd read and reread the case notes. As a parolee Simmers was normal enough, considering that not many people went inside for murdering their mothers.

When, after the brief shower, Steve arrived at Chris Simmers's front door, it was wide open to the returning sun. He noticed the ivy had been neatly clipped back from the tiled footpath. Raising his hand to knock, he saw that the old iron knocker was rusting and the paint on the panelled door was blistered by years of weather. There was no point in knocking, he thought. He could see straight through the house and out of the back door into the small yard. Simmers was bending over the frame of a bicycle. Steve decided to walk through without knocking. He called out as he crossed the kitchen. Chris looked up.

'Afternoon, Mr Watson,' he said, with no trace of surprise.

'Afternoon, Chris. Call me Steve. I've asked you before.'

'Steve,' said Chris Simmers, but on his lips it didn't sound any more familiar than 'Mr Watson'. Pleasant enough, but not familiar. Or even friendly. 'Would you like a coffee?' Chris went on.

'Thanks.'

Steve followed him back into the kitchen and leaned on a cupboard as Simmers scrubbed the oil from his hands at an old white-glazed earthenware sink, filled the dinted, battered whistling-kettle through its spout, heated it on the gas stove and made two mugs of powdered coffee.

Following his own thoughts, Steve said, 'You don't seem to mind being in here.'

Simmers turned his head sharply.

16

'In here? Oh! You mean in the kitchen.' He paused, then said in a low voice, 'You forget that I didn't see her here.'

Steve couldn't help being affected by his parolee. The man didn't come over as hostile, only withdrawn, but somehow Steve felt himself goaded into crassness, into lack of sensitivity. Who the hell expected him to exercise sensitivity anyway, with a brutal murderer?

'You say you don't remember, but, let's be accurate, you must have seen her.'

Simmers picked up the two mugs of coffee carefully and led the way out of the kitchen, into the corridor and then the front room of the house. He set down the mugs of coffee, went out of the room again, and shut the front door.

'The whole house smells musty,' he said, explaining his actions. 'That's why I had the doors open, but I don't like being overheard, if anyone should pass.' Steve said nothing, but the noisy shutting of the difficult old door had made him uneasy in spite of himself.

After a second, Chris went on, 'Steve, it must be in my notes and I've said it to you, I have no memory of any of it.'

There was a three-piece suite in the front room which looked out of date but not yet antique. Steve Watson sat down on the settee. Dust rose around him in clouds. The table on which Chris had put the coffee mugs looked like an Edwardian piece cut down to modernise it—definitely a mistake on someone's part. Impossible to tell what wood it was made of through the chipped black varnish. The fireplace was the original black iron and tiled confection put in when the house was built. The wallpaper was stained and tired. The light coming in from the brightness of the day was filtered to a grim greyness through dirty glass and decayed lace curtains. Steve thought it a sad little room, pretentious without having anything to be pretentious about. He reached out and picked up the mug. The coffee was hot.

After a sip he put it down.

'A lot of'—he bit back the word murderers—'...people...say that they don't remember. The brain seems to wipe it out. Sometimes they think the crime has been a dream sequence or something they've watched on TV, not something they've done.'

Simmers looked fixedly at the floor. 'The last thing I remember of my mother on that night is saying goodbye to her as I left the house early in the evening. I went with my pals to the pubs for a party; it was partly a send-off for a friend, an American lad who was catching a late train, and partly to celebrate my twenty-first birthday which was coming up. At the end of the evening I must have been very drunk. The next thing I remember is being woken by a police officer the following morning. I was asleep in bed. Even that doesn't seem real. Then I must have lost consciousness again. After that I remember lying in hospital, being treated for alcoholic poisoning. They were pumping my stomach out, and that's not very nice let me tell you. Then I must have drifted off again, but I came to properly later in the day and was transferred to prison. That's it. The kitchen doesn't seem any different to me to the way it's been all my life. Otherwise that night's scene would haunt me, I suppose, and I wouldn't be able to use the kitchen, or live here.'

No, Steve Watson thought. You wouldn't be able to use it quite normally, the way I saw you, if you remembered seeing the body and the blood and remembered raining down blows, the way you did, Simmers.

'We won't mention it again,' he said.

'The trick cyclists said I was perfectly normal mentally.'

'I've read the reports.'

'I felt I had to come back, you know. You meant it for the best, Steve, suggesting I make a fresh start somewhere else. But

I've got to come to terms with things here first.'

'All right. When are you planning to look for work?'

'Not yet. A day or two, perhaps. There's a lot to do here, but I must sign on and see about getting some money from somewhere.'

'Has that bike been stored all this time?'

'Yes, it's been in the shed. I can get it right again. I'm going to need it.'

'You mean you won't be able to afford a car.'

'I don't want one if I can help it. Apart from affording it, a bike is more practical in the city centre, and I like cycling.'

They talked generally for another half-hour, and both drank their coffee, before Steve got up to go. 'Don't forget, Chris, I'm here to help you adjust in any way I can. You may meet a lot of prejudice in this city from people who know you, or even have only heard of you. You've got my home telephone number. Don't hesitate to contact me any time.'

'I appreciate that, Steve.'

Simmers was of medium height, and had to look up slightly at Steve Watson, who was over six feet tall. When Steve had left, Chris Simmers closed the front door again and this time turned the key. Having people walk in unannounced was over. He was damned if he was going to stand it. No one had the right to come in here and walk all over him, no one. Not any more. He'd had twelve years of screws walking into his cell and he wasn't having Steve Watson or any other toffee-nosed git walking in unannounced and that was that. As he went back through the kitchen what Steve had said recurred to him, but he let it fall away out of his mind. He couldn't make himself imagine his mother lying here in her blood with her shattered head on the floor near the sink. He couldn't imagine her dead.

Back again in the yard he carried on patiently, persistently, cleaning and oiling the many different parts into which he had stripped down the bicycle. As the sun began to dip in the sky he felt hungry, but went on with what he was doing until most of the bike was reassembled. Some small parts he left soaking in a dish of oil overnight. It was already late evening when he stopped work and went in, scrubbed his hands again, put on the immersion heater for hot water for a bath later, and began to cook his meal. Food had been the first thing he'd had to deal with when he'd arrived. There had been a fresh bottle of milk sheltering under the buddleia. He'd gone into the small streets nearby in search of a corner shop. Where once there'd been corner shops galore now he could only find one and its stock was limited but he'd bought potatoes and tins of corned beef and peas, some bacon and eggs.

It was while the potatoes were boiling that the yard door opened. He was busy examining the potatoes and prodding them with a fork and did not look up, though his heart sang. He heard footsteps crossing the yard, the back door being opened, and a young female voice calling out, 'Cooee, Chris! Can I come in?'

'It's not locked, Annie.'

Anne Atkinson, the girl next door, walked into the kitchen. 'Hi!'

His head had been bent over the saucepan.

'Hi, Annie,' he said abstractedly, before turning to face her. A happy look of greeting was on his face, but when he saw her it faded, to be replaced by an almost stony expression. She put a large, professional-looking tape recorder down on the kitchen table, then a slim zip-top black document case bulging with papers. She had no doubt of her welcome.

'I couldn't get round any earlier,' she said.

He made no reply. At last his lack of response penetrated. She looked at him in surprise.

22

'What's the matter, Chris? You expected me, didn't you?'

'You said you would come my first evening, in your last letter.' But his voice sounded flat and cold.

'Well, then.'

He had been staring at her, helplessly. He had been living for the moment when he saw her again. When he went inside she had been twelve years old. He had known her since her birth and always thought of her as his little sister. In the dreary years he had been living through it seemed to him that the world outside was also standing still. He had felt suspended in time, for prison is not a real world and time there is not a real time. Working from a hostel in Wakefield had gradually acclimatised him to fiendish traffic and new fashions in clothes, His mental vision of Annie had not changed. But she had. Now she was twenty-four.

'You've altered,' he said at last.

'Don't you recognise me? I haven't altered that much.'

'I think you've changed completely.'

'Oh, come off it, Chris. Actually I've grown hardly at all. I was the tallest girl in the class, you remember how it worried me? But I don't think I've grown an inch since. Well, maybe one inch.'

'No, you're not much taller. You've

grown up, though.' My little sister has disappeared, he said to himself.

'What did you expect?'

'You sounded just the same, in your letters.'

By now Annie was sitting in one of the kitchen chairs and gazing up at him. It was quite true. From being five feet tall at the age of twelve, she was now five feet one inch. Also bust thirty-four, waist twenty, and hips thirty-six. The phrase 'pocket Venus' had been used to describe Annie Atkinson. She'd also been living for this moment, when the most important person in her young life came back. He stood there, ignoring his potatoes, which smelled as though they were boiling dry, and there was no warmth in his manner or speech for her, no gesture or words of welcome.

'I'm still a red-haired little nuisance,' she said. 'Everyone calls me Anne nowadays. But you can go on calling me Annie if you like. It sounds nice. Almost like we used to be.'

To his surprise, her lovely hazel eyes brimmed with tears and she looked down hastily.

This wasn't right. With Annie he could be open, surely? Talk without watching every syllable. Smile, even laugh, perhaps. Not make her cry, never that. Not his little sister/friend, not even this new version.

'So you've brought your homework round for me to help you with it?' He tried to sound the way he knew she would remember.

'What, that?' She glanced at the tape recorder and document case on the table. 'No, I don't want any help with that, thanks. It's something I do, and a session was arranged for this evening. I had to go there straight after tea, and I've only just got back.'

He longed to ask her what it was she had been doing but he felt ill at ease with this vibrant, attractive young woman. Annie, his little friend, with the ginger plaits and the school uniform including socks, he had been desperately looking forward to seeing again. He had looked forward to teasing her until she lost her temper and thumped him as hard as she could, and then apologised and wanted him to go with her to buy fish and chips, or lend her one of his collection of pop music tapes, or plan some sort of expedition. He should have realised—he had only himself to blame. Twelve years old and twenty-four coming up twenty-five are centuries apart. Even more centuries between an old lag, a lifer, and a young woman like this.

'You've grown up,' he said at last, grudgingly, but he had to make some kind of explanation of his apparent unfriendliness. 'I'm sorry if it takes a bit of getting used to. I want to thank you, Annie—Anne—for your letters. You were the only person who wrote to me.'

'Oh well, if that's all that is the matter,' said Anne, and was silent again.

It occurred to Chris that he too had probably changed. Twelve years in prison does change a man. He conquered his aversion to intrusiveness, and asked her what she had been doing.

'What's this all about?' He waved his hand at the large tape recorder.

'It's an oral history project.'

'Come again?'

'There's a group of us doing it. We visit old people in their homes and talk to them about their lives, recording the conversations. We've published several booklets with things they've told us about Old York. I'm visiting a dear old lady on Kyme Street once a week at present. Oral, because it's spoken, history, because that's what memories are, Chris.'

Chris thought that in the old days, the ones he had memories of, it had always been him telling her, and her listening and saying, 'Yes, Chris.' He remembered her being born. That was history, too, he supposed.

'What about a coffee?'

'No, thanks. I hope you don't mind me

mentioning it, Chris, but is your potato pan dry?'

He whipped round to the stove and caught up the saucepan. 'Some of them will be all right,' he said, peering into the pan.

Anne got up to go. 'Mother is expecting me back. She didn't want me to see you, you know.'

'I'm not surprised.' She didn't need to say that, he thought. It used not to be like Annie to be hurtful. Perhaps she didn't mean to be, was only putting him in the picture. Steve had told him to expect prejudice, antagonism.

'Does it seem very different?' asked Anne in a low voice.

He deliberately misunderstood her. 'The house looks exactly the same. Dirty, of course.'

After a pause, she said quietly, 'The police arranged to have this kitchen cleaned up in the first place. Then the solicitor arranged for a cleaning person to come. Before she arrived, there was a break-in. Things were all strewn about. So Mother and I came in before the cleaner did, put things as straight as we could and tidied all the ornaments away into drawers and cupboards.'

'I thought it looked a bit bare. Thank you, Anne. It was good of you. Thank your mother for me.'

'You should be able to find everything.'

'I'm sure I shall. Did whoever broke in take much?'

'We didn't think so. They were probably looking for money or jewellery.' She hesitated. 'You wrote to me once that you couldn't remember anything about it—the murder.'

'That's right. Apparently it is quite a usual thing for criminals not to remember the crime. The mind rejects it. So they keep telling me.'

Annie picked up the tape recorder and the document case. 'It must have made it difficult.'

'If only I could see her grave—take flowers—stand there and look down at it—I might be able to believe that it really happened, that she is really dead.'

Anne knew him in her bones and where others would have missed it, she could hear anguish in his voice, and he seemed to force out the words.

'There isn't a grave,' Anne almost whispered. 'After the cremation the ashes were disposed of at the crematorium—put in the garden, I expect. There is no stone or anything.'

Chris turned away quickly to his pan of potatoes. He poked a few out on to a plate.

'See you tomorrow,' Anne said brightly and went out of the door.

'Goodnight,' he called after her. 'Thank you for coming.'

He put his meal on the table—corned beef and plain boiled potatoes and tinned peas. He would have to discover where to shop, how much to buy, learn how to budget on Income Support, all those kind of things which had not exercised his mind these twelve years, for the self is not an active agent in prison. He held down his thoughts as he had been used to there. This was not the time. There was only one time to think—when you were alone in the dark and the blanket was over your head—then, if you dared, you could allow yourself to think.

After eating and washing up it was time to bathe and go to bed.

First he carefully locked the doors, front and back. It was ironic, surely, to be so anxious about locking himself in. Then, turning out the downstairs lights, he made up his bed after taking the sheets from on top of the hot water cylinder, where he had put them to air. Later, in the narrow bedroom over the hallway which was the only bedroom he had ever known—for he could hardly count the cells he had shared—he locked the bedroom door.

Suddenly he relaxed as he had not done

all day. He looked down at the brass lock, as old as the door, and remembered how his mother had hated him locking it. She felt neglected, shut out—not only literally but also metaphorically—if she could not share his space. Strange that he should need to lock himself up now, in order to feel secure. He slid into his bed. With his hand on the switch of his bedside lamp he lay a few minutes, looking round at his room and listening. The road outside was very quiet. The room was very full. The narrow bed, the narrow wardrobe, and the narrow chest of drawers had been supplemented by shelves he had made himself. In this small room existed the record of his life, up to that fatal night. This was one place where Annie and her mother had not tidied things away—he supposed they had not known where to start. Then he remembered that the room door had been locked when he first went upstairs that morning. Probably they had decided to leave it locked. He could see the ears of his childhood teddy bear poking up behind the guitar he had bought so proudly with the first money he had ever earned, in his teens, doing a paper round. There were the rows of tapes, with each separate musical craze entombed in its little plastic box. The rows of books, some dog-eared and tattered, some pristine, all much loved.

On the walls were the posters, faded now, once brightly coloured; the original wallpaper could hardly be seen anywhere in the entire room.

Chris was about to turn off the light. The evidence at his trial. He was back again in the courtroom, listening. The voice was plain in his ears. On the wool rug by the bed the blood-covered axe had rested, next to his trainers, which were soaked in blood.

He left the light on a bit longer.

Here it is, the record of my life. No mystery in it, even in those few hours I cannot dignify by remembrance—their events are well known enough. Straightforward. Plain sailing. A boring life on the whole, to any outside view. The adventures all those of the mind, which knows no frontiers.

Since he could not remember the bloodstained axe and trainers, they faded at last out of his head; he turned off the light and slept.

2

Anne Atkinson promised her mother, that first night, that she would not call to see Chris again until two full days had passed.

'I would stop you seeing him altogether if I could,' Mrs Atkinson said. 'Filthy murderer he is.'

'Chris is Chris,' Anne answered. 'I've known him all my life, Mother. I've written to him all the time he's been in prison. I'm free, white and over twenty-one. You can't stop me seeing him and you're not going to.'

'If your poor father was alive!' Her mother often used this as a trump card. Anne had dearly loved her father. 'You wouldn't hurt his feelings like this. But you don't care about me.'

Anne sighed. Here we go. After about half an hour of tender reassurances she might agree to shut up about Chris, but first I have to go through all that performance. Emotional blackmail, that's what it is. Mothers!

Mrs Atkinson had a good many arguments she intended to use before she allowed her daughter to 'get round' her. She reached for her hankie. Half an hour, she reckoned, ought to be long enough to rehearse all the anti-Chris arguments and reduce Anne to the right level of grovelling devotion. Then she could stop and switch on the television, in nice time for the ten o'clock news on ITV.

Just before ten o'clock that night Anne finally promised not to see Chris for two full days, by which Mrs Atkinson meant forty-eight hours, and not a minute less. Not that it made any difference to anything. Anne had decided for herself already, before her mother's emotional hysteria. It would take Chris that long, she thought, to grow used to the idea of a grown-up Annie. Then by degrees she could work towards bringing about a relationship which held the old comradely feeling but which was more equal than the old one had been. Yes, two days. He would have plenty to do, plenty of adjustments to make, to keep him busy that length of time without missing her.

Chris began next morning by putting the rest of the bits back on his bike. Towards the end of the operation, Steve Watson walked in on him through the yard door.

'Just passing,' Steve said. 'Thought I'd say hello. I'm not stopping.'

Chris thought he had better try to look and sound welcoming.

'Everything's okay,' he said, and went on tightening screws and generally going over the bike for last adjustments.

After five minutes or so, Steve nodded at him, remarked, 'Great, see you later,' and went.

Chris stood back and looked at the bike, feeling pleased with his work. He was tingling with the anticipation of riding it again, feeling free and independent. But that morning, what there was left of it, he thought he would walk to do his shopping on Micklegate and later, in the afternoon, he had an appointment with his solicitor at three. He might ride his bike to that.

Micklegate—the long, beloved street which runs from great Micklegate Bar, the royal gateway to the city, where once human heads decorated the outer surface to strike terror into the wayfarer who came with less than honest intentions. Micklegate, which from the Bar rises up a little then over and down the hill, and runs helter skelter at last down a cobbled slope towards the river. A long street. A street with two churches, Trinity and St Martin's cum Gregory, to protect it from harm. A street with an ancient pair of stocks under the churchyard trees of Trinity to remind the passer-by once more of days when punishment for crimes was very definitely physical. A street with public houses a-plenty amid a mixture of shops. A street still unspoiled, where the citizen holds his breath and hopes with crossed fingers that long may it continue to be itself. Micklegate, which is one frontier of Bishophill, where Chris and Anne had both been born and raised.

As Chris turned into it with a carrier bag in his hand he felt a sense of homecoming greater than he had felt as he stood, the previous day, smoking a cigarette and noticing the changes in his own terrace. There were changes here too, but he didn't mind them so much—they didn't seem to matter. The shop on the corner still had good cream cakes and good cream cakes were not to be had in prison. He bought bread too. There was a delicatessen where he bought cheese. He looked in the windows of Oblong Books and the other bookshops, and the charity shops with their range of cheap second-hand clothing. He went inside the fruit shop and bought a bagful of fruit and veg. He went out of Micklegate at the bottom end as far as the butcher's, and treated himself to a steak and some chops. He turned round and made for home feeling cheerful. No one had spoken to him. No one had recognised him. Or so he thought.

35

He thought he had grown used to modern traffic, but in the narrow street, what with parked cars and delivery vans and general clobber, where each side was built up, noise resounded from one cliff wall of façade to the other. Chris could not help feeling thrilled and exhilarated, enjoying every step. There was one fascinating thing to see after another. The people themselves intrigued him; their fatness, their thinness, their hairstyles, their babies in buggies and teenagers in jeans, their mothers in jeans, their fathers in jeans. To judge by one lady, their grandmothers in jeans. He was pleased that his own jeans still fitted him after twelve years and that his black bomber jacket looked fashionable enough. He wouldn't stand out because of his clothes and that was good.

Back home the exhilaration still bubbled in his veins. He had salad and cheese for midday and saved the steak for evening. Another bound of exhilaration thrilled through him as he relished organising his own life. There was no one to tell him what to do and dictate his actions. There was a purpose in his life and objects for his activity. For the first time ever he was self-determining.

Later, at a quarter to three, he travelled down Micklegate again, this time swooping downward on his bicycle towards the church of St John's Ousebridge End, past it and by Ouse Bridge over the river, left—walking now and pushing the bike—along Spurriergate where once men had made spurs for horses, then on to Coney Street, the street of the king. Off the street, passing under an arched passageway, he was suddenly in the secluded courtyard of an old Georgian building. Here he fastened his bike to a wrought-iron railing and went in.

'Mr Hale is expecting me,' he said as soon as the receptionist could spare time from her switchboard to speak to him.

'I'll let him know you're here.'

'Do sit down,' added the receptionist.

Chris didn't want to sit down. He moved from one part of the waiting-room to another, examining the old water-colours on the walls. He admired the Victorian upright mahogany chairs without wanting to sit on them. The constantly ringing switchboard provided plenty of aural interest.

'Someone will be coming down for you,' the receptionist said.

Footsteps descending the old curved staircase in the entrance hall told him his escort had arrived. She was young, buxom, and cheerful. Chattering, she preceded him up the stairs and into a room he remembered seeing before.

It looked exactly the same. Humphrey Hale, tall, thin and angular, with his fine mouse-coloured hair brushed across his head, rose to his feet behind the desk and offered a hand.

'Mr Simmers! Good to see you. Do sit down. This is the time of day we normally take tea—will you have some? Good. Judith, an extra cup for Mr Simmers, if you please.' As the door shut behind Judith, he went on, 'And how are things going? Did you find everything in order at the house?'

'Yes, thank you. The electricity, gas, and water had all been turned on. The milkman had delivered a pint of milk and another came this morning. The phone is connected. Everything seems to be fine. I'm grateful to you for arranging all that for me.'

'Not at all, not at all. Here's our tea,' said Humphrey as the door opened. The girl Judith put the tray on the desk, smiled, and went again.

Humphrey Hale poured out, and handed Chris a fine china cup full of rather weak steaming hot tea, and then a small plate of biscuits. In some ways it was like being in the presence of the prison governor, but in other ways there was all the difference in the world, the difference between being a prisoner and being a free man, treated like a human being.

'So! You are back with us again,' Hale said pleasantly. Chris felt gratified and soothed by the solicitor's manner. He might have been away on holiday, not in prison.

'What a good thing you have a house of your own,' went on the solicitor.

'I am very conscious of that. Most people I knew were going to have a helluva job finding accommodation. And the probation officer did all he could to persuade me not to come back here.'

'Really?' Hale leaned back in his chair, balancing his cup on his fingers in front of him in a leisurely fashion. 'Why was that?'

'He felt I would encounter a lot of prejudice.'

'He may well prove right, you know, Mr Simmers.'

'Yes. I shall have to face it when it comes.'

'If you recall, when you first...went in...I tried to let the house furnished, but there were no takers, although it had been thoroughly—er—cleaned...'

'You explained to me that you had tried.'

'Hmmm. It was a pity not to use an asset like that. As things are it will, I am afraid, have deteriorated.'

'There's a lot to do at it,' said Chris, unconsciously echoing Steve Watson.

'Are you aware that I have the deeds here?' asked Hale.

'Deeds? Of the house? I hadn't thought about it.'

'Oh yes. It belonged, you will recall, to your grandparents, Mr and Mrs Nournavaile.'

Chris stared at him. 'My mother told me that my grandmother had left the house to me. She was rather bitter that it had not been left to her. I barely remember Grandfather. I always called Grandmother "Grandma Nourny". The name you said—Nournavaile, was it?—sounds quite unfamiliar.'

'An unusual name. On your mother's side, presumably. Your grandmother inherited the house at your grandfather's death and then left it to you.'

'Good old Granny,' said Chris.

'A very useful capital asset, when it has been put in order.'

'Yes.'

There was a pause, and Humphrey Hale sipped his tea. Chris seemed to be sinking into a reverie so to rouse him, Hale went on making conversation.

'I saw the name, oddly enough, quite recently in another connection.'

'Really?'

'The *News of the World* is not my usual Sunday paper, of course, Mr Simmers. Not at all. I am rather fond of the *Observer*. But there were no *Observers* at my newsagents on Sunday morning—I take a walk down rather than have it delivered, it is good both for me and the dog. We were a little late. So, deprived of my usual prey, I bought a *News of the World*. Most enlightening. Amongst other things, there are advertisements of the type which say, "Any descendants of Walter Clarke please get in touch with Blank, Blank and Blank and they may hear of something to their advantage." Quite amusing to speculate upon. There was one, in fact, with the name Nournavaile. Rather unusual. Any connection, do you think?'

Chris was looking surprised. 'I don't suppose so,' he said. 'I don't remember hearing the name before you said it a few minutes ago.'

'I'll tell you what I'll do. We should still have the newspaper at home. I will put the advertisement in an envelope and post it to you. We won't have thrown it out. Throwing out day is Saturday, invariably, in our house.'

'That's very kind of you, but what would I do with it? I don't know anything about the Nournavailes.'

'You could find out,' said the solicitor

41

bracingly. 'It would give you a change from painting the woodwork. Nice hobby, family history.'

'I am hoping to find a job.'

'Splendid. There aren't many of them about though, you know. What were you before? Banking, wasn't it? Of course you weren't in for fraud or anything of that kind, but they might hold your career during the last twelve years against you.'

'I'm sure they would.'

'I'll do what I can,' said Humphrey Hale unexpectedly.

Chris looked at him in surprise, struck dumb.

'Yes. I have a good many connections. If I hear of anything I will tell you. They would have to know, of course. I would inform them, to see if it made a difference, before contacting you.'

'The probation officer would insist on them knowing in any case.'

'How wise.'

'That is very kind of you, sir,' said Chris, getting up to go. He felt both surprised and elated. The *News of the World* advertisement for someone of the name of Nournavaile meant so little to him that he had already half forgotten it, but that this man should offer to help him find a job, now that really was something.

'We will be sending you a bill, shortly,'

said Humphrey, rising also and walking round the desk.

Chris was glad that he had been made to save when he was a child and had carried on saving, still having a residue in the bank, which money earned in prison had at least added to.

'A large bill?' he asked.

'You settled all our legal expenses at the time of your incarceration. This is only for recent work for you—charged at secretarial rate, because it was my secretary who made the arrangements with the water board, milkman and so on.'

'That was kind of her.' Chris wondered if he ought to seek out Judith and thank her personally.

'Not really. Only part of her job. Sometimes we have to take dogs to kennels and goodness knows what odd kind of things we sometimes do for clients. When they're dead, that is, mainly.'

Chris shook hands, glad that the firm were not having to arrange things for him on that basis, escaped downstairs and unfastened his bicycle in a mood of unaccustomed joy. He was mentally prepared for hostility, overt or covert. Humphrey Hale's helpfulness and friendliness got under his guard and made him feel human again. It wouldn't last; in fact he mustn't let it last. The world was too fearful a place to allow himself to be relaxed and happy in it. But for a few minutes—while he pedalled home through the spring sunshine and the daffodils blew golden yellow round the ancient walls of the city—for a few minutes he would let himself dwell on the fact that he had met kindness this afternoon—unwarranted kindness which he had done nothing to deserve, and that was the best kind. He had completely forgotten about the newspaper advertisement.

In this mood he decided to confront Mrs Atkinson. It would have to be done sooner or later. After putting his bike in the yard he went out again, a few feet along the back alleyway, and into Mrs Atkinson's yard. As he tapped on her kitchen door he could see her outlined against the lace curtain.

'What do you want?' she greeted him sharply.

'Just to say hello.'

'You needn't think you're getting round me, young man.'

'I'm not all bad, Mrs Atkinson. We're going to be neighbours. Annie doesn't mind speaking to me.'

'You can guess what I think about that,' she said. Looking at Chris, she felt herself giving way. He looked older and sadder—grim-faced, in fact—but still the lad she'd known all her married life, since first she came as a bride to live in the terrace and he was seven years old, the little boy next door. She hesitated. 'You can come in for a minute,' she added ungraciously.

Mrs Atkinson was the only one left of the old neighbours. She had kept up with the changes in the terrace. Outside her front door were matching tubs of daffodils. In the kitchen, Chris looked around at the unfamiliar fitted units. The room looked like something out of a glossy magazine. He hadn't seen anything quite like this before, in real life. It was always shining and spotless because Mrs Atkinson's passion in life was her house, but now he felt you needed to be a film star at least to feel at home and cooking would be too gross an activity to take place in it.

'Sit down and have a coffee,' said Mrs Atkinson, still frosty, perturbed by the withdrawn aura he carried round with him. She remembered him as quiet, but responsive. Chris sat carefully on a stool. She put a mat on the table and made him a powdered coffee. He sipped at it, petrified in case he spilled a drop, or made a mark on the mat.

'I don't approve of Anne having anything

to do with you, but I can't stop her.'

'She's grown up now, Mrs Atkinson. I was surprised when I saw the change in her. We won't be able to be friends as we were when she was a little girl. You needn't worry. I'm not going to push my company on to her. She can't be my little sister any more. It's all quite different.'

'That's good. You see my point. I don't want her life spoiled. If it gets around she's seeing you, no one will want anything to do with her either.'

It was the 'either' that Chris found particularly daunting.

'I was wondering if you would tell me how to clean windows,' he said after a pause. 'I need to do them.'

'That house has been a disgrace for years.'

'I'm very grateful for what you did— Annie told me—twelve years ago—putting ornaments away and that.'

'Yes. Well,' said Mrs Atkinson.

'The shammy leather is all dried up,' Chris went on. 'I found it under the sink, but it's useless.'

'You can get really good cloths for windows in Sainsbury's.' Mrs Atkinson's eyes lit up. 'Like this.' She bent down and extracted a thing from a cupboard which Chris felt was neither cloth nor chamois leather. He touched its odd texture.

'These are good, are they?'

'I've got a spare. You can have it.'

The spare was still in its wrapper.

'This is very helpful of you, Mrs Atkinson. Let me pay you.' Chris fished out his wallet.

'No you won't, Chris.' For a moment she sounded as she used to do. 'You'll have to go now. I want to get dinner on for Anne. Take the cloth. It's all right. It'll be worth it to see those windows cleaned.'

'Use warm water and vinegar,' she called after him as he walked away through the yard, before she seized his cup and washed it up vigorously, as if to wash away the stain of his presence.

After inspecting one window Chris decided that they could wait until tomorrow. For now he'd cook his meal and have a quiet evening. He hoped Annie would not appear—he needed time to think, where she was concerned. The phone rang at about eight o'clock.

'Steve here,' said the probation officer.

'Hi, Steve.'

'I thought you might ring up before this. You have my home number. We didn't have time for a real talk this morning.'

'There hasn't been much to ring about.'

Steve obviously wanted to know how things were going. Chris searched about for something to tell him, and at last told him everything more or less—leaving out his own sensations.

'You'll have to be careful with this friendship with your neighbours, Chris. I would like you to keep me informed how it goes on. You don't need me to remind you that we will be keeping an eye on your relationships in the community—particularly with women, and particularly older ones.'

'I like older women,' said Chris.

Steve made an odd kind of noise.

'Oh, you know what I mean,' Chris went on, 'as people, as friends, as neighbours. I've always got on well with them.'

Steve's silence was eloquent. Chris decided not to try to answer it. After what seemed like a long wait the voice came again, elaborately casual.

'How about a drink tomorrow night? I'll call for you about eight o'clock.'

'Fine,' Chris replied, 'except that I don't drink. I decided after—after the crime. I shall never touch another drop.'

'Good for you.' Steve sounded almost falsely hearty. But how could he have sounded, Chris thought, after his own remark? 'You can drink juice or something,' Steve went on.

'As long as you don't mind being seen with someone who's on the wagon.'

'Eight o'clock, then.'

'See you,' said Chris.

That destroyed the tentative peace of mind he'd been feeling. It started his thoughts on the old rat-trap round of speculation. I don't remember murdering my mother. Perhaps I didn't do it. Perhaps I'm being punished and I'm innocent. How can I be innocent, I must have done it. Why did I do it? She was my mother. I loved her. Did I love her? Perhaps really I hated her. I can't remember hating her, only odd times for a few minutes. I must have done it. How horrible a person I must be. I deserved to be in that stinking place. I deserve to kill myself, too. But I don't remember murdering...

Chris shook his head to get those endless speculations out of it. For twelve years they had tormented him. He'd lain awake night after night wondering. He had nearly been driven mad. Perhaps he deserved to be driven mad. Oh Lord, here we go again...

He had another bath. He didn't think he'd ever have enough baths, hot, private, not like anything he had in that place, prison. Had a bath and washed his hair and went to his bedroom in reasonable time, then sat on the edge of the bed and looked at his rows of books, taking one after the other down from the shelf and fingering the worn pages of his boyhood favourites.

At last he turned back the bedclothes. Then suddenly he felt a horror of the bedside mat. It came back to him in a rush that all the night before he'd had nightmares about that mat, seeing it endlessly with a blood-soaked pair of trainers and a bloody axe lying on it. He'd have to do something about it or he'd have another night of horror.

He'd been standing on the mat without thinking but now he jumped off as if it had burnt him. He rolled it up, touching it as little as he could with his hands. He rushed downstairs and unlocked the back door and found the dustbin, his bare feet on the rough old tarmac of the yard. He pushed the mat inside—it would hardly go in—almost in a frenzy he pushed it down, and it reared up again, too long, too big—hardly able to touch it he nevertheless shoved at it—pushed the dustbin lid on top of it—pressed down to hold the thing within as if it was trying to escape, trying to rise out and *get* him—as if the long woolly roll could come up out of the dustbin and handcuff him and take him off again to that place...

Chris climbed into bed at last. He was sweating. Trembling, too, or rather shaking as if he would never stop. He pulled the sheets and duvet and blanket up to his chin and then over his chin up to his nose although it was warm, warm enough not to need anything but the duvet.

Far away in the office of a London genealogist there had been a conference that day, about the advertisement in the Sunday papers.

'Is it to be renewed?' the new secretary, Margaret, had asked.

'Let me check. Yes. We have to maintain the search for another six weeks. Renew the advert for a fortnight at a time. The solicitors deal with any applications. If they need our expertise, they'll let us know.'

'Any other action?'

'All that can be done has been done. We came to a complete dead end. As far as I know no new info has come in which would help us with this.'

'I could go through the file again, in case there is anything,' offered the secretary.

'Margaret,' said her new boss, sitting informally on the corner of her desk, 'you did well, tracing your own family, didn't you?'

'Oh yes! There was that block when—'

'All right, all right. You were an amateur. You could spend what time and money you liked. But we are professionals and we have to operate on a different basis. I'd better

51

explain. We get a tremendous amount of work from America. Many Americans are descended from British migrants. If one dies intestate—without a valid will—there is often a search for kinsfolk over here to inherit. If there is a will, there may be a bequest for someone over here. Time has often passed and the relatives have died themselves or moved house. Results are achieved through long hard slogging through records. These searches are of no personal interest to us. There are so many of them it's become business—in fact our bread and butter. How would you like to spend a fortnight reading every single entry in the census for Essex?'

'Hard on the eyes, I expect,' said Margaret, looking interested.

'This search has had all we are prepared to give it. We have to balance the probability of a result against the time involved, and believe me, the clients are only ever interested in paying for our time if we get a *positive* result. Present them with a negative result and point out that it's as useful in the long run, and send them a big bill for the time taken—and you'll see the back of one dissatisfied client. We can't afford to do it. Sorry. We want you here, we know you're good, but you will have to adapt to our different ethos. The firm hasn't done badly out of the Nournavaile search, but every fruitless hour now brings down our profit average on it. It's possible that one of these American firms—there were several interested, I know—might press on and get somewhere. Tough.'

'For my own satisfaction, though?'

'No, repeat, *no*. More than your job's worth.'

Margaret had been unemployed for a year before finding her new job. She filed the Nournavaile papers away.

3

Chris was to remember the next day as the last calm one before the troubled waters. It was a day of fleeting clouds across the sunshine so that old York was filled with lovely vagrant shadows and was a photographer's dream.

It was the day he signed on at the Job Centre and the day he cleaned the windows.

The Job Centre first, and they weren't very hopeful about him finding anything.

Then he thought he'd start with the outside of the house, and before doing the actual glass he'd give the whole thing, frames as well as glass, a rinse over with soapy water. He'd examine the woodwork and see how sound it was, and then go over the glass again with the warm water and vinegar as recommended by Mrs Atkinson. There was a ladder in the outhouse and he remembered seeing the attic window cleaned by his mother. He'd always been terrified in case she fell out, because it was a sash window and she used to sit on the windowsill with only her legs inside the attic and the rest of her busy cleaning the outside.

Chris found, after having a bash at cleaning the sash window of the attic for some minutes, that he wasn't getting very far. So he copied the way his mother had done it, sitting on the sill with his torso outside, one sash down on his legs to give him some feeling of security. After the first uneasy seconds it seemed a fairly sensible, natural way to clean windows, and with a little juggling with the two sashes he cleaned it fairly well. He decided that all those Victorian housemaids who were said to have met their deaths by falling out, had been rather careless—or perhaps the stories were exaggerated.

The attic was an old playground of his and he had looked round at the suitcases and cardboard boxes with a comfortable feeling of reassurance. They had not changed. Memories of games played up there came into his mind, jumbled like bits of old dreams.

Chris was beginning to feel his solitariness, alone in the house.

There had been no doubt about his mother. When she was anywhere around, you could hear her. Even shut away in his bedroom he'd become used to the background noise of radio or television, often both at once, with his mother's voice raised in raucous song or arguing with the commentators, who fortunately could not argue back. Sometimes she held noisy conversations from an open bedroom window, or outside in the street, sounding as though she was challenging the neighbours to a duel, probably audible for miles around. It hadn't been very lonely in the nick, either. Not sharing three to a cell. There had more often been times when he had longed for privacy, longed agonisingly for it. Now he'd got it, and it seemed strange.

On the whole the woodwork had survived well. They had always kept it well painted, so that in spite of twelve years of absolute neglect there wasn't much rot. His penknife went in too easily in places, where flaking paint revealed dark rotten wood, but patching ought to see the frames through at least one more winter, and Chris thought he could do that. He had worked with his hands during the twelve years, including carpentry. It would be something to occupy him. Then by the next spring his life might have sorted itself out.

The window cleaning was a tedious task and by the time it was finished evening had arrived. He had hardly time to cook and eat and make himself respectable before Steve Watson knocked at the door—this time he found it locked against him—and they set off together to find a pub. There were plenty of pubs on Micklegate, they were spoilt for choice. On Friday nights the teens and twenties of the city made the street their Cresta run, a test of stamina and endurance. Starting at one end they would attempt to drink in every pub until they reached the other end. Steve casually chose a nearby establishment. He went first, barging through the double doors into the dark crowded interior, assuming his parolee was following close behind.

Chris had got no further than the pavement.

When Steve went in, a great gale of noise swept out, of loud music and male voices, carrying the stench of beer and tobacco. It swept past Chris and overwhelmed him. He stood there wondering if he was going to be sick. He could no more go into that pub than fly. The door banged shut in his face and for a second he couldn't hear the noise as clearly and the air was sweeter. Full of exhaust fumes, but sweeter.

Inside, Steve turned to ask what kind of orange juice Chris wanted, and found that he was alone. Annoyed, he walked out into the street again, and saw his parolee pale and shaking on the pavement.

'What's up with you? Why haven't you come in?'

'I don't know—I only...'

'You're as white as a sheet, Chris.'

Steve, concerned, was thinking, I don't like the way Simmers is taking this; it's not a good symptom; is he going to break down?

And then what, would it be the precursor of violence?

'Felt ill for a minute,' Chris mumbled. Underneath, in his subconscious, he knew what had been the matter. It was one of the pubs where he and his friends celebrated his twenty-first birthday. Most of the evening had been spent there and in retrospect he had a horror of the place. He was always to fight back this knowledge from the light of day, keeping it shrouded, one of the memories he was unable to face.

Deciding he would let the incident blow over without pressing for an explanation, Steve remarked that it was a bit noisy in there anyway. 'Would you rather go somewhere else?'

'There won't be any quiet pubs,' Chris answered with conviction.

Steve came close to him, turned him by placing an arm casually across his back for a second, and said, 'We'll have a look-see.' They walked side by side, not speaking. Evenings were still dark fairly early, and the street was busy but not as busy as it would be later. Traffic was sparse. Light beamed out from the fish and chip shop, the Italian restaurant, the pubs. Steve chose a pub with an austere frontage and two steps up to the front door. It looked as though it catered for commercial gentlemen of the most boring kind and unblemished behaviour.

'Try this one?'

'All right.'

'You're looking a bit better. They don't have music in here,' said Steve as he went up the steps and opened the door.

'Thank God.' Chris was still shaky.

'Sit down, I'll get them. Britvic orange juice?'

'Right.'

They talked of nondescript things. The price of fish. The political situation. The Cup Final. Asked what football team he supported, Chris said York City. Steve was a southerner and favoured Arsenal. Somehow they passed a couple of hours. It was towards the end of the time that Steve asked, 'Were you worried about meeting old friends in that first pub?'

'It wasn't that. I don't know what it was. I can't think why but I felt peculiar.' As usual Chris sounded withdrawn, but he felt he had to give some sort of explanation.

'Have you been in contact with any old mates?'

'No. I last saw them twelve years ago when they were all in the witness box, one after the other, testifying to the evening we'd spent. None of them kept in contact when I was inside, and it would have been appreciated. If they haven't cared for twelve years—if they all agreed with the verdict and thought I was guilty—then that isn't how friends are supposed to behave and I don't care if I never see them again.'

It was the longest and most open speech Chris had ever made to Steve, and it wasn't so much a confidence as something forced out of him by circumstance.

'You wouldn't have expected them to disagree with the verdict. The evidence was overwhelming.'

'I know that. But if just one of them had said, "I can't believe it of you, Chris, you wouldn't do anything like that"—but none of them did.'

They dropped the subject and soon after left the pub. They walked together as far as the end of Priory Street. Steve said he was parked in Nunnery Lane, and they said, 'Cheers, mate,' both vaguely raised a hand in a wave, and parted. Steve was pleased on the whole. It had been worth making the effort, though Simmers was as much of an enigma as he had been before.

Chris unlocked his front door wondering if he was going to be all right tonight. Was he going to have another experience like the one with the bedside mat, or would a sense of well-being visit him as a benison?

As he lay in bed his mind reverted to the window cleaning, not the outside, but the inside work. It was the bedrooms he thought of now as he lay waiting to go to sleep. Not his own, but the other front bedroom, which had been his mother's and long ago his father's too. It seemed a forbidding, strange room to him. Earlier that day he had walked into it boldly as if he owned the place. He had to remind himself that he did own it, literally, and had every right to walk in. He walked over and took down the curtains, which were black bright, as they say in York. Cheerfully he sloshed water about, feeling every moment as though he was intruding. He decided the dressing-table resented him. Well, he resented it. It was a fussy, meretricious piece of furniture. The surface was stained by years of scent bottles and cosmetics. The veneer was lifting. The decoration of brass curlicues had looked cheap when it was new and now looked revolting. Suddenly he realised he could throw the thing out if he wanted to. The pink shiny bedspread gleamed unpleasantly—he'd never liked it. The carpet, a shaggy pile in some inferior man-made fibre, tried to trip him up. He looked round, remembering his parents' purchase of each piece, and a feeling stirred in him that every item had ousted something he preferred, that once this had been a pleasant room, and he had liked being in it.

The back bedroom felt no better. By then his nerve ends were tingling, red raw with emotions he couldn't understand or control. Chris's memories of his childhood were patchy and under all the analysis in prison he had been made to realise how patchy they were, how great lumps of his life seemed to be lost to him. This back bedroom had been his grandparents' and Grandfather Nourny was now only a tobacco-scented presence far, far back in the past. Granny Nourny was much closer; he retained little pictures of her, fragments. This had been her bedroom. For the first time he wondered why, when she died, he had not been given her room instead of staying in his little shoebox over the hall. Perhaps he hadn't wanted it; perhaps his love for his own space had been too strong. Certainly through years in prison it had helped sustain him. He had lain in his narrow bunk on sleepless nights and gone over in his mind the contents of his room, mentally running his eye item by item over every shelf and ranging through the contents of every drawer. His possessions had formed a sort of litany.

He caught his breath as he wondered how he would have reacted if he had found the bedroom cleared out and everything destroyed. It must have been Annie who locked the door, keeping it safe. She shared his memories. They had sat side by side on the edge of the bed—there was no space for chairs—listening to the music of his tapes, because his bedroom was the only place he was allowed to play them. When she was very small he had read stories to her as she sat on the floor, or perched somewhere. When they went out and sat on the grassy bank opposite the house, under the trees, she would choose a book to take with them.

Chris wondered how it was that he had started to think about the front bedroom and somehow worked round to thinking about Annie. He supposed that it was because they were both only children that they had become so close. If they had both had real brothers and sisters, their relationship would probably never have developed at all.

The back bedroom. It was still very much as Granny Nourny had left it, but his mother, too impatient to climb the stairs to the attic, had taken to using it as a boxroom. She had pushed all kinds of oddments in there—cardboard boxes which might come in useful—bundles of old curtains which gradually began to smell of dust—pairs of worn-out shoes which she couldn't make her mind up to part with.

He woke feeling fresh and alive next morning, but was hardly dressed before Annie was knocking at the back door, exactly as she might have done twelve years earlier.

'What are we doing today, then?' she asked brightly as he let her in. She was wearing slim, well-cut stone-coloured trousers, flat shoes, and a jumper of emerald green. Her hair hung down her back, fastened at the top, the rest flowing free and bright. Chris felt as he had before, acutely embarrassed by this vibrant young woman. He couldn't sound natural with her, although she seemed unaware of his inhibition and spoke to him as she might have done long before.

'Aren't you at work?' he asked.

'It's Saturday, silly.'

He shook his head to get some sense into it. 'I've lost track of the days.'

'It's too nice to stay inside.'

He was at a loss. Awkwardly, he said, 'I ought to be making a start on the window frames. They need a lot of work. I'll have to buy some tools.'

'You never did woodwork before.'

'I did some in prison. But I haven't the

right tools for the windows.'

'Where are we going, then? To shop for tools, then a coffee?'

'I was going to have breakfast.' He felt as though he was verbally fending her off, shutting out her cheerfulness and friendliness.

'I've had mine. You carry on while I buzz round.'

Anyone would think, to hear Annie, that they had never been separated by those twelve growing years. This wasn't how Chris had meant things to go when they met again, he thought grumpily. He'd been looking forward to bacon and egg but decided instantly on toast and marmalade. Quicker, and less trouble, less messy. As he stood by the toaster he could hear Annie moving about in the rest of the house. As he ate the second piece she reappeared, carrying a letter in her hand.

'Haven't you finished yet?'

'Now look here, Annie...'

'There's a letter for you. I heard the postman struggling with the letterbox. You'll have to see to it, oil it or something.'

He licked a lump of marmalade from his finger and reached for the letter.

'You'll make it all sticky,' said Anne. 'I'll open it.'

'You've grown up awfully bossy,' grumbled Chris. He had meant to take a lofty and slightly unfriendly tone with her, and she was making it impossible. Annie found a vegetable knife in the kitchen drawer and slit open the envelope, then peered inside.

'It's a newspaper cutting,' she said with some surprise.

'Oh, I know. It's from my solicitor. He said he'd post me a cutting. It isn't anything important. You can look at it.'

When she had read the cutting through Annie looked at him seriously. 'Did you know what it was?'

'Some family history thing, Mr Hale said.'

'Why should he send it to you? It's about some family called Nournavaile.'

'It seems that was my Granny Nourny's proper name. She died while you were still in your pram. No. You were at junior school.'

'You ought to follow this up,' Anne said. It was slightly irritating that Chris reminded her so often that he remembered her childhood. She was busy living in the present.

'It doesn't interest me.'

She flopped down into the other chair. 'But I'm interested. This oral history project I'm on means I've met a lot of

66

people who're in the York Family History Society. I've even bought a book on how to trace one's family. It's really fascinating.'

Chris said nothing as he finished his toast and poured a second cup of tea.

'Go on, Chris. It would be interesting to trace your grandpa's family. Is there any chance of you getting a job?'

'I doubt it.'

'Well, it would give you something to do. We could start today and you could carry on next week while I'm at work.'

Anne studied the cutting again and Chris looked across, noticing the differences between the old Annie and the new Anne. Eyelashes for one thing. She'd always had them, he supposed, but now that she darkened them a little they showed up as they never had before and made fan-shaped shadows on her cheekbones. Her skin was clear and fine, her red hair gleamed with golden highlights in the sun. Her pert little nose was as cheeky as it had always been. Her emerald green jumper, perhaps a shade too bright, reflected the cheerfulness of her personality. He had seen her furious, seen her weeping, but ninety-five per cent of the time Anne was the most cheerful person he knew. Too much so, at times.

'I'll tell you what I'll do,' he said. 'On Monday morning I'll ask Mr Hale if he'll write to these people for me and ask them what it's all about.'

'Nournavaile. Will anyone able to prove their descent in the male line from Thomas Nournavaile, twin brother of Joseph,' read Anne, 'baptised the first of November 1785, please get in touch with Donne, Donne and Flight (of an address in Chiswick which I won't bother reading) when they may hear of something to their advantage.'

'It can't possibly apply to me.'

'Why not?'

'That business of the male line. Doesn't that mean anyone with the surname Nournavaile?'

'Yes, I suppose so.'

'Mine isn't, as you might have noticed. My mother must have been a Nournavaile before she married, so they won't want to know about me.'

'It's worth checking. If they can't find a male line descendant they might settle for a female line one.'

'I'll ask Mr Hale to write, as I said. But I don't see any point in wasting time on it.'

Anne knew a barrier when she saw one. 'Oh, all right.' But she could not resist having a last little try. 'We would have to start with your birth certificate, and then look for your parents' marriage certificate, I suppose.'

'What were you doing upstairs just now?'

'I thought I'd take the ornaments out again and stand them about, since you haven't done it.'

'There hasn't been time.'

Anne sighed in a resigned way. 'If you want to get on with your window frame repairs I may as well go and do a bit of shopping of my own.'

'Nice of you to call round, Anne,' said Chris formally.

She felt damped, almost snubbed. 'See you, then,' she said, downbeat, and went out of the door.

He could have kicked himself, but it was for the best. Even though she behaved and spoke to him as if she was still twelve, in all the innocence of childhood, sooner or later she had to accept that their relationship could never be the same as it had once been. The days when they felt like siblings had gone for ever. She was now a very attractive young woman, old enough to have been married and given birth to children, had she chosen to do so. When they met again she might easily have been a wife and mother. Then her husband would certainly have objected, as her mother now did, to her staying friendly with an ex-jailbird. Chris wondered idly about the many boyfriends she must have had—had still, he expected. He himself was no loss to her. Mentally, sternly, he cut himself out of any part in her romantic life.

He went upstairs for his wallet and counted his money, guessing at how much the tools would cost. The list of what he would need went into his jacket pocket. After locking up the house he rode his bicycle into Priory Street, paused at the end, as soon as the traffic allowed turned right on to Micklegate, and in less than a minute was threading his way between parked cars and moving ones, then as the downward slope steepened he began to freewheel down the hill.

It was the third time since coming home that he had had the joyous flying sensation of freewheeling down towards the Rougier Street traffic lights. The first time they had been at green and he had dashed through at full speed. The second time, going to the Job Centre, they had been at red and he had not liked having to slow down quickly from that delirious movement. This time they were green as soon as he came within sight of them, and he was slightly worried in case they turned at the last minute. He decided to shoot the amber if necessary. Tearing down the hill with one eye on the lights, Chris saw them turn to amber when he was travelling fast. You were supposed to stop unless it was dangerous to do so—Chris decided it would be very dangerous to stop now. He would be through before they turned red.

He was still some yards off when the lights turned red. Too late to shoot the amber. He jammed on his brakes and nothing happened. Harder. Nothing happened. He couldn't believe it and the traffic was moving now round the right-angled junction. Instead of gripping, the brakes were spinning round. He tried to steer into the kerb but a car was parked in the way. He put his feet towards the ground and the cobbles—or setts—seared as if they were red hot. The momentum was too great for him to turn left and join the stream of traffic along Rougier Street. There was nothing he could do except hold on and pray. The street ahead was almost flat, rising slightly to Ouse Bridge over the river, and if he passed across the junction unscathed the bike would automatically slow down.

How could he expect to get through unscathed when traffic in two directions was moving rapidly across his path? He did not expect it. The only conscious thought to flash across his brain was that his last moments had come.

The double-decker bus looming up ahead had seen him with half a second to spare. The driver jabbed on his brakes so fast that a stout lady with two shopping bags fell over in the aisle. The other passengers could see him and were saying, 'What the heck does he think he's doing?', 'He must be tired of living!', 'Stupid idiot!'

Both Chris's feet were now jammed down on the ground, jarring his whole body as they slid over the surface of the road. He had been incredibly lucky with the bus, but the second line of traffic had not had the half-second's warning. They could not see him until he was amongst them. He collided with the back end of a car as an old truck, coming up fast enough itself to run into the car, caught him a slanting blow with the bumper. This threw him, falling towards the nearside, where he was caught again by the bumper's sharp projecting end. The headlamps and wing mirrors were the right height to hit him hard on the hip and the side of the head. He was thrown on to the farther pavement with the bike in a tangle on top of him. The Saturday shopping crowd fell apart as he landed amongst them.

'You all right?' asked an anxious man, bending over him. 'I'm a first-aider, can I help?'

'Wants helping into the nearest lunatic asylum if you ask me,' shrieked the truck driver from his cab.

Everything had come to a halt.

The driver of the car in front of the truck got out to inspect the back of his saloon.

'You'd better give me your name and address,' he said aggressively to Chris. 'There'll be a bill for you to settle. Look at the back of my car!'

'Hold on,' said the helpful man, grabbing Chris's wallet from where it had flown on to the pavement and standing with it in his hand. 'First things first, you know. This man's been hurt. I think we ought to phone an ambulance. Give me your name, sir,' he went on politely to the car driver, 'and I'll see he is in touch with you as soon as he's had medical attention.'

The car driver wrote down his name and address on a piece of paper torn from his pocket-book and the first-aider tucked it into Chris's wallet before giving the wallet to Chris. The truck driver climbed down into the street and inspected his bumper, headlamp and mirror. Then he stood looking down at the man who lay on the ground.

'Anything to say for yourself?' he demanded aggressively.

The last thing Chris wanted to do was to speak. His head had taken a nasty crack on the pavement, he wasn't sure what had happened to the rest of him, and the bike he had spent a whole day putting into first-class order was bent up into a lump of scrap metal.

'My brakes failed,' he whispered at last.

'You're lucky it was no bloody worse,' the truck driver said, every bit as aggressively as before. Most traffic was now moving on. Cars behind the truck were still held up and drivers began to lean out of their windows and swear at the truck driver, who swore back. Someone had darted into the large shop, once the York Co-op, which filled the whole corner, and phoned for an ambulance. It arrived with a cacophony of sound, barging through the other traffic on the junction. Cars pulled in to make way. Chris was lifted up and loaded in, but his bike, what there was of it, was left on the pavement. The first-aider picked it up and stood it tidily next to the shop window.

There was a certain peace in lying in Casualty and handing over all responsibility for himself to the doctors and nurses. After cleaning him up a bit they decided that his body had probably escaped with nothing worse than bruising, though they couldn't rule out the possibility of some internal damage. His head was examined and X-rayed. Although there was a hair-line crack in his skull, it didn't seem to worry them.

'You could have been killed,' they told him.

'I'm going to live?' he asked.

He was kept in overnight for observation. For different reasons, his night's sleep was as bad as any since coming out of prison. This time it was the pain that kept him awake, allowing only fitful dozing in spite of the medication he had been given. Nothing dogged his short dreams, although he did find himself thinking in the darkest part of the night that if he had done as Annie wished and gone ancestor hunting with her, the accident would never have happened.

The next morning, worried sick, Anne rang first the police and then the hospital. She turned up in mid-morning when Chris was being brought back from Physio and waited anxiously.

'Have you come to take him home?' asked the nursing sister at last.

'If he's fit to come.'

'Yes, I think we can release him now. A few days' rest at home is what he needs. If there's any cause for concern, see that he comes straight back to us, Mrs Simmers.'

Chris heard this. 'She's only a neighbour, and her name's Atkinson,' he said from the trolley.

'I'll pack your things if that's all right,' Anne said politely.

'I haven't got any things. Look the other way. I want to get dressed.'

'Be careful,' warned the nurse.

There was no need for the warning. He ached too much to want to be active. It was all he could do to put on his clothes, but he indignantly refused help from Anne and the nurse.

Anne went to phone for a taxi.

'We think you've suffered slight concussion,' the nurse told him. 'If you have a headache, dizziness, or vomiting, then come back here or see your doctor, at once, immediately, forthwith. We've observed you for twenty-four hours and think you should be all right, but take things very easy for a few days. Are you working?'

'No.'

'That's all right, then, you'll be able to rest.'

Anne walked out of the hospital with him. She was ready to lend a hand if he wanted to lean on her, but he was in the mood for managing alone, no matter what.

'You didn't need to come and fetch me, and I'm not going to bed,' he announced when they were back at the terrace and she had unlocked the door with his key. 'I'll stay downstairs, in the front room, and watch the telly.'

Anne decided he was best left alone. She saw him settled with everything he might need within arm's reach, then went home, promising to return with regular meals. As soon as she had gone he telephoned the probation officer's home number and asked to speak to Steve.

'He's out, can you leave a message?'

'Ask him to ring me when he comes back, please.'

Steve rang half an hour later.

'Someone tried to kill me yesterday,' Chris said.

'Nonsense, Chris.'

'No, really. Someone must have loosened the nuts holding the brake shoes on my bike. I was going really fast down Micklegate, and the brakes just spun round instead of holding.' He went on to tell Steve about his night in hospital, and his present condition.

'I'll come and see you tonight,' Steve offered. 'Where's the bike? I'd like to have a look at it.'

'The last time I saw it, it was lying on the pavement outside the Co-op.'

'Victoria House,' Steve updated him automatically.

When Steve arrived that evening, he had the bike with him. 'Where do you want this heap of junk?' He edged his way in at the sitting-room door.

Chris reared up in his chair and looked at the tall probation officer with his arms full of twisted metal. 'Not much I can do with that, is there?' he remarked.

''Fraid not. I would have taken it to the police for fingerprinting but so many people seem to have handled it there wouldn't be any evidence left, I shouldn't think.'

'Put it in the yard,' said Chris. 'Please,' he added.

When Steve returned he said seriously, 'There's no doubt that it was tampered with. The screws holding the brake shoes were almost out, and I saw you tighten them up myself.'

'I've been thinking. I did put the brakes on, gently, at the end of Priory Street.'

'Gently, they would hold, I suppose. With full force, definitely not.'

'You warned me I wouldn't be popular.'

'It's going a bit far to sabotage your bike. Any idea who might have done it?'

Chris shook his head. 'Apart from you, the solicitor, who is a real gent, Mrs Atkinson next door, and Anne, I haven't spoken to anyone who knows me. I've been shopping, but all the people I knew have retired or moved from the shops round here. As far as I know, no one else has recognised me.'

'Someone has.'

4

It was not very pleasant to think that someone had seen and recognised him without making themselves and their hatred known. Chris could have understood it if someone had challenged or confronted him, reviled him publicly for the thing that he had done, spat at him in the street or knocked him down. Anything like that would have been what he was half expecting, and what the probation officer had foreseen. Or some whispering campaign, so that the folk of Bishophill turned their backs when he was near—that would not have been surprising. Neither of them had thought of this method of making him feel unwelcome in his native place.

'Have you been locking the yard up?' asked Steve.

'I never thought of it. It's something we've never done.'

'You had better start locking it, and the shed.'

Strictly speaking the outbuildings in the yard, which were brick-built and had once been the coal-house and outside WC, were not sheds, but the name suited them and most people used it. Long ago with the introduction of the Clean Air Acts most inhabitants of the terrace and the neighbouring terraces had changed to gas for cooking and heating, and had indoor bathrooms and toilets put in. Some outbuildings had been pulled down to make bigger back yards, some had been enlarged and made into kitchens with bathrooms over, some had become conservatories, but most, like the Simmerses', were general-purpose covered areas where tools and bikes, paint tins, old toys, and a million other things were stored.

Chris remembered that it was Sunday. 'Tomorrow I'll go out and buy some padlocks and catches for the doors. I expect I'll need three, and something for the yard door.'

Outside the sitting-room window the tree-covered bank rose green to the ivory-coloured stones of the city wall, with nothing but blue sky visible above, as though the world ended with the sheltering ramparts.

Steve knew that Simmers had the reputation in prison of being a hard man, but he had obviously been badly shaken by the damage to his head.

'Do you think you'll feel well enough in the morning?' Steve asked.

'I hope so.'

'Pity you couldn't have done it earlier today. The do-it-yourself stores have been open.'

'On a Sunday?'

'They're all Sunday trading these days.'

'I'll go to Stubbs'. I don't know these new shops.'

'Well, make sure you do it tomorrow. Are the Atkinsons looking after you while you recover?'

Chris felt amused at Steve's change of tune. After saying a few days ago that he would be keeping a stern eye on the relationships between Chris and the neighbours, now the probation officer was hoping the contact would be close enough for them to care for him. His own voice was reassuring as he answered.

'They've been very good. Anne fetched me out of hospital this morning. I'd rather be independent, actually. As soon as I can manage, I will be.'

'Rome wasn't built in a day.'

Steve left. There was nothing he could do, and his wife liked a bit of his company at the weekend. Chris lay there in the most comfortable armchair, his mind barely occupied by the television programmes. Tomorrow he intended to walk into town—not that he had any alternative to walking. He would make the house into a fortress if necessary, but

81

why should he? He had served his time; his dues were paid; he was a relatively free man. The thought of an unknown enemy was disturbing.

Monday morning. The beginning of the working week, for those lucky enough to have work to go to. Cloudy, rather dull after the brilliance of the last few days, and slightly cooler. Chris walked carefully through the town streets, anxious not to jar his head, to buy his padlocks and door fasteners, and the tools he needed to tackle the repairs to the window frames. Stubbs' was an old-established shop with long mahogany counters, where men in overalls dropped in for things they wanted in their work. The friendly assistants advised Chris on the best padlocks for his purpose and the most useful sizes of screws and screwdrivers. He was reassured to find one establishment that had not changed, when so many old names were missing from shop fronts.

On his way back he picked up fresh food. When he was in the house again, he felt that his expedition had been quite long enough. Every bruise had started to ache. He rested for a while, then found the energy to go into the yard and busy himself with the screwdrivers. Soon all three doors in the yard were capable of being locked.

There didn't seem to be any need to lock the door into the back alleyway during the day when he was at home, but Chris thought he would keep the two shed doors locked except when he wanted to be in them. If that precaution had been taken earlier, his bike would still be in good and ridable condition.

Mrs Atkinson herself brought round a tray of food for him at tea-time.

'Anne is out all evening,' she said. 'And I don't believe in coddling ex-convicts.'

Chris thanked her and said that he would manage to feed himself after this. When he had washed up and returned the tray he locked the yard door and decided to have an early night. Then, he was positive, he would be right as rain in the morning.

When he was in his pyjamas, he came out of the bathroom, turning off the light as he did so. He stood on the landing in the dim greyness of the last of the day. If his eyes had not become accustomed to the near darkness quickly, he would have seen nothing. As it was, outlines became visible and he began to walk about, drifting into the front bedroom and over to the window. For a while he looked down into the quiet road and then watched the outlines of the trees opposite. Moonlight grew slowly. Soon he could distinguish tree branches and soft outlines of growing leaves blurring the clarity of the twig masses, as they moved in the breeze in front of the pale city wall. By the time he turned from the window the moonlight had strengthened to such an extent that it fell on the ornaments and toilet things which Anne had taken from the dressing-table drawer and set out on the stained, roughened top surface. They were reflected in the dusty silvery mirror, ghosts of themselves. Chris picked up the framed photograph which stood there. He knew what it was, a wedding photo of his parents. The light was not strong enough to see it properly so he took it with him when he drifted back to the landing and then towards his own room. There was a quiet excitement in walking slowly, silently, round the unlit house.

Once with his own door locked behind him and the curtains closed, Chris turned on the bedside lamp and stood looking at the photograph. He knew it well. Although he had not seen it for twelve years it was as familiar as ever. The young woman who was later his mother stood, barely recognisable in her youth and slim freshness, hanging on to the arm of the young man who had become his father. She carried a bouquet of mixed flowers, most of which looked like roses, and he had a carnation in his buttonhole. His hair was dark, like Chris's own, and he looked ill at ease in his best suit. Chris remembered him better in his overalls; he had been a mechanic in a local garage. It was his teaching that enabled Chris to take a bicycle to pieces and reassemble it expertly. He had died, as quietly and unobtrusively as he had lived, when Chris was nearly fifteen. Chris had become so lost in thought as he stood gazing at the photograph, busy tracing the years, that time passed by unnoticed. At last he realised that his feet were freezing and shuffled them about to restore the circulation. His gaze, which had gradually become abstracted, sharpened again on the photographic image and he noticed something that was different about it, something he had never noticed before, though he had held the frame like this many times, and seen it nearly every day of his life until he went to prison. There was something underneath the photograph, showing by almost an eighth of an inch at one corner, thinning to nothing by the time it reached the next corner. He could see a narrow white border, some sixteenth of an inch in width, and a grey patterning inside it, which was only visible at the extreme corner where the thing underneath showed the most. Chris was convinced as soon as he saw it that it was a second photograph, which, due perhaps to the unusual movements involved in laying it in a drawer and then taking it out again, had slipped—or the one in front had slipped—so that for the first time that he could remember, it could be seen. It seemed odd to have two photographs, one underneath the other, in the same frame, but he supposed there was some perfectly simple reason for it. The frame itself was a thin one of oxidised metal, dull grey-bronze in colour, decorated by a small motif in each corner. The edges were rather sharp and unpleasant to touch, where they lay on the glass. Chris turned it over in his hands. He had seen the back before—it was usually reflected in the dressing-table looking-glass. There was a long dull grey piece of cardboard which folded out to form a support so that the frame could stand upright, and two small side rings to be used if it was to hang. The backing was of the same cardboard as the support, and held in place by a small moving catch of thin metal and several ears of metal projecting from the frame. It was the work of a moment to turn the catch, lift the cardboard using the support as a handle, and slide it out from under the projecting ears. Once the cardboard was out, Chris could turn the photograph frame horizontally on its back and he felt the two photographs drop from it on to the palm of his hand. They were both the same size, almost as large as the frame itself. In the frame, their edges must have usually coincided, barely hidden by the frame's overlap on to the glass. Chris felt curious, and that was all. He put down the remainder of the frame carefully. Now he was only holding the two photographs, and these he separated and took one in each hand. He turned on the main light, the bulb hanging from the centre of the ceiling with a paper shade, and examined them under it, half expecting they would be two prints of the same image. At first sight this almost seemed to be true.

They were both wedding photographs and they were much alike. The grooms were both dark-haired, reasonably tall and about the same age. Neither of them was fat, although the image which had been underneath was of a slimmer and more handsome man. Both wore dark suits with a carnation in the buttonhole. They both stood at the right hand of their brides. The brides were more riveting for Chris. At first he thought they were both his mother. He noticed that the dress worn by the bride who had been hidden looked a few years earlier in date than the one with which he was familiar. Was it possible that she had been married twice? That was the startling idea which first came to him. His mind raced. Of course if she had been married to someone else before his own father, and presumably the man had died, that would explain why she had hidden the old wedding photograph with her new one, reluctant to throw the earlier one away, unable to quite forget, but anxious not to offend her new husband by having it on view.

He stood until his feet grew cold again, thinking about this possibility. Then he turned off the central light, and getting into bed while still holding both the photographs—a very skilful operation—he leaned on his elbow and laid them side by side on his bedside table, which was actually a folding shelf he had long ago contrived for himself so that he could read comfortably in bed.

The more his eyes went from one bride to the other, the more convinced he became that they were two different girls. They were very alike, and he began to wonder if they had been sisters. His mother had never mentioned a sister, and he felt sorry about that. It would have been fun to have an uncle and aunt, and even cousins of his own age. Perhaps they were still alive, and he would be able to find them. For the first time a slight interest stirred in his family background. Would the brides have been twins? No, he soon dismissed that idea. The underneath photograph was definitely older by some years, judging by the clothing. He remembered his father's wedding suit, which had still been worn occasionally in his own boyhood. It might still be hanging in the front bedroom wardrobe.

The other man's suit looked more old-fashioned. The girl in the underneath photograph was like his mother, but her hair was piled up in a beehive and she was wearing a skimpy white shift which must have been the latest thing at the time. As he went on looking, he saw that her chin was more pointed than his mother's square one, and the way her hair sprang from her forehead was different to the distinctive sideways curve his mother's always had, no matter what she did to it.

'I think it was her older sister,' Chris said to himself at last, putting the two photographs down and turning out his lamp. They had probably quarrelled, he thought. His mind was so intrigued by the possibilities that unwelcome thoughts of bedside mats and gruesome things standing on them were kept away.

The next morning, Tuesday, he went round to talk to Mrs Atkinson.

'What do you want?' she greeted him.

'It won't take a minute. I found a photograph yesterday and wondered if you knew who it was.'

She dried her hands and reached out for it.

'It was under this one of my mother's wedding,' he explained, passing one to her and keeping the other.

'At first sight it looks like your mother.'

'But it isn't. Compare it with this one.'

After a pause, she said, 'No. You're right. There is a strong family likeness. Perhaps it's a cousin.'

'Or a sister.'

'I never heard your mother mention a sister.'

'No. I didn't either.'

'Sorry I can't help you. Goodbye.'

Chris recognised the brush-off, and went. The photographs were intriguing, but they didn't really matter. He was quite happy with the way Mrs Atkinson was treating him. She had never been out to work since her marriage, and long ago, before he went to jail, her habits of thought had been set, and they were familiar to him. He could have impersonated her if he had been a woman of her own age. It gave him a painful kind of pleasure to anticipate her reactions.

He didn't feel well enough to start

on the window frames, although he had bought the tools when he was at Stubbs'. After lunch and drinking several coffees—it was a pleasure to be able to make a drink whenever he liked—he decided he would walk along to the reference library on Museum Street. To stop the constant debate in his head—did I do it—I must have done it—he was determined to look back at the newspapers of the time and read the reports of the trial. He knew what had happened, almost by heart; but there might be a different slant somewhere—he hadn't read the newspaper reports while it was all going on.

The central library looked exactly as it had done twelve years before, a pleasant modern building created before the days of brutalist architecture. It was made of brick and stone and bronze. Chris entered with a grateful feeling of reassurance and safety. There was a double staircase, rising from two sides of the foyer. He walked up the shallow treads, revelling in the graciousness, admiring the arched and coffered ceiling, the colour scheme, the lighting fitment, the whole ambience and smell of the place.

The large reading room with its oak tables and comfortable chairs reassured him that intellectual and cultural life still existed. The assistants at the counter were busy, but in a short time one of them was free and he asked to see the newspapers of twelve years before.

'*The Times* is on microfilm, you would need to book a reader. The *Selby Times*, the *Gazette* and *Herald*, and the *Yorkshire Evening Press* are on microfiche, you could see those now,' the assistant told him. She was a pretty girl with long blonde hair.

'Yes, the local ones will be fine.'

'There is a vacant microfiche reader over there.' And she indicated a small thing like an early television set. 'I'll bring them for you.'

When she came with various microfiche he looked at them, and then the machine, uncertainly.

'Haven't you used one of these before?'

'Well, no, I haven't, actually.'

'Pull out this glass screen, put the microfiche in between the two plates.' And she inserted a black piece of film negative, which is what it looked like to Chris. 'Push them back, turn on the light, look, the text comes up on the screen, move the handles to and fro until you find the part you want to read. If you would like a print-out, come and ask and I'll show you how to do that.'

'Thanks.' Chris smiled radiantly at her. Here was someone who knew nothing about him, and the casual polite contact was heartening. He wriggled the handle of the machine until he found the front page headline, then after reading, wriggled it again until he found the continuation of the story on an inner page. He had not realised that he was such a villain. The little niggling doubt that he could have committed the murder shrank away into nothing. The evidence was so damning no doubt was admissible. He found himself flinching away from the calm letterpress on the screen, hardly able to read it, the import was so horrific. Whoever had done this crime was a brute beyond redemption, and it was an open and shut case. It must have been the talk of the town, while he was locked away from all the furore. He knew now why he had been rushed out of the prison van with a blanket over his head, into the courtroom. The newspaper reports were far worse than the actual trial proceedings, which had that judicial tone and police vocabulary to tone down the horror. This was put into plain everyday language and shocked him afresh.

When Chris rose from his seat he looked haggard. He returned the fiche to the assistant without a smile, and pushed out of the swing doors blindly, stumbling down the elegant stairs and gasping as he reached the outside air. He walked along looking down at the pavement. If ever he had begun to forget the events of twelve years ago, they had come back now in full force. For the first time in years he could clearly visualise the face of his friend, the American. He had only known Tom Bell for some six months, but in that time they had become unusually close.

This had partly been because Chris's mother had taken a liking to Tom, which was not something she had ever done before. She happily asked the lad into the house and invited him for meals. They found subjects of common interest to discuss and several times Chris had arrived home and found his mother and Tom sitting one each side of the fireplace with papers in their hands and cups of tea cooling unnoticed on the table, eagerly discussing something or other. As soon as he came in they had always fallen silent.

'What's all this, then?' he had asked once, only to be told that he wouldn't be interested. All the papers had been shuffled away. He was pleased, not put out, by this strange friendship, feeling that it was good for his mother to have a new interest and to make a friend.

The newspaper reports told how Chris had got drunk at the party and Tom had helped him home. Chris, who had never been drunk before, had shouted and sung and many of the neighbours had been disturbed by the noise. They told reporters how Chris had banged on the door, and his mother shouted she was not letting him in in that state.

Then they heard Tom saying, 'Oh, do open the door, Mrs Simmers,' and at last she did. After a few minutes they had heard Tom saying goodbye as he hurried away, and her voice in reply. Chris remembered helping Tom take his luggage to the station before the party. He was off on a tour of Europe before returning to the States. The night staff in charge of Left Luggage, and the ticket inspector, had both seen and spoken to Tom.

Thinking all this over, Chris had turned right from the library and walked down the road and over Lendal Bridge. One of the minor pleasures of York was a conical roof straight out of a fairy tale, covered by the rich texture of weathered handmade tiles, topping a tiny round building, once the terminus of a ferry.

This little roof was at eye level, but today Chris walked past without a glance in its direction. He had turned without thinking towards the railway station, because this alternative route home made a pleasant change. Being a Scorpio Chris liked to approach his home from different directions, sometimes with stealth, as if to surprise it.

He wondered what interest there had been in common, between those two ill-assorted people, his friend and his mother, that they had not wanted to share with him.

Chris passed the station on the opposite side of the road and was walking towards the junction outside Micklegate Bar, where he intended to turn left, when the car, going too fast and then over-compensating as it rounded the sharp upward bend in the road, drove out of control up the kerb on to the pavement and straight towards him from the rear.

5

Chris never knew, afterwards, why at the crucial moment he had flung himself forwards and escaped the oncoming rush of the car.

He could remember no conscious warning, no change in the note of the vehicle as it reared up on to the pavement and roared towards him. He could only think that he must have developed some sixth sense during the twelve years in prison, some abnormal awareness of events around him, which had taken over and saved his life. As it was he found himself lying on the pavement with a pain in his leg which made him think at first that it was broken. In flashes in his head he retained the split-second images of speed, of the small shin-high wall at the back of the pavement being crunched over, of the bright red bonnet of the car colliding with the trunk of a flowering cherry which grew in the flat grass which ran to the daffodil-covered rise of the city wall. Wheels spinning under the now stationary car, daffodils apparently spinning in the heavens, a stone which had been knocked from the small wall and lay within a fraction of an inch of his temple, made a kaleidoscope he could have done without. The car engine stopped. He shut his eyes and heard the grate of a car door opening over bent bodywork, and the sound of voices. They were speaking in French, loud, idiomatic, rapid French. He opened his eyes to slits, moved his head, and found he was now looking at the road. Then a police car drew up with a squeal of brakes, and an English voice broke in, and an English pair of policeman's feet appeared in his line of vision.

'Are you all right, sir?' asked the policeman's voice with concern, and a fresh young face bent over Chris. He opened his eyes fully.

'I think so. My ankle hurts.'

There was a policewoman, who stood next to the wrecked car, and the young policeman who squatted down by Chris.

'Let's have a look.' He ran his hands over Chris's ankle and Chris had to grit his teeth. 'I think it's only twisted,' said the policeman, moving the leg to a more comfortable position. 'Try standing up.' He pushed an arm under Chris's shoulders and heaved, raising him by degrees. The two foreign-looking men who had been in the wrecked car were talking to the policewoman, still in French, still in loud voices. Chris's French was not equal to their fluency, but the policewoman seemed to be doing all right. As far as he could tell it was all about not being used to driving on the wrong side of the road and the iniquities of the hired car.

'You will have to give a statement, sir,' the policeman said to Chris.

'I think I'm all right. Is a statement really necessary?'

'Oh, I'm sure it will be. Don't worry, we'll drive you to the station and then home again afterwards.'

Chris wanted to visit the police station like he wanted a hole in the head.

Lucy Grindal had been asked to deliver some leaflets. Only because she'd said, 'Can I do anything to help?' Her feet ached, she was tired and in need of a cup of tea, and the old army advice rang through her head, Never Volunteer. How could she help volunteering with no proper job and a conscience the size of a house about service to the community?

So she worked her way along the terrace of small houses inside the old wall of the city. Near here the Roman approach road had led down to the ford, and she remembered how the memorials to their dead had been excavated. They once lined each side of the road. A Roman civilian trading settlement had grown up, here, across the river from the fortress. Drat this letterbox. Lucy struggled with the rusty black iron flap, which had no intention of opening, on the badly weathered door. Just when she was on the last section and she'd been enjoying a little day-dream and—nearby a car pulled up and someone got out.

'Are you going to be all right, sir?'

'Yes, thanks.'

A limping footstep behind her told Lucy that whoever lived in this disreputable-looking house had arrived. She turned with a sheepish expression and found herself nose to nose with a slim, dark man, probably in his early thirties, who was looking at her with an unfathomable and none too friendly expression.

'Good morning. I am delivering leaflets,' said Lucy.

'What about? I don't want to buy anything.'

'Oh no, nothing like that. It's for the church. St Mary Bishophill. To raise money for the work they do in the community.' She tried to speak brightly, fighting against the feeling of being very unwelcome indeed.

The man felt in his pocket and produced a key which he put into the lock, then as he moved the key he turned white and clung to the knob as if he would faint. In about a second he had recovered. The event was so fleeting that if she had been looking away even briefly, Lucy would have missed it.

The door needed a firm push to open it. When he stood safely on the threshold and was looking sideways at Lucy, the man said, 'You can give me the leaflet now, if you like.'

He seemed so much softer and gentler than before that Lucy, who always dashed in where angels fear to tread, asked, 'Are you sure you're all right? Have you been in an accident? Could I make you a cup of tea?'

Saying nothing, the man looked at her. He saw a middle-aged woman with turbulent wiry hair, thickset, in sensible clothes and flat-heeled walking shoes. The clothes, though, were nicely matched in toffee colour, and at her neck she wore an agate brooch with the bands of colour in the agate picking up the toffee shade. The brooch's silver mounting gleamed against the fabric of her shirt. Her face was an open, honest, pleasant face and Chris liked it. He regretted the hard way he had spoken to her at first.

'If you've time, then, and will you have one yourself,' he said, still sounding unfriendly.

Lucy followed him inside. He limped

ahead and she soon found herself in the kitchen, where the man drew out a chair and collapsed on to it. It was not a modern kitchen, but neither was Lucy's at home. She half filled the kettle and found the teapot and some tea-bags. Neither of them spoke again until she had the teapot standing cheerfully on the table and sat down herself. She had lifted two mugs from their hooks under the wall cupboard, sure that mugs were what this young man would prefer.

'I *was* in a slight accident,' Chris said at last, after he had drunk some tea, rolled an exceedingly thin cigarette, and lit it. 'I am only shaken, not stirred.'

'Well, that's good,' replied Lucy, and handed him the leaflet. 'You are almost the last house on my round, and I was ready for this tea.'

Chris studied the leaflet. 'A jumble sale, is it?' he asked.

'Not exactly jumble. Or at least, not only jumble. We like to have a lot of books donated, they are rather a feature of the thing, and anything unusual.'

'For good works in the parish?'

'Better than bad works.' Lucy smiled at him.

'Do you live in this parish?' asked Chris.

'No. I live next to the Minster. My

father's one of the canons, the governing body I suppose you'd call them. Our house goes with the job.'

'I'm Chris Simmers.' And Chris held out his hand.

'Lucy Grindal,' responded Lucy, shaking his hand with all seriousness over the untidy kitchen table.

On finishing his cigarette, Chris took a tin out of his pocket and carefully put the slight remains inside. They sat companionably until they had both drunk their tea. Then he saw Lucy to the door.

'I'll have a look for something suitable for your sale,' he said. 'For next week, is that right?'

'We're coming round collecting on Thursday. If you're out it doesn't matter, you can leave your contributions in a dustbin bag outside the front door, with a label.'

He was alone. He looked at the clock and realised how late it was. Giving that statement at the police station had taken ages, and it was all useless anyway. He couldn't blame the foreigners for having an accident, and he wasn't much hurt—the ankle felt better already than it had earlier. Hot food—that was what he needed, and he was in the middle of cooking when Annie put in an appearance.

'I can do without you just now,' he told her curtly.

How he has changed, she thought. He was a boy of twenty-one, though he seemed so old and wise to me then. Now he's a man of thirty-four, and rather a hard nut.

When she said nothing he felt constrained to add, 'I've had another road accident.'

'I don't remember you being accident prone.'

'I wasn't, and I'm not, dammit. Some bloody tourists who didn't know which side of the road they were supposed to drive on and weren't used to the wheel on the wrong side either.'

'What happened to you?'

'Luckily I jumped out of the way in time, but I fell, and my ankle got twisted. Then the police wanted a statement and then when I arrived home there was a woman delivering leaflets.'

'We've got one too.' Annie looked at the leaflet, which was still lying on the kitchen table. 'They have this sale every year.'

'Anyway, I said I'd try to find something for it. It will give me something to do tomorrow if the ankle still hurts.'

'You ought to tell your probation officer about the accident.'

'What for?'

'He'd want to know. It's strange, two in a week.'

'Only a coincidence, I told you.'

'Was your head banged again?'

'Not to cause any damage.'

'I'm going to ring the probation officer, if you don't.'

He might have resented this interfering attitude if he had noticed it, but her words brought something else to mind.

'I'm supposed to be going round to the Probation Office in the morning.'

'Ring him. It isn't far. He won't mind coming to you, in the circumstances.'

'I don't want him here all the time.'

Anne proclaimed by her silence that this was not the attitude at all. He also said nothing. It was as though a silent debate was going on between them. At last Chris capitulated, with, 'If the ankle still bothers me tomorrow I'll ring him.'

'All right.' It seemed to her that it was time to change the subject. 'What did you do today?'

He told her about his visit to the library, about reading through the newspapers' versions of his trial.

'Wasn't that a bit morbid?'

He couldn't help feeling irritated with her, although her presence cheered him, and although he knew she was right. Before, she had never questioned his

105

actions. She had looked up to him then. Now she was a woman and independent. She had grown used to deciding things. The freedom with which she told him what she thought galled him while at the same time he admired the general air she had of thinking for herself.

'Look, all the time I was in jug I've been telling the trick cyclists that I don't remember doing the murder. Again and again I kept saying it. I've had them up to here.' He gestured angrily at eyebrow level. 'All they reported was that they found me sane. I know I'm sane, but it nearly drove me mad, not really knowing. There was only one way to tackle it—I shut it out of my mind. But now I can't do that any more, girl. This is my home. How can I live here, not knowing? How can I live anywhere, outside prison, not knowing? That *is* going to drive me mad. What a way to die! Poor Mother! If she only had a headstone, I could kneel there and say—whatever happened and whoever did it—I'm sorry...'

'So did reading it up make you feel any better?'

'No, worse.'

'Waste of time, then.'

'I'll tell you something, Anne—I'm going to find out. I'm going to go back over it again and again and find out, no matter what I find. There's got to be something everyone overlooked at the time. There's got to be some way of knowing. I left the library convinced I was the worst monster ever but now I don't feel so sure.'

'It seemed as if the police were pretty thorough.'

'Not thorough enough. They jumped to the conclusion I'd done it and their other investigations must have been a bit skimpy when they were so convinced. Why waste police time on an open and shut case? The same with my brief. Defending a case of obvious matricide—not the job you're going to wax all enthusiastic about, eh?'

There didn't seem to be an answer to that.

'I'll help all I can,' said Anne.

'You've got your own life to live.'

Anne shrugged her shoulders.

'I am seeing everything with a fresh eye. You know that sentence—isn't it L. P. Hartley's—"The past is a foreign country, they do things differently there." Or is it "another country"?' He paused. 'That's how it seems, only more so. You aren't a schoolgirl any more, Anne. I'm not the person I was, and my mother has been dead these long years. I'm going to venture back into that other country.'

'I'll help.'

'Are you sure? Look, I appreciate

everything you've done and are doing. You're the only friend I have outside, that's the fact. But we have to get to know one another all over again. I'm not in the business of expecting anything.'

'I am sure. Two heads are better than one if they're only sheep's. Are you sure you won't mind living here?'

'It's way ahead of a prison cell.'

'Even on your own?'

'Thank God, yes, on my own.'

'You've started with the newspaper reports of the time, right?'

'There's something else as well, which I know by heart but you don't. In my suitcase is a transcript of the court case.'

'How did you get that?' asked Anne in surprise.

'Us criminals do get them.' He was laconic.

They looked at one another.

'Do you think I did it?' he asked at last.

'I've always been sure you didn't.'

'On what grounds?' He couldn't help sounding like prosecuting counsel.

'Because I've known you all my life and because though Mrs Simmers—let's face it, Chris—was often unpleasant, I've never heard you say anything against her. I never knew you be anything but considerate and kind towards her.'

He was looking at the floor and tracing the pattern of the old linoleum with his foot.

'I told you I remember nothing of the murder. But you see I do remember some things,' he said, softly and gently. 'I remember when I was a little boy. I remember fairly well up to the age of six, but only very babyish things. Other people were more presences than observed. Can you understand that? From that early time I have no mental picture of Mother or Father, only a sensation of their loving presence. All the time and care and money they must have lavished on me has left nothing concrete in my mind. Toys, playmates, experiences like starting school, like falling down, like eating ice-cream, those are the kind of things which have stayed clear to me.'

Anne tried to think back. 'Perhaps that's all any of us recall from early childhood,' she said. 'Why is it important?'

'Because there is a blank for me after the age of about six. And that early blank may be connected in some way, which no one understands, with the later blank. I know, because I gathered this afterwards, that for a time Mother and Father went away and I was left here, in this house, in the care of my grandmother and grandfather Nourny. Then Mother came back and later Father

109

must have done so too, because when my memory starts again they were both here and we were all living together, and soon after that Grandad Nourny died, I remember that very clearly, and everything from then on. Your parents coming to live next door, you being born, daily life, school.'

Anne didn't have any comment to make so she waited for him to go on.

'When Mother came back, in the time which has gone from me, it seems that she had changed in some way, and she went on changing, Anne, changing into the person you remember. Perhaps it was some dreadful experience she had had. But I could never forget how she had been when I was small, that she had been a loving presence and my refuge.'

'Someone killed her,' Ann said flatly. 'Whoever it was.'

'She was murdered. Someone killed her. If it was me—well, all right. If that was the case I must accept it, which I haven't managed to do yet. But if it was someone else...'

A look came over his face which startled Annie Atkinson. She felt herself shiver as if a goose had walked over her grave. It was a look which told her that this man could kill. That was not something which had entered her head before. But this evening

Chris was different from the other times they had been together since he came out. She felt almost frightened.

'Mother will have my meal ready.' She prepared to go.

'It would have made me feel better if the police had found my friend, Tom Bell. But I don't think they even tried. I'd really like to talk to Tom.'

'Do you think he could exonerate you?'

'No. But there might be some scrap of evidence he could give which would put a different complexion on things.'

'I saw him leave, did you know?' she asked. 'I knew him by sight, he'd been at your house a lot. That night I was woken up by your front door opening.'

'You didn't see me arrive home drunk?' Chris felt the blood rising to his face for the first time in years. He thought he'd stopped feeling the emotion of shame. But he would have hated her to see him like that. 'Other people in the road saw Tom bringing me home.'

'It's possible that had disturbed me a few minutes earlier, but it was as he went that I woke. Your mother had opened the front door and she stood on the step. I opened my bedroom window, dying to know what was going on, and put my head out. I could see the top of her head and see Tom. He was going, but because he was talking to her he was half turned round even though he was getting farther away.'

'You don't remember what was said, I suppose?'

'Perfectly. She said, "I'll tell him in the morning, then, Tom. It's a pity you won't be there, to see how pleased he'll be. A lovely birthday surprise."'

Chris could do nothing but stare at Anne.

'Then Tom said, "I wish I could be with you both, Mrs Simmers, after all our hard work on the project."'

'And?' Chris choked out, hoarsely.

'Your mother said, "Trust him to get drunk and spoil our plan to tell him tonight. Goodnight, then, Tom."'

'I didn't read this in the papers,' he said.

'I didn't tell anyone.'

'And you remember so exactly.'

'It was a beautiful calm clear moonlit night. I've always loved moonlight. The voices were so close. Then, the events of next morning must have fixed that conversation in my mind. Later events can, you know. By making you remember something instead of forgetting it, it registers permanently.'

'It wouldn't have made any difference to the trial,' he said, 'but it sure makes

112

a difference to me. They had some project—that was obvious. I didn't like being excluded. But if it was being saved as a birthday surprise—I wonder what it was. Nothing important, or it would have come up later.'

He was gentle and softened now, but the fierce look he had worn earlier had made an impression on Anne. She thought she would go.

'You are a bit worked up this evening, Chris,' she said consideringly as she paused at the open back door. 'It's probably due to the accident. You should have had a sedative from the doctor. Don't forget to tell your probation officer about it tomorrow—promise?'

'Promise,' he said, and smiled as she remembered he used to. It was the first time she had seen him smile like that since he'd been home. Perhaps he's been in a chrysalis, she thought, and now he's slept his sleep and is breaking out of it. Or perhaps he's only over-excited by these accidents. He should have had his temperature taken, he's probably feverish. He'd talked more to her, taken her into his confidence. Then, her bit of information had pleased him. She ought to feel happy about that, but she felt anything but happy as she walked into her mother's kitchen.

Steve Watson was seriously upset the next day when, in the Probation Office on Priory Street, Chris told him about the second accident.

'You should have rung me.'

'What good would that have done?'

'I could have told the police your circumstances,' Steve said.

'That would have made things worse, don't you think so?'

'Last week your bike was sabotaged, deliberately.'

'Yes.'

'This week someone drives off the pavement straight at you,' Steve said.

'Coincidence.'

'It looks like that. How could there be any connection? All the same, I'm going to have a word with a detective inspector I know, on the quiet. He'll have a discreet look at the records of the accident and see if there's anything fishy about these tourists.'

'If anyone's got it in for me they will be locals, not bloody tourists.' Chris was more forceful than he had dared to be, yet, with his probation officer.

'That makes sense. But an accident a week doesn't make sense.'

'It was the moving finger of fate,' said Chris.

'It's changed you, whatever it was. You

hadn't two words for the dog when you came out of prison. Today you've been quite loquacious.'

Chris sat and thought about that. 'You're right. I was talking more last night, too, to Anne Atkinson. I got out of the way of talking much, in jug.'

'You're shaken up by the accident. It might not last.' And Steve smiled, implying that it wouldn't matter if his parolee lapsed back into quietness.

All the same, pure coincidence or not (and how could it be anything else?) Steve went down to the door of the building with Chris and stood watching him as he limped out of sight. He reached the corner quite safely. Back in his office Steve paused, looking at the phone, then decided to walk over to the police detectives' office in Castlegate. There were still police offices near the magistrates' courts and the Assize Courts, although police headquarters had been at Fulford for some time. Steve wanted a word with Detective Inspector Dave Smart, a man he knew. But before going over he gave Smart a quick ring, to be sure that he wouldn't be taking a wasted journey.

'You just want a word?' repeated Dave Smart. 'Right, then, come on over. No, I'm not busy, only typing up reports. I'll be glad to be interrupted, if you want to know.'

Even by Steve Watson, who occupied that uncomfortable no man's land between the police force and the social workers.

Lucy Grindal had been making coffee for herself and her father, Canon Grindal, in their rambling old house next to the cathedral. They were in the breakfast room, which faced south and had a wonderful sideways view of the east end of the great cathedral building. This room caught the sun and was particularly pleasant at mid-morning.

'I hardly saw you yesterday,' Lucy said to her father.

'You were distributing those leaflets.'

'But you dashed out in the morning, you weren't in for an evening meal, and you were tired when you did appear.'

George Grindal smiled, his ugly, bumpy, squashed-in face lighting up with generous affection. It was the shape of his nose which made people infer, wrongly, that he had been a boxer in his youth. The lovely thing about Canon Grindal which people did notice was his voice, which sounded like chords rather than single notes, and with which he could still sing beautifully. His soul was beautiful too.

'You are quite right, Lucy. I'm not

getting any younger and do tire more easily. A day out of the house, like yesterday, does exhaust me. Are you going to tell me to slow down a bit? Is that what all this is about?'

'You wouldn't take the slightest notice,' replied Lucy, returning the smile. 'No, I only wanted to exchange news. I had an odd encounter when I was out, as you so accurately remember, delivering leaflets.'

'What sort of an encounter?'

'Originally with a letterbox. I was struggling with one that didn't want to open. Hadn't been used much for years, judging by its stiffness and the state of the house. Then a young chap arrived who was delivered by police car. I caught a glimpse of it as it rounded the corner, going away. He had been in a road accident. He asked me in and we had a drink of tea.'

'That doesn't sound very unusual. You're always having tea with somebody.'

'I think he had recently been in prison,' Lucy said thoughtfully.

'What makes you think that?'

'Rolling cigarettes...putting the stubs in a tin...'

'Common enough habits, no indication at all,' said Canon Grindal.

'A certain way of looking and speaking, not a trusting, normal way.'

'What you mean is, your father does a

lot of work with young men in one kind of trouble or another, here's a case which might interest him,' said her father in his deep, beautiful, chord-like voice, which was a pleasure to hear.

'Yes, Daddy dear.'

Canon Grindal drank his coffee slowly. 'I can't descend on him and insist on being taken into his confidence,' he said at last, obviously taking Lucy's intuitions seriously.

'No, of course you can't. I suppose nothing can be done.'

'Give me his address. Do you know his name?'

'Yes.'

'And name, then. I can't do anything at all out of the blue. But I can keep an eye and an ear on the alert on his behalf and if anything comes up...'

'Bless you, darling,' said Lucy.

'I only wanted to talk to you about two traffic accidents,' Steven Watson said to Dave Smart when they were sitting comfortably in the office Dave shared with the other detectives. Dave was as tall as Steve, but a good deal more heavily built, red-faced, with dark crisply curling hair. They hadn't met since Dave had been on that case concerning a murdered girl he'd found by the river early one morning—the girl all in black apart from her red suspenders.

'Traffic's not my department,' said Dave stolidly.

'No. Well, look. You could ask to see the police record of the second one. As far as I know there was no report of the first.'

'I could do that thing. Now try to persuade me that it's a good idea and wouldn't be a waste of my time.'

Steve persuaded him.

Across the Atlantic, in a typical small town in America, the Director of the Nournavaile Institute for the Study of Ageing was chairing the weekly meeting of the management committee.

Dr Albrick was a handsome elderly man, silver-haired, who would have been retired years ago if he had not been unsackable as head of the establishment. He was probably the most able person on the staff. He was immensely learned and cultured as only an old-fashioned American can be, and was respected world-wide. 'Before we close our meeting today,' he said, looking round the men sitting at the long polished table, 'I'd like to tell you of a somewhat disturbing incident which happened to me yesterday. You are all so busy with your respective departments, the nursing wings and the research labs, that it has probably slipped your minds, but we did commission a genealogist in London, England to check into the present-day descendants of the Nournavaile family. Time is nearly up for us in this quest and we don't seem to be getting any results. So I gave them a bell and as it happened the head of the firm was out and I found myself talking to a new assistant there, a lady called Margaret. What she said was most enlightening. They have, in effect, stopped looking. Margaret herself has done well, tracing her own family, and she was eager to work on our case but her head man would not allow her to do so.' There was a murmur of surprise from the rest of the committee. The Director rose from the table and strolled to the window to gaze out over the beautifully landscaped grounds of the institute towards the bustle of the interstate highway, which ran along the perimeter. A row of tall trees rising from a bank of shrubs screened out much of the noise and pollution. 'Hire someone else immediately,' he heard from the table behind him. 'Send someone over to find out what's going on,' said someone else. 'That is my own inclination.' The Director strolled back and seated himself once more in his chair. 'Who could we send? Is there anyone in our organisation who knows a bit about the subject? I gather these old British records are tricky to use, that's why we employed a local specialist in the first place.

'We owe a lot to old Arthur Z. Nournavaile,' went on the Director in an almost dreamy voice. 'I want us to achieve for his memory what he was not able to do in the flesh. Without his intervention we'd never have got the state funding. That's why we bear his name. Thanks to his unfailing support we were able to do good work and we're still doing good work.'

'We finished our annual accounts yesterday,' said the Head of Finance, 'and I have a bright young man I could spare for a couple of weeks: Dwight Brisling.'

'Sounds good,' said the Director. 'I'd like to meet him and put him in the picture. After all, a free trip to Europe is an attractive proposition, if he's right for the job he'd have to do.'

The telephone rang on Steve Watson's desk in the Probation Office in Priory Street.

'Watson,' he said into the handset.

'Smart here,' said Dave. 'You asked me about a traffic accident.'

'You've had a look at it? Great!'

'The tourists were as normal as they come.'

121

'Oh.'

'Why, did you want them to be international crooks?'

'I suppose not.' But Steve sounded rueful.

'Two perfectly normal blokes from Boulogne. Used to seeing English tourists over there and thought they'd like to see what the English were escaping from, so they set out on a tour, starting in York, which was to be their farthest point north. They had only taken over their hire car a couple of minutes before the accident. They did breathalyse positive, but apparently they always have wine with their lunch and they had been drinking on the train. They weren't much over the limit.'

'Coincidence, then.'

''Fraid so.'

'Thanks, Dave.'

Chris's ankle was still swollen and stiff so he spent the time, between putting on cold compresses, searching for things for the local jumble sale, as he called it. The back bedroom was the obvious place to start, and he turfed out the old curtains, pensioned-off blankets, and antediluvian sheets, and stuffed them into a black bin-liner. That made quite a clearance. Then, with something of a pang, he sorted through his mother's cast-off shoes. Some were no good and had to be thrown away, but others looked as though they might still be useful and these were put with the sheets for the sale. It did not take long for the bed and the corners and most of the floor to be cleared. Chris looked around and realised that the room now looked much more as it had when Granny Nourny was alive. It had suddenly begun to look pleasant instead of forlorn. He humped the bags downstairs. Then he sorted systematically through the cupboards and drawers in the room. Everything in them seemed to be cast-offs once belonging to his mother, or else the indeterminate kind of rubbish which accumulates in most households if it is allowed to. He turfed a lot of that out as well, then finished by fetching the vacuum and giving the place a good clean, including the mattress and bedding, all of which were dusty. He found himself enjoying the rather mindless task, and looking round for other things to run the nozzle over. He cleaned all the drawers and cupboards with it, took the good bedding and decent curtains down to the kitchen to wash later, and gave the furniture a rub with a duster.

Although he'd been trying to stand with his weight on his good foot, the sprained ankle had decided enough was enough and was throbbing. With a new cold compress soothing the pain, he flopped into an armchair and put his foot on the coffee table. As he rested, he mentally thanked Lucy Grindal for her visit. Without it, he would hardly have tackled the clear-out, and he was feeling a pleasing glow of virtue. What else, he wondered, could he find to give her for the sale?

Things in his own room were staying, no danger. He hadn't the heart to tackle his mother's room. Wait a minute, he said to himself. There's the attic. Mentally he ran over the various boxes and suitcases. Must be something in those which he would never want, but someone else might find interesting. He thought of Anne Atkinson and her recording of old people's memories. He'd have a look—as soon as his ankle recovered a bit—and if in doubt, he'd ask Annie. For the first time his thoughts of her were more natural, without the trepidation and unease which had bedevilled them. He was gradually moving towards accepting that she was no longer a child and his substitute sister, but an adult who knew more about some things than he did, and could become a close friend.

Annie, he thought as he looked wistfully at his ankle. Annie will know what sort of old junk people will want to buy.

6

'Come up into the attic,' Chris said to Anne when he next saw her, after she finished work that Wednesday. They were a little uneasy and on edge with each other. As a result they spoke in a carefully casual, offhand, even jokey way. She could not forget what she had seen at their last meeting—that this man had a capacity for violence, if certain emotions were aroused; that he was no tame pussycat.

'Ooh, I thought you'd never ask.' she said.

The evening sun was bringing out the bright glitter of her hair, and Chris thought it was a pity to take her into a fusty attic and risk getting it dulled, even perhaps cobwebbed, but he might need her expertise. Anyway, she looked so excited at the prospect that he hadn't the heart to change his mind and rescind the invitation. He led the way up the narrow bare wooden stair, still limping slightly.

'I like the attics in these houses,' Anne said when she arrived up there beside him. 'I always wanted to have ours for a bedroom but Mother wouldn't hear of it.'

'We used to have all kinds of games in the attics, me and the boys from school. I don't remember you and I coming up much, Anne.'

'No, we didn't, though I do remember watching the tourists from this window.' She crossed over to it. 'Nice and clean,' she added.

'After all my hard work I should think so.'

She seemed to be absorbed in the view so Chris tackled the nearest suitcase. It was rather disappointing to find it full of shoes, far older than those he had found downstairs.

'Any good, Anne?' he said doubtfully. She came to look.

'How quaint! Yes, they might be interesting to a collector of costume. I'll dispose of those for you.'

'Costume's the word.' He put the case ready to take downstairs.

The next was a box of papers, mainly, he found, relating to himself. There were all his school reports going back to the year dot by the look of it, in a large brown envelope.

'Keep those,' said Anne.

'You needn't think I'm going to let you read them!'

'What do they say? Must try harder? Should not shout out in class?'

'Watch it. You might get your hair pulled.'

'Those are your school exercise books.'

'Looks like.' He lifted them out and put them separately on the boards. There were various other records of his schooldays, things which he had forgotten, but which looked familiar. At last he found a piece of paper which Anne caught from his hand.

'Here's your birth certificate!'

'Big deal.' Chris was scrabbling about in the bottom of the box.

'No, really, Chris, I told you we needed it if you are to trace your family tree and find out if you're connected to those Nournavailes.'

He sat back on his heels. 'Don't I keep telling you, Madam Annie, that all I want to find out is more about my mother's death and try to solve the puzzle of how and why it happened?'

'This won't help us much, anyway,' she said in a disappointed tone as though she had 'lost a tanner and found a sixpence', as the saying is.

'It's what you said you wanted.'

'It's only a short certificate. That's no use if you're tracing your family. You need a full one.'

Chris looked. The certificate gave name, sex, date of birth and that was about it.

'What do I do to get a full one?'

'This was issued by the Registrar General from an address in Hampshire, so the same address will be able to issue you with a full certificate, if you were born in that area.'

'I was told I was born in this house.'

'That's funny. I'm not sure if you can be registered in an area you weren't born in, but there's no problem. As soon as your ankle feels well enough for the walk, go along Bootham to the Register Office and ask. You will have to pay for a full certificate. Take this with you. Usually for people born in York they can go straight to the original and make a copy. They sometimes do it the same day, if they aren't busy.'

Chris had exhausted the contents of the box. 'Give it to me, then.' He folded the certificate and slid it into his pocket. 'I'm putting these schoolbooks and things back again. They aren't any use for the sale and I'd quite like to keep them. Are you ready for a break, because I am. A smoke and a mug of tea.'

'We've hardly started.'

He hesitated. 'One more box, then.'

Anne saw that he looked tired. His face had lines she had never noticed before, and he was pale. It had been rough on him, two accidents in a week.

They turned to the next box along the wall.

'These look more interesting,' said Anne.

'Postcards, only old postcards.'

'Don't you know that old postcard albums fetch high prices in salerooms nowadays?'

'Really? Well, I'm looking at them first before you get your mitts on them. This one isn't a postcard album, it's more like a scrapbook.' The thick pages had been covered with newspaper cuttings. 'Anne,' he said, 'you're on about the Nournavailes. This is all about them. But the cuttings look very old.'

'Nineteen fifties and sixties,' said Anne over his shoulder. 'Are they in date order?'

'Seem to be. I bet this was Granny Nourny's, and it must be about relatives of hers.'

'Are you settling down for hours up here, Chris? You were on about a mug of tea a minute since. Come down, bring that with you, I'll make one.'

It was while they were drinking their tea in the dining-room that the cat arrived. Anne's attention was absorbed by a postcard album she was examining, and Chris had been studying the outside of the album of newspaper cuttings before opening it again. There was a soft thump at the narrow window on to the yard, and they turned their heads to see an old cat, a large old cat with shaggy grey fur. It was a cat of indescribably battered appearance glowering in at them, through the window, with huge golden eyes. An indignant, demanding, primeval howl could be heard even through the glass. The animal stretched its jaws wide and howled at them again.

'It's that stray,' said Anne. 'An old tom. We've seen him about, a time or two. No one can get near him. A few people have put food out.'

'He came and looked down at me from the wall, while I was doing the bike. Do you think he's hungry?'

The cat glared malevolently and yowled again.

'That seems to be the message,' said Anne.

'I don't know what you feed cats on. We haven't had one since I was little.'

'Tins of cat food. But a saucer of milk will do, I should think, if you feel kindly disposed towards him.'

Chris laid down the album and went to feed the cat, while Anne watched through the window, too lazy to move further. The dining-room was small and crowded, with a table, four upright chairs, and the two small fireside chairs with wooden arms. A sideboard fitted into one alcove and some shelves into the other. The carpet was in shades of brown, the paintwork brown and the walls had an old dim paper of cream, the pattern nearly faded away. She guessed it had not been redecorated since the old lady, Chris's grandmother, died. As long as Anne had been popping in and out of the house it had always been the same, and it felt like home.

Chris glanced up at her as he put down a saucer of milk for the cat and a dish of pilchards. While he was close the cat stayed on the windowsill, but when he came back into the house and rejoined Anne, the old tom approached the food and at last ate voraciously, looking round warily from time to time.

'He's a battle-scarred old warrior if you like,' Chris said.

'A lovely colour, though, that soft even grey and with long fur. He looks as if he has some Persian in him.'

'His fur's matted and full of burrs and tangles and he's been fighting, there are bleeding claw marks on his head, and old scars.'

The cat looked round as if he could hear them and gave them a vicious glare through the window before turning his head back to the dish.

'I wonder where he sleeps.'

'Any old place,' Anne informed him.

'It's a pity I have to lock the sheds. I'll make him a shelter. There's some old wood.'

'I must go soon, do you realise it's getting late? And I'm not going before I know what you will find in that album.'

'All right, Madam Annie. I'll make a shelter later.'

'He probably won't use it.'

Chris shrugged. He had taken a liking to the cat, to his demanding food as of right, like a highwayman or a pirate, not joining but preying on society. He hoped he would shelter under the wood he meant to rear against the wall in one corner. There were some old sacks which could go underneath.

Then he forgot all about the cat as he finally began to read the pages of the album. He opened it at the beginning and looked carefully at the inside of the cover, and the first page.

'You haven't changed at all, in some ways,' smiled Anne. 'You always did begin at the beginning and read to the end, with books. First the introduction or preface and then Chapter One and straight through to the adverts at the back.'

'That's how you are meant to read them,' Chris said.

'It isn't how I do it.'

'I know all about you. You open a book

in the middle and read a paragraph and either say, yes, I can read this, or no, I can't read this, no way.'

'At least I don't carry on like a girl at work. She looks at the end.'

'That's dreadful. Don't you realise the author and the publishers spend a lot of time planning the sequence in a book? You are meant to read from front to back to get the proper effect. Anyway, this isn't a book in the real sense, though it is chronological. It starts, if you want to know, with this bloke, Roger Nournavaile, getting some prize for being Action Photographer of the Year for the *Yorkshire Post*. There's a picture. It looks like a rugby match.'

Anne came and leaned on the back of the chair so that she could look over his shoulder. Chris turned the pages very slowly, because he was reading all the text and the bits written in by hand. These were usually the name of the newspaper and the date. He thought he could recognise the elegant formal handwriting of his Granny Nourny. It was obvious that the young press photographer had gone on to more exciting things than the local rugby match. He had become a war correspondent, and chased the theatres of battle round the globe. They had hardly progressed a third of the way through when Anne sighed, straightened up and said that she must go.

'I won't see you again until Saturday,' she added.

'More oral history?' he asked.

'Tomorrow, yes, then I'm going to see a film on Friday.'

'On your own?'

'No, with Graham. He used to work in our office but he was moved to the Acomb branch.' Anne worked in a building society in York city centre.

Chris froze for an instant, then said casually, 'Do you go out with him often?'

'Now and then.'

'I expect you've had lots of boyfriends, Anne.'

She picked up the light jacket she had arrived in and slipped it on. 'Quite a few.'

'Serious?'

She laughed. 'Depends what you mean by serious.'

'Serious I suppose is when you sleep with them.'

Anne shrugged in the way she seemed to have acquired in the last years.

'This is the nineteen nineties,' she said. 'Sleeping with a man is hardly classed as "serious" these days. See you Saturday. If your ankle's better we'll do a bit of ancestor hunting. It'll stop you getting into any more road accidents.'

It was only what I expected, Chris

134

thought when she had gone. I was sure she had had relationships, she's an attractive girl. 'This is the nineteen nineties.' That's what she said. He examined his conscience to see if he was disturbed by the idea of Anne's 'serious' relationships (they would be serious in his book, anyway, if they involved full sex), but found that he was not.

He asked himself if he would like to be going to the film with her instead of this Graham, and knew that he would hate it. In the darkness an enemy could attack—no, he was better where he was, at home. Safe. Perhaps.

Before it grew too dark he wanted to make the shelter for the cat, who was nowhere to be seen. He might come back, and if he did, Chris wanted him to feel welcome. Going out into the yard, he reared up an old cupboard door against the wall, near to a corner but not quite in it, so that there was an escape route at the back. The sacks were ancient but they were dry and should be quite acceptable, Chris thought, to the battered angry old warrior tom. Then he locked up carefully and went inside, to the excitement of the tale unfolding in the album of cuttings.

He was soon enthralled by the stories and the pictures of far-off wars and floods and famines. The pictures were usually credited to Roger Nournavaile, the articles if they had a byline were normally by one Peter Smith. The two men appeared to have worked as a team. The worst shock came when he turned a leaf and was confronted by a wedding photograph, the twin to the one he had discovered under that of his own parents. The handwriting underneath said only, 'Roger's wedding to Prue, August 1958.'

They are, he whispered to himself. They are connected to me, in some way, these two. I knew they must be. How, though, and who, and what relation? Only by marriage, I suppose. He sat alone in the plain little room with the old furniture and the old-fashioned centre lamp which shone harshly on the few dull brass ornaments on the mantelpiece, ornaments which had once twinkled so brightly, and the economical old gas fire. Solitary, alone, he yet felt caught up in some mysterious web of time and space and blood links, and the curdling howl of the tom-cat outside echoed his mood of strangeness. His heart beat strongly and he felt as though he could transcend the unknown, rend the veil, shatter the glass through which he could now only see darkly.

It was Mrs Atkinson who lost her sleep that night. She used the back bedroom,

Anne the front. Chris next door was snug in his boxroom, with its window over his front door. He heard nothing, but Mrs Atkinson came round early next morning to complain bitterly. 'Anne tells me you have been feeding that stray cat,' she began, without the preliminary of a greeting or a comment on the warmth of the sun.

'Yes.' Now what, he thought.

'You shouldn't do that, Chris. It only encourages him. I didn't get a wink of sleep.'

'I'm sorry you didn't sleep. Do you mean because of the cat? Were you lying awake thinking about it?'

Chris sounded concerned but she wasn't letting him off like that. 'You must have heard that howling he set up in the small hours. I'd managed to drop off at last and it was a dreadful shock to wake like that, at two in the morning. No one would think a cat could make such a noise. And then there was the shouting. I'd blame you for that but it wasn't your voice.'

'I didn't hear a thing.'

'No, neither did Anne. I sleep at the back, I had to suffer it all.'

'Tell me about it. Would you like a cup of tea?'

Mrs Atkinson was soothed by the concern in his voice and nearly agreed until she remembered that in Chris's kitchen...

'No, I have work to do. Can't stand gossiping all day. But I'll tell you about the noise before I go. First there was a scraping and scratching kind of sound, like a cat makes but louder, like sawing wood, that's what it was like, so that I was lying awake and listening. Then a louder noise like a bang but not a bang. Then all hell broke loose with that cat, squealing and screeching he was, and a man's voice swearing at him. That went on a long time but it really wasn't as long as it seemed. I'd put my light on and looked at the clock. At first I was going to get up and look out the window but then I thought, better not. After a bit the cat shut up. The noise went sort of quiet and gradually died away.'

Mrs Atkinson had impressed even herself with her scene-painting. She nodded a few times in self-congratulation.

'I wish I had heard it.' Chris was uneasy. 'Are you sure the noise was from my back yard?'

'Oh yes, quite positive.'

'Thank you for telling me. I'm sorry the cat disturbed you but I like him and I'm going to go on feeding him, no matter what.'

'Oh well,' said Mrs Atkinson, who had

no active dislike of animals, although she would not have one in her immaculate house.

Chris was glad afterwards that she had told him of the disturbance. It put him on his guard. He looked for the cat but there was no sign of him, although the old sacks had a round hollow in the middle of them, and he found a wisp of grey fur on a sharp raw edge of the wooden cupboard door he had used to make the shelter.

He was planning to make a start on the repairs to window frames today although emotionally he was exhausted after Wednesday, and his ankle still hurt a bit. First he heaved out the ladders from the place at the back of the shed where he had stored them after washing the windows. Once the two lengths were standing up in the yard, he decided to raise them to the bathroom window, in the extension over the part they used to call the scullery. No one had sculleries any more. He would have to remember to call it the utility room. He had a feeling of predestination, of fate. Before mounting the ladder he paused, and examined every rung. The first time he'd used the ladders he had taken this precaution and the whole thing had been perfectly sound; he'd felt a bit of a fool. But when someone will sabotage your bike, they might also sabotage your ladder, and once again he checked it.

This time, he found that several of the rungs had been cut through at one end, near the uprights. It had been done so stealthily that the casual glance, even the careful survey, might well have missed it. There was nothing to prove that it had been done at two o'clock in the previous night, of course, but for the first time Chris felt scalded by a mixture of fear and fury. Couldn't he be safe in his own home? And he felt that a nebulous something or somebody was threatening his life. They—whoever they were—wanted to kill him.

A shudder ran through his slender body. He'd faced hostility in the nick. He wouldn't kowtow to the boss-prisoner on his landing and it had taken months of passive resistance, and active resistance too, before the other man accepted it and left him alone. From then on he'd been regarded as something of an outsider. He molested nobody unless someone molested him first, but neither did he toe anyone else's line. He had lived in a strange isolation in the midst of hundreds of other men, affable with everyone but only making a few friends, and even with those few he had been reserved, keeping his innermost being, his thoughts, his wishes, close hugged in the secrecy of silence. Then he realised that he could perfectly well mend the window from the inside, and, shaking slightly with the strength of his anger and revolt against the turn of events and their influence upon him, he set about doing that. It took him the rest of the day. The evening, except for the absence of Anne, was not very different to the previous one. There was the album to finish reading, and the cat reappeared as darkness fell. Well before that, he had reached the end of the cuttings, reading each with fascination. It was only at the end, when he found that the last page of all had been roughly ripped out and was missing, that he felt defrauded and empty. At the cat's first ear-splitting howl he went out and gave him half a tin of the food he had bought at the corner shop. On the whole the cat seemed to have preferred the pilchards, but began to eat. It was only when Chris, wanting to see how bad various wounds were, stood a little nearer, that the old tom left the food and with a growl launched himself at Chris's ankle.

Shrieking with fury he lashed into Chris with teeth and claws, clinging on with both ears flat back against his skull. Involuntarily Chris cried out and, reaching down, intended to tear the cat from his flesh, but before he could touch him the creature had jumped off and now stood a yard away, glaring and still hissing.

'That's exactly what it was like in the night,' called Mrs Atkinson from over the wall between the two back yards.

'Mrs Atkinson! Was it? Is that what it sounded like? He's been kicked at some time, there's no doubt about that. He's terrified of feet if they come too near.'

'That's exactly what it was like, only it wasn't your voice, of course.'

'No wonder it woke you up.'

'I was washing the pots in the kitchen just now. If I'd been in the lounge watching telly I'd never have heard it. Have you still got that cat there? You'd better have him put down.'

'That would be a pity. He's fought for his life, better let him have it while he can. You should see the state he's in.'

'Don't say I didn't tell you,' warned his neighbour as she went inside.

'You and me together, eh, old tom?' said Chris softly, but the cat retreated a few steps. 'What shall I call you? Sam. That's your name. Understand me? Sam.'

The cat hissed. Chris felt it politic to leave. Once he was in the house and out of sight the cat went back to the food and milk.

The night was still young. He thought he would read the album through again.

It had raised all kinds of thoughts and queries. Although it had never occurred to him before, he considered now that he would have liked to be a photographer, one of the best (obviously), travelling to exciting places which were under the stress of war and revolution. What had he ever done with himself, when he had the chance, before that night so many years ago? Home and school and then a job in a bank, mundane if anything ever was, this quiet domestic street with its decent friendly terrace houses, and only the silent barrier of the old city walls opposite to make the inhabitants feel that they lived somewhere special. There was that, of course. He'd always been intrigued by the history of his ancient home town. Once he'd spent his summer holidays on one of the archaeological digs which had formed a continuous saga as first one site and then another had gradually unfolded more and more of the history of the city. Anne had gone with him to watch the excavations on Bale Hill, further along the road, when she was only a toddler. He'd told her stories of the old Romans and Vikings and the Middle Ages and the Tudors and the Council of the North and then the Civil War with Cavaliers and Roundheads. He'd read her Kipling's *Puck of Pook's Hill,* still a vivid representation of different eras, and when she was older, Rosemary Sutcliff's books—but by then she preferred to read them to herself.

Thinking of Anne reminded him of his birth certificate. He'd go along first thing in the morning and order a full one.

7

Now that spring was advanced enough for daffodils York was crowded with tourists, as anxious to see the dancing yellow heads on the green banks which ran up to the old city walls of creamy limestone as they might be to see the same flowers along the margins of Wordsworth's lake, or along the river banks in Farndale, where the dainty small-flowered wild daffodils spring up here and there in the grass.

After squeezing past the bin-liners he had filled with surplus items for the jumble sale and put by his front doorstep the previous day, Chris walked along to Priory Street, down Micklegate, then left along Rougier Street before crossing the River Ouse by way of Lendal Bridge, thinking as he did so that in York in the spring there was no escaping from daffodils. They had been in every front garden of the terrace except his own tiny scrap, which was two square yards of dismal earth, apart from the ivy and the buddleia. They were in the leafy tree-shaded churchyard of Holy Trinity, Micklegate, and in sheaves in the windows of the greengrocer's. They were gilding the archway which had once been cut through the city walls to allow the access of trains to the old station created by the Railway King, George Hudson. The trains no longer came inside the city wall, but the arch was now used by a busy road and across the head of it was a walkway and a flower bed full of daffodils. They were evident in sprays of colour in the Museum Gardens as he walked past and an exaltation of them sang out bright yellow greetings from the flower bed in the centre of the road at the Blake Street junction. The gracious curve of St Leonards Place was enhanced by tubs and window-boxes of daffodils and they could not even be escaped as Chris turned away from the city centre and headed up Bootham towards the Register Office. Here the stately Georgian town houses, now used for so many different purposes, rose straight from the pavement, but here and there a window-box, a tub, the tiny public garden with silver birches and seats, a bunch of flowers in a girl's arms, all called out the same message, daffodils.

Although Chris was sated with the message, he had taken in little else on his journey. Every sense had been alert for attack.

His ears, straining to hear any untoward sound amongst the myriad, his eyes, seeking always to view in the near-circle only possible to owls, his mouth, slightly open as if the heavy air he breathed carried the scent and taste of danger, were only parts of the tenseness of his whole body, tense as though through the skin itself he could recognise the approach of murderous intent.

It was a relief to reach the Register Office, just past the house where W.H. Auden was born, and mount the shallow steps to a pillared door. He moved into the shadowed gracious hallway. At a hatch in the wall, he explained his errand and proffered his short birth certificate. 'It says some other county, but I was born in York,' he ended.

The woman who took the short certificate and gazed at it obviously had experience in these matters.

'I'm afraid I can't help you here, sir,' she said. 'You will have to buy a full certificate by post from Southport. I can give you the forms.'

'Well, if you could do that, please.'

She passed him a Form 18b and a copy of Leaflet 20 which gave charges. Crossing neatly through one section on the back of 18b, she said, 'That address is no longer in operation. Send to this other one.'

'Thanks.'

She gave him a pleasant smile and a

'Good morning', and turned to deal with the next person.

On the way back Chris called at the library and photocopied his short birth certificate, thinking he could put in a copy with the application form; it might save whoever dealt with it a lot of searching. Then he decided he had better visit the bank and arrange to have a cheque book and a current account. He had put off going because, years ago, he had opened his account, naturally enough, at the branch where he used to work. Would anyone there still remember him? It seemed unlikely. His contemporaries would have moved up the promotion ladder long ago, and that almost always meant moving to another town.

But it was difficult to make himself go into the bank. The shining floor, the gleaming glass of the partitions, the neatness of the assistants pointed the difference between himself and the staff on the other side of the windows. No, he could not see anyone he knew. The girl behind the counter thought his account was too unusual altogether for her to deal with, and fetched a supervisor.

'This current account has been idle for a long time, then only a very few small deposits over the last year,' the new girl remarked. 'Have you been away, sir?'

'Yes,' answered Chris. 'Working abroad,' he improvised.

'There isn't much in your deposit account, either.'

'Regular payments will be going into my account.' He did not feel the need to explain that they would be from Income Support. 'Could you move all the deposit over into a current account? I can't see that I will be able to keep anything on deposit for the time being.'

'Certainly.' He felt like heaving a sigh of relief that all was going well, but made a conscious effort to breathe slowly and silently, and look impassive.

'We will post your cheque book to you, sir,' said the girl at the end of several minutes of keying characters into a computer.

'Oh! That's a blow. I wanted to send off for something.'

'We can issue you with a Sundry Person's Cheque, if that will help.'

So with a cheque for fifteen pounds with which to apply to the Registrar General for a standard certificate of birth, death or marriage, Chris left the bank feeling relatively cheerful. Safely negotiating the journey home, he filled in the form as far as he could and found an envelope. Copying off the Southport address, he noticed idly that the address the woman in the Register Office had deleted was that used for postal applications for adoption certificates.

She must have thought I might make a mistake, he decided, as he stuck down the envelope flap and walked back to the post office on Micklegate to buy a stamp and drop his application into the letterbox.

So far that day nothing untoward had happened, and in his relief Chris felt like buying someone a bunch of daffodils. They should, he supposed, be for Annie. At the greengrocer's lower down Micklegate where earlier he had noticed sheaves of them, he managed to buy the last few bunches, and then decided to call in on his way home to see his probation officer.

Steve was in, and free.

'For the office,' Chris said, proffering a bunch of daffodils.

'It's not often one of you brings us flowers,' said Steve, astonished.

'Not personal, just for the office,' Chris said. 'Everyone else has got daffodils, so why not the probation service?'

And then he told Steve about the sawn-through rungs on the ladder, which he believed had been done by whoever put the fear of hell into the stray cat, Sam, during the night of Wednesday, or, strictly speaking, the early hours of Thursday.

'You can't shrug this off any longer, Chris,' Steve said sharply when he had heard the tale. 'The car driving at you might have been coincidence but this damn well isn't and you know it.'

'Someone out there doesn't love me.' And Chris could not help sounding flippant. Okay, so he was terrified, but he wasn't about to tell Steve that.

'How did you feel when you found those sawn-through rungs?'

'Bloody mad.'

'We ought to get some forensic work on this. Apart from your fingerprints there might be those of whoever did it.'

'On rough wood?'

'Nowadays it's surprising what they can do.'

Chris thought of the axe handle of twelve years ago, when the evidence at the trial had been that because the wood was rough there had been no traceable fingerprints. Where was it now, that axe? Would they still be able to pick up fingerprints, after so many years? No doubt it was in a black museum somewhere and had been handled by half the police forces of England and Wales. It was too much to hope that this new ability to take fingerprints from rough wood would be the breakthrough he had been looking for.

'Have you any objection?'

How could he object? 'If you think it's a good idea.'

'What did you do with the ladder? You handled it yourself, obviously.'

'Yes. After I found the damage I put it back in the shed until I decided what to do. Actually I thought that if I can afford it, it would be a good idea to buy a metal ladder. Meanwhile maybe I can borrow or hire one.'

'Don't touch the damaged ladder again until I've had the chance to speak to CID about it.'

'Right.'

There wasn't much of the afternoon left by this time. It was too late for a proper lunch, so when he reached home Chris took out some cheese and biscuits and ate them with a drink of milk. Then found that he had an acute repugnance for going on with the repair of window frames. One had been done; a change was as good as a rest; why not have a go at the front garden? The sacks of items for the jumble sale were still outside the front door, and once again Chris had to squeeze past them. He took out into the sunshine a border fork and spade and stood looking at the solidified earth inside his little boundary wall.

'Oh, you've put something out for us, how kind,' said a familiar voice. He looked up to see the friendly middle-aged woman

152

who had given him the leaflet on Tuesday.

'I thought you were collecting yesterday.'

Lucy wondered how it was she always seemed to get on the wrong side of this young man. 'Mostly they did collect yesterday. This street was left till last and in the end not done, so I said, having the car with me today...'

The car was a Morris Minor so old that even Chris, partly out of touch still with the changes in the streets, stared at it in amazement. A dog's head poked out of the window. He recognised it as a dachshund. Its dark eyes gleamed brightly. He hoped it didn't spot the battered old cat, who was sitting on the low boundary wall.

'Cup of tea?' he offered.

'I won't, thanks, time is short. You're going to have a bash at the garden, then?'

Chris put his foot on the border fork and pressed down hard without making any impression whatever on the compacted soil.

'Not easy,' commented Lucy.

'You can say that again.'

'What were you thinking of doing with it?'

'Daffodils...'

'I'll just pack these sacks in the car.'

'I'll give you a hand.'

'Oh, thanks... Mr Simmers...'

'Chris.'

'Of course. I remember now. Mine's Lucy, in case you've forgotten,' said Lucy, extending her hand. 'Lucy Grindal.'

Once more they shook hands solemnly.

'It is good of you to find so much for us.'

'You're doing me a favour.'

After these courtesies they stood and smiled at one another.

'Don't you get rather tired of the standard daffodil?' asked Lucy. 'I hope you'll plant something with a little more imagination and variety to it.'

'What do you suggest?'

'It's fun to have the very earliest. February Gold is one of those. Terrific one-upmanship on the neighbours. Then later there's Mount Hood, a pale whitish one, which is supposed to be the longest lasting of any. And why not wind up with a few Pheasant's Eye or something similar—old-fashioned but very scented and spreading the daffodil season nearly into summer? Narcissi we should call them, of course.'

'They won't want planting yet, will they?'

'Not till autumn. You've got all summer to knock some sense into that bit of ground of yours. Would you like me to write you the names on a bit of paper and push it through your letterbox?'

'Please. I am going to rub the rust off it and oil the hinges, you should find it usable.'

'Next time I'm passing, then.'

Together they packed the bulging black dustbin bags into the back seat and boot of the Morris Minor. As Lucy Grindal drove off she caused some alarm amongst other drivers as she certainly wouldn't be able to see through the back window and Prince Rupert was bouncing around in the front.

Chris wondered why it was that some people had the power of making you feel good, without being either young, or beautiful, or anything else you could put a name to, except, of course, themselves.

Chris had gone inside again before Anne Atkinson arrived home for her evening meal. She had to be at the Odeon for seven, but she was ready in good time and decided she had a few minutes to spare to chat to Chris. As she pushed open his yard door softly he came out of the shed.

'You gave me a shock,' she said.

'I've been tidying the garden tools away. Did you notice I'd had a go this afternoon?'

'Not really. At the front? I snuck down the alleyway to the back.'

The stray tom-cat was already tucking into a brimming dish of food.

'Oh, you've still got him,' said Anne, at the same moment as Chris exclaimed, 'Don't go too near—'

Anne screamed.

Her slender ankle had suddenly turned into a large grey ball. The ball hissed and growled angrily and loudly through teeth that were biting into her tender flesh. She lifted that leg off the ground and screamed again.

'—him with your foot,' finished Chris, bending down quickly and grasping the cat, ready to pull him away. As soon as he felt himself held, the tom let go of Anne's ankle with his teeth and claws and turned all his aggression on to the hands round his midriff, bringing up powerful kicks with his hind legs and trying to bite. He had problems as Chris had caught him behind the front legs and held him firmly in spite of the convulsive efforts of the furious cat, carrying him two yards then dropping him on the ground next to the wooden shelter. The tom turned his head and glared at Chris through eyes like angry burning gold, then unfurled into the air what had once been a thick Persian plume of soft grey, but now looked like a bit of chewed string, and stalked in a huff under the reared-up cupboard door and on to the sacks.

Chris moved the dish of food near to the shelter.

'Who are you concerned about,' asked Anne hotly, 'that dratted *animal* or me?'

'He's terribly thin,' replied Chris, 'and you aren't, as far as I can see.' And he twinkled a smile at her.

'I'll have to go home again and change these tights.'

They were certainly in ribbons and she was bleeding from various long scratches and bites.

'Is your anti-tet up to date?' said Chris in a concerned but practical tone.

'Yes, as it happens. I had a booster a few months ago. What about you?'

Chris's hands had been lacerated by the cat's hind legs.

'I had a course of injections before they let me start work from the hostel. As you know I was on a nursery, a tree nursery, dealing with earth and seedlings all day, so they thought it was important.'

'It's a nuisance,' Anne complained. 'These scratches will have to be properly cleaned. I did have a few minutes to spare and wanted to hear more about the album.'

'I've found it very exciting. It was a let-down to find the last sheet ripped out.'

'Oh, it wasn't, was it?'

'Yes, unfortunately. Someone wanting to

destroy the evidence of something—what, I wondered—his death, perhaps. Makes you think, Annie, the sort of life some people lead—the horizons, the adventure, the things he must have seen, the places he'd been. My life has been changed by that album. I've never even taken a photograph, never been interested, but now, all of a sudden, I feel as if there's a window, or perhaps a door, more accurately, and I could walk through it and away into a different kind of life altogether.'

In the fading light Anne looked wistful. She had only just got him back. She didn't want him walking away through any doorways, however exciting the horizons. Then she said firmly that she must go, she didn't want to be late, and she limped slightly as she walked out of the yard.

'Oh, and I sent for that full birth certificate,' Chris called over the yard wall after her.

'Good,' came the reply.

'I'm going to have a bath and meal and then bring some flowers round for your mother,' he went on.

Her voice was farther away now. 'Good,' she said again, and he heard the Atkinsons' back door close. Chris went inside, put out the food he was to cook later for his meal, and went upstairs for his bath.

Although the darkness of night was gathering over the city of York, it was still full day in middle America, midday and lunch time at the Nournavaile Institute. The Director, tall, handsome, energetic even though he was in his seventies, intended to stroll round the grounds for a little exercise. He made a point of taking exercise whenever he could build it into his busy daily schedule. He walked round the end of the building and ran into Dwight Brisling, the promising young accountant who had shown so much competence—in fact flair—during his career with the Nournavaile, and had been suggested by the Head of Finance as a suitable person to visit England and do a bit of genealogical research on behalf of the institute.

In appearance Dwight had a good skin, was neatly dressed, his thick mid-blonde hair was combed back, and he wore a pair of large dark-framed spectacles. As he had twenty-twenty vision the lenses were clear optical glass. Bumping into the Director like this was making him nervous.

'I thought you had gone to Europe before this, Dwight,' the Director said, rather unreasonably, and the displeasure on his face made the young man even more nervous.

'It isn't possible to go without some

159

preparation, sir,' he answered. 'I'm booked on a flight to London tomorrow. Meanwhile I've been in communication with our representatives there on the ancestor quest. They are to brief me when I arrive and produce a report on the present state of the enquiries.'

Albrick's expression lightened.

'Tomorrow, eh? See you're on that flight.' He patted the young man's sleeve. 'I envy you, Dwight. It's many years since I was in Europe. And if you manage to trace a descendant, you will certainly have done what none of the people we've hired have been able to do. Nothing would please me better than to fulfil our founder's wishes. Founder is perhaps an exaggeration, but as you know, Dwight, without Nournavaile's say-so we would not exist, the good work we do would not have been carried out. That's why we bear his name, in his honour. And of course we have him to thank for a substantial income over the past years. Yessir.'

Dwight Brisling had heard this so often that he did not bother to listen. He was only waiting for the moment when he could make respectful noises and slide away.

'Promotion if you succeed, Dwight,' finished the Director.

'Thank you, sir.'

When Annie Atkinson arrived home after seeing the film at the Odeon the house next door was in darkness, except for the bathroom.

'Good film, dear?' her mother asked.

'Very good. You ought to go, Mother. The performances start at twelve, if you'd rather go in the afternoon.'

'I'll think about it.'

'Have you had Chris round?'

'He knows better than to show his face.'

'Funny. He said he was bringing you some flowers.'

Mrs Atkinson perked up a little. 'He hasn't been.' She was sorry to have missed the chance of flowers. Buying your own wasn't the same, somehow.

'The last thing he said was that he was going to have a bath, then a meal, then bring you some flowers.'

'He had his bath,' said her mother, 'because when I went out to the dustbin I noticed the light on in the bathroom. You ought to tell him to invest in some new curtains, our Anne. Those hardly pull across the window. It isn't decent.'

'You can't see anything. You'd have to be up a ladder to see in.'

'If he'd been near the window, shaving, I could have seen him.'

Anne failed to see that such a sight would have been very shocking, but she wasn't going to argue. Instead she went into the Atkinson back yard and looked across at Chris's bathroom window. The light was still on, behind the skimpy pink curtains. Sure enough there was an open space where they didn't quite meet, but it was not more than an inch or so wide.

'He can't still be having a bath,' she said, mainly to herself, as she went back into the cosy elegance of their own house. 'I'm not happy about this,' she said to her mother. 'The bathroom light's still on.'

'It's time you stopped worrying about that young man. He's no good to anybody.'

'I'll ring and see if he answers the phone. Surely, even if he'd gone to sleep in the bath, he would have woken up by now and come downstairs.'

Anne stood there, listening through the Atkinson handset to the phone shrilling out in Chris's hallway, for about two minutes.

'I'm going to ring his probation officer,' she said at last.

'He won't thank you for a telephone call at this time of night.'

'I don't expect to be thanked,' said Anne, finding the probation officer's home number in her address book. She had made a note of it when she happened to see it scribbled on Chris's notepad, which had been lying on the dining-room table, when he went out to feed the cat two days before. She had felt no compunction about copying down the details.

'Mr Watson? I'm very sorry to disturb you at this time of night.' When she wanted to, Anne could produce a voice which would charm the birds off the trees, and she produced it now. Briefly she explained the situation. 'We have a key,' she added, 'we've always had one in case of emergencies, and I could have gone in, but it seemed a good idea to speak to you first.'

Steve Watson was seriously worried. Enough odd and unexplained things had happened since Chris Simmers was released from jail to make him on edge about even the slightest suggestion that things were not right with his parolee.

'I'll be with you in quarter of an hour, Miss Atkinson. You did the right thing to ring.'

'I could borrow his ladder and climb up to look through the split in the curtains to see if he is all right,' volunteered Anne.

'No! Don't do that...' Steve hesitated, then added, 'Chris said something about his ladder not being safe.'

'All right, then. I'll be outside the front

door in fifteen minutes.' A slight crispness had crept into her tone.

'She's worried,' Steve said to himself. 'And, my stars, so am I.'

He was already undressed, intending to have an early night, and had been cleaning his teeth when the phone rang. Now, with a few quick words of explanation to his wife, he pulled on his clothes again, grateful for the fact that he had left the car out in the drive instead of putting it away in the garage when he arrived home at tea-time. Pure laziness, as his wife had remarked. Maybe it had been premonition.

Steve had not met Annie Atkinson before, although he had been carefully monitoring Chris's relationship with her and her mother. So he did not know quite what to expect when he drew his car up outside Chris's terrace house. Anne was waiting for him, standing on the pavement, still wearing the clothes she had put on to go out with Graham, a well-cut though casual suit, floating elegant silk scarf, pretty shoes. Shapely legs showed below the longish skirt. A soft informal hat with a brim was pulled down to eyebrow level. The effect was like an illustration in an Edwardian novel.

'It's the front door key. Now you are here I'll open it,' she said. The lock was stiffish. 'Chris is supposed to have oiled this.'

She inched the door open and Steve reached past her and flicked on the hall light switch. There was no sound at all in the house. Together they walked along the hallway and, as they passed, peered into first the sitting-room then the dining-room, Steve flicking on the light switches as they went, and calling out, 'Hello, Chris! Anyone in?'

Then into the kitchen. Steve flicked on the light again, and they stood side by side looking at the work counter where, neatly laid out, they saw a packet of frozen peas, some oven chips and a couple of chops. A fly was sitting on the chops and Anne waved impatiently at it. It took flight and found refuge on the ceiling.

'He didn't have his meal,' she said in a low voice.

'You said the bathroom light was on?'

'It seems to have been on all evening. Well, at least since about seven.'

They turned with one accord and made their way upstairs. The bathroom door was the first they came to. The bathroom was built out at the back, over the scullery—or utility room, as Chris was learning to call it.

'Let's hope he didn't lock it,' Steve said to Anne. He turned the handle gently and pushed, encountering some resistance when the door had opened about a foot. Steve stopped pushing and edged his way in. He turned to stop Anne coming but she was so close behind him that her head was already round the edge of the door.

Chris lay face down, sprawled diagonally across the floor, one of his knees bent and the foot still up, resting on the wooden rim of the bath. Steve crouched down and took Chris's wrist in his fingers. Anne struggled round the edge of the door and compressed herself into as narrow a vertical column as she could. She daren't ask the vital question. Her lips were pressed firmly together to stop any sound coming out and only her eyes showed her distress.

Then Chris moved his head slightly and groaned. His eyelids flickered a little, then closed again. Steve took his hand from Chris's wrist. He stood up carefully and turned inch by inch to examine the bathroom. All at once he grabbed Anne's sleeve and said, 'Look at the chain to the bath plug.'

Anne could hardly believe her eyes. The chain looked as though the metal of which it was made had melted. Water was still in the bath. It looked too clean for any bathing to have taken place in it. The walls were covered with a film of moisture, but the bath water looked too cold now to give off steam. It was obvious that somehow the electricity was faulty. Nothing else could explain that melted metal chain.

'Don't touch anything.' Steve's voice had the edge of command. 'Wriggle out of here without touching anything. Me too. I'm getting a doctor and the police. We'll have to move him with care. Thank God he's alive. But we'll have the electricity off at the mains before we do anything. Have you got a torch? Do you know where the meter is?'

'We've got to move him,' said Anne, 'quickly, quickly. He might touch something live.'

'As soon as the juice is off.'

'I won't be a second fetching a torch. We keep one inside the front door.'

Anne darted off and true to her word was back almost at once with a strong torch. Steve was standing in the hall. She showed him the door under the stairs, leading to the cellar-head where the meter was, the area just inside the door before the cellar stairs began. He nervously took hold of the big old-fashioned meter switch and turned it to OFF. Anne put on her torch and the strong beam struck through the sudden darkness. She sagged against the wall. She could only see one thing in her mind's eye; Chris lying there, sprawled, helpless, and, over, under and round him, the gay golden flowers of the scattered bunches of daffodils.

8

Steve and Anne stood in the pitch-black hallway, Anne's torch beam the only light. For a few seconds neither of them said anything. Steve clicked shut the door to the space under the stairs which held the meters and shelves for food, and where the cellar steps led down into even blacker blackness.

'We'll get used to it in a minute,' said Anne, turning the torch to let its strongly directional beam flash for a moment over banisters, walls, the hall-stand with its load of coats and oddments and the linoleum-covered floor with a strip of carpet. 'Let's move Chris.'

'Who's his GP?' asked Steve.

'I haven't a clue. He probably hasn't got one.'

'Who is the nearest, then? Or had I better call the police doctor?'

'Why are you on about doctors? Look, can't we fetch him out of there? You and I can lift him between us. He'd better come into our house for the night. I'll go in the spare room, he can have my bed, it's the most comfortable.'

But Steve was in no hurry.

'I want a doctor to see him before he's moved and as well I want a word with the police.'

'He could be dying, lying there!' Anne was beginning to lose all patience with the probation officer. She turned to run upstairs to Chris, but Steve reached out and caught her sleeve once more.

'This is serious,' he said. 'You don't realise how serious. But a few minutes won't hurt. He's alive. You saw him move his head. You saw me taking his pulse. It's steady. He's breathing normally as far as I could see. The glimpse I had of his eyes, they look all right. He felt warm to touch. Stop panicking.'

'You're completely heartless!' exploded Anne. 'He's been lying there for hours! If he moves he might electrocute himself!'

'He can hardly electrocute himself now the juice is off. I don't know how much he's told you, but it looks to me as if someone is trying to kill him. What's caused this incident tonight I don't know yet, we'll have to get it checked. It may be a freak accident.'

'You don't believe that and neither do I,' spat Anne.

'Look, if someone is trying to kill him we need evidence. Then I can act to stop it, put the police on the trail. You and

I can't do that, it isn't our job. Barging about in that bathroom we might destroy vital evidence. See sense, girl.'

'Vital evidence is a bit academic if he dies,' said Anne. 'We're standing here arguing. Let's *do* something.'

'I'm going to contact CID and take their advice,' said Steve, walking to where the phone was fixed to the wall.

'Let me ring our doctor first,' said Anne. 'She lives close by and I'm sure she'll come and say if he can be moved or not.' She did this, leaving an urgent message at the doctor's home—the GP herself being out on call. Then, handing the torch and phone to Steve, she slipped out of the front door and went home.

'Mother,' she commanded as soon as she was in her own house, 'Chris seems to be hurt. I've rung our doctor. The probation officer is ringing the police now. He wants them to take charge. As soon as they give the word I want to move Chris. Unless he needs hospital attention I think he'd better stay with us. He can go in my bed, it's comfortable and warm. Will you make up the bed in the spare room for me? And switch the electric blankets on in both beds? Say on control 2. Boil a kettle, make a flask of something hot—tea, coffee, soup, whatever you think best—there's a dear?'

Before her mother could object, Anne

stepped across to her, gave her a hug and a kiss, and was out of the front door again and back into Chris's hallway before Mrs Atkinson could recover from the shock.

Steve was on the phone, but not speaking. He looked as though he was waiting to be answered.

'Mother's making preparations,' Anne told him quickly. She was sure that her mother would not let her down. Steve nodded, and went on listening intently. He had dialled the police office on Clifford Street, where Dave Smart and his boss, Robert Southwell, were usually based.

'Detective Inspector Smart is off duty,' a voice had told him. 'Southwell? Acting Superintendent Southwell is off duty too.'

'This is a case of attempted murder,' Steve had said, desperate at these obstacles. 'I need guidance from CID before we move the victim. He's semi-conscious.'

The voice got its act together. 'In that case I will notify DS Southwell immediately, sir. Probation officer, you said? Stephen Watson?'

It was at this point that Anne had come back in through the front door. Although it seemed to her like eternity it was only four or five minutes since they had found Chris on the bathroom floor.

Bob Southwell, Acting Detective Superintendent, was at his home on Ouse Avenue, Clifton. He'd had a busy day at work and a hectic family evening with his two children, Susan and Paul, and his wife Linda. After the children's bedtime he'd had a quiet hour with Linda listening to music and reading, watched a programme on TV, then prepared for bed. Now he was relaxing, sinking into sleep. He'd been Acting DS since his boss went sick in late February with a massive heart attack, at the end of the chocolate factory murder case. While filling the DS job in a temporary capacity, Bob Southwell had gone through the hoops of applying for it himself. There'd been a long selection procedure. It hadn't been the easiest period of his life, and you could say that again. In a way it was even worse when the results came through and he found he hadn't been chosen. A chap from Sheffield was appointed—Bruno Hallam. As soon as Hallam could be released, he would be taking up the post and Bob Southwell would be reverting to Detective Chief Inspector.

Bob turned restlessly in bed and wished Linda would come up. What did she find to do down there last thing at night? He wanted to turn his thoughts away from Bruno Hallam taking over. That would come soon enough. He heard Linda's step on the stairs, and at once shut his eyes and pretended he was dozing.

He found a comfortable position and, through barely open lids, watched his wife preparing for bed. He loved to see her serious expression as she went through her ritual of brushing her hair and taking off her make-up, the little she used. Then she went into the bathroom and he could hear energetic tooth-brushing noises and the snap of the lid of the linen basket as she dropped in her underclothes. In a few seconds she'd be sitting on the edge of the bed to take off her slippers, then sliding into his arms...

The phone rang.

'Duty officer here, sir. Probation officer Stephen Watson just phoned about an attempted murder. Needs advice. Is remaining on the scene. No CID in the office at present, sir.'

Bob Southwell sat upright then sprang half out of bed. His wife Linda might as well not have existed for all the thought he had to spare for her now.

'Number?' he asked crisply. 'Right, I'll speak to Watson. Where is everybody? No. Don't tell me. Try to locate them. Get uniform manpower if you can't find CID. Attempted murder? Get a photographer from the scene of crime team to the incident, pronto. Now connect me to Watson.'

'Steve?' he said as soon as he was through. 'Southwell here. Put me in the picture.'

At this point the doctor Anne had summoned arrived at the terrace house where Chris Simmers was still lying in the bathroom. Anne opened the door and began to explain the situation. In spite of himself, Steve was reassured by the sight of the doctor, a calm, competent middle-aged woman, and also by finally having made contact with Acting DS Southwell.

'I have a parolee, a murderer, came out of jug ten days ago,' Steve was explaining. 'A number of incidents suggest someone is trying to kill him. Tonight it looks as if an electric current was connected to his bath. The chain to the waste plug has melted... No, he's not dead, sir. He's semi-conscious on the bathroom floor. I don't want to destroy evidence by moving him but he ought to have treatment as soon as possible—'

'How long has he been there?' put in Bob Southwell.

'Since about seven o'clock, I think. If this sort of thing is allowed to continue he will be killed in one of these incidents, that's why I wanted to contact you, sir,' finished Steve. 'The neighbour's offered him a bed, and a GP is here.'

'The photographer's on his way,' said Southwell, 'and I'm coming. If the doctor says he can stay put for a few more minutes, I'd like to see the scene as it is.'

The doctor and Anne had gone upstairs with the torch. Steve called up to ask the doctor not to move Chris if she could help it, during her examination. The doctor edged out of the bathroom as Steve climbed the stairs in the darkness. She spoke to him at once. 'I can't possibly approve of leaving an injured man without aid, for the sake of what exactly?'

'Catching whoever is attacking him, if we can,' said Steve. 'I know it's unusual.'

'I have examined him superficially,' went on the doctor, 'and perhaps a few more minutes won't matter, but I don't like this semi-consciousness. Beyond minutes I won't be answerable for the consequences.'

When Bob Southwell arrived at the front door it was at the same time as a plain-clothes man festooned with video and still cameras.

'Thank goodness you're here,' Steve Watson said. 'I couldn't have kept the poor man where he is much longer or I'd have had a riot on my hands. Sorry it's so dark but we had to turn off the juice.'

Bob quietly produced a torch of his own. Glancing round the hallway he intercepted a flashing and indignant look from the red-haired girl who was holding her torch high, to illuminate the area. Bob and the photographer went upstairs, Bob seeming to know where the bathroom was without anyone telling him and exchanging a courteous word with the doctor as he passed her. He inched round the bathroom door and took in the scene at a glance.

'We could do with a photograph of this,' he said, but, looking at the prone body of Chris Simmers, he shared the concern felt by the doctor and Anne. 'Video and stills, be as quick as you can, two minutes maximum.' Inching out again, he left the photographer to it.

'I take it you're the police,' the doctor said from the shadows of the landing. 'I can't take responsibility for leaving an injured man all this time.'

'I agree with you completely,' said Bob. 'But we will move him very shortly now. The probation officer was afraid of destroying vital evidence if he and another lay person moved Mr Simmers. Can you give me your opinion on his medical condition?'

'For now I want him in a warm bed,' the doctor said. 'It won't hurt him to be lifted.'

The photographer was experienced and took very little time to carry out his task.

'Right, Steve,' Bob said. 'You and me to lift and carry him?'

'I'll do that,' said Anne with such firmness that no one argued. She and Steve worked together as though they'd been doing it all their lives. Anne had fetched a blanket and they rolled it round Chris, Steve took him under the shoulders, supporting Chris's head on his arm, and Anne took him by the knees. They moved backward down the stairs with the doctor holding the torch and now and then putting out a hand to guide them. Chris's eyelids fluttered again and Anne breathed out a sigh of relief. She had been tormenting herself with the idea that he might have died. They left a trail of daffodils behind them on the stairs, and carried Chris next door.

As soon as the probation officer returned to the house Bob Southwell said, 'I'd like you to fill me in on what's been happening. Now. Tonight. But as far as the rest of the investigation goes, it will be better postponed until morning. We'll go back to the station as soon as things are fixed up here.'

The photographer came downstairs.

'Stewart, thanks for coming. We'll do the rest tomorrow. Can you be here at eight o'clock? Right, off you go then. Any uniform lads turned up?'

Steve Watson had passed them on his way back into the house. 'Sergeant Diamond and PC Clark,' he said. 'They're standing at the front.'

Southwell went out to have a word with them. 'I'd like two constables on guard for the rest of the night, Sergeant,' he said. 'PC Clark will do for one. One in the yard at the back and one at the front door. We'll be back about 8 a.m. It might be best to have another team to relieve your men at the end of the shift, we'll be here all morning.'

Southwell took Steve Watson back to the station on Clifford Street. Once in the office, Steve could relax. He realised how much tension he'd been under. Bob was anything but relaxed. He pulled a pad of paper towards himself and found a ballpoint, with short jabbing movements.

'You realise', he began aggressively, 'that your parolee (has he got a name, by the way?) could have been staging these accidents to draw attention to himself, or for some other obscure psychopathic reason?'

'That's been worrying me. That is exactly why I was—am—so keen to have a proper investigation.'

'Right. As long as you understand we

will be investigating that angle as well as everything else. Now fill me in on the background and what's been happening.'

Steve briefly outlined Chris Simmers's history and went on to deal with the strange incidents which had taken place since his release.

'You saw him tighten the nuts and screws on his bike but he could have loosened them again afterwards.'

'Yes, sir, but rather a strange way of committing suicide.'

'Then this incident when he was nearly killed by a car driven by foreign tourists. You checked it out at the time, you say?'

Steve told how he'd asked Dave Smart to check into it for him and the result.

'Hard to see how he could have staged that,' said Bob.

'Impossible, I would think.'

'I expect we have a record of your enquiry. Right. The next thing. Sabotage to the ladder rungs, is that it?'

'Yes.'

'Hardly a professional hit-man's job. On the other hand, exactly the kind of thing one might stage oneself if looking for sympathy. Is he getting sympathy from that red-haired girl?'

'The neighbours are giving him a surprising amount of support, even the mother.'

'No other neighbours?'

'On the other side of him it's a student house and they've gone home for the holidays. Be back at the start of the summer term.'

'And the rest of the row?'

'Most of the inhabitants have changed since he went inside. The Atkinsons are the only ones in his part of the terrace who knew him before. But there is another terrace, starts a bit further on, which is more or less an extension of his. There may well be people still there who remember him.'

'Sad, the way we all move around so much these days. It looks such a settled, domestic kind of area. Probably someone's already planning a theme park or museum there, and a multi-storey carpark, and a few supermarkets, and hey presto, the character of the place, the mixture which gives it its character, will be gone for ever.'

'That's right,' agreed Steve Watson.

'But it is this latest incident which is the serious one, the one you've called us in on.'

'Judging by the fact that the chain to the bath plug had melted, I concluded that the electricity had been wired to the bath or the water mains in some way, and that he had only escaped electrocution by the skin of his teeth.'

'He has as many lives as a cat, your parolee. Most people lean out of a bath to alter the radio station and touch a faulty wire and die, just like that.'

'I have heard of a case like this before, sir. That's why I feel this is a copy-cat murder attempt. There was a lot in the papers about the other. It failed, too.'

'Not a good example for a murderer to choose, then, Steve. And how did they get into the house? For the matter of that, how did they get into the outhouse to sabotage the ladder, the other day? That's where the rub is, and we start thinking, he's doing it himself.'

'If you could go over the house for fingerprints...'

'Oh, we will be doing that, the full investigation, as if he had been killed.'

'Good.'

The doctor examined Chris thoroughly when he was safely in the well-lit front bedroom of the Atkinsons' house. She came to the conclusion that the electric shock he had received had been a slight one, that he had been incredibly lucky. There was some evidence of burning on his leg.

'He obviously didn't touch anything which would have earthed the connection,' she said.

'But he still hasn't come to properly,'

182

Anne protested. 'Why is he like this?'

'Didn't you tell me he's had two other accidents recently and one of them left a hair-line crack in his skull? If he knocked his head again, as he fell, it wouldn't do him any good on top of all that. It is my opinion that what he needs in the first place is a good sleep. I'm going to administer a sedative, and I'll call in the morning. It might be as well to have a hospital check on his skull tomorrow. There are a number of tests I'd like to have carried out to try to eliminate possibilities, but simple home nursing might be the best answer in the end. We'll see. Meanwhile, stop worrying, Anne. He's pretty tough. Get to bed yourself.'

Anne left the flask of hot tea her mother had prepared on the bedside chest of drawers, in case Chris woke in the night, and adjusted the softest light so that it illuminated the flask and not his face, then she tiptoed out and left him. Her mother looked excited, but Anne felt whacked. It seemed like a lifetime since she had been at the pictures with Graham. She gave her mother a kiss as they parted on the landing, and went into the spare room, where the narrow bed had become nicely aired thanks to the electric blanket. Like Chris's room in his own home, it was over the hallway and the front door of the house. She snuggled down into the unfamiliar bed.

When Chris drifted up from a long sleep he opened his eyes on to something so unlike home that he thought he was still asleep, and dreaming. The heavenly softness of the bed, the comfort of the pure cotton sheets and the down pillows, was better than anything he had ever experienced. He had no desire whatever to wake up, so he allowed himself to drop down again into the depths of oblivion. He woke later, stretched gently, absorbing the amazing comfort, turned his head, and before he knew it was asleep for the third time.

It was not until morning was well advanced that his eyes snapped open on the world, his longing for rest satisfied at last. Then he realised that he had no idea where he was. He turned his head luxuriously and saw the window, the same size and shape as the window in his parents' old room. Even from where he lay he could see that the outlook was virtually the same as from his own house, he recognised the trees. So he could not be far from home. At that moment he did not care in the least where he was.

Later he saw a little more, when he moved his eyes from one side to the other, and a good deal more when finally he pulled his body higher on the pillows. The room was provided with expensive fitted furniture finished in eggshell enamel in a delicate ivory colour, a fitted plain carpet in a shade of biscuit, ivory curtains and cushions with a light, discreet pattern in a soft, deep clover pink. All the fittings looked exclusive and there was a vase of flowers in a recess. Next to the bed he saw an incongruous thermos flask, and although the room was full of spring sunshine a lamp was burning, casting a different kind of glow on to the top of the piece of furniture where the thermos was standing.

Chris thought that if it was full of tea he would like some. He wriggled his way over, enjoying the sensation of moving through the light warm bedding, and sat up to investigate. It was tea. He poured some into the top of the thermos and found it was the best drink he'd had for ages. He lay there puzzling over his surroundings, and then the door opened and Mrs Atkinson walked in.

'You're awake then,' she said.

Chris felt it was impossibly corny to say 'Where am I?' so he smiled and said nothing, sure that he would find out sooner or later.

'Anne had to sleep in the spare bed,' Mrs Atkinson went on severely.

Chris's feelings changed completely. It was one thing to wallow in anonymous luxury, another to be in Anne's bed. He flushed, feeling hot all over. Although the old relationship had almost vanished already, it would be irretrievably lost if they allowed sensual attraction to enter the equation of feelings between them. The main thing he was determined on was that she was not going to be contaminated by a murderer and jailbird. She had to be defended from herself. He could see the danger, if she couldn't.

'I'm sorry about that,' he said.

'Anyway, the doctor's here to see you, and the police are coming if she says it's all right.'

Chris was back in the real world with a vengeance. Mrs Atkinson went before he could ask for explanations. The doctor appeared with her no-nonsense manner and put him through various tests and a careful and thorough examination. Chris had the feeling that he had met her before.

'No more of these escapades, young man,' she said. 'Even a cat only has nine lives. I would like you to go for an X-ray at the hospital, but you seem so well it needn't be today. No headache?'

'None at all.'

'You can get up when you like but

I would advise staying put until this afternoon.'

By the pretty clock at the bedside Chris could see that it was already eleven, so that was not much of an imposition. He felt quite happy to do as he was told. He realised that he would need a GP, and he liked this one.

'Can I register with you, Dr er...' he asked.

'If you haven't registered with anyone else, yes, I can take you on my list if you wish,' the doctor said in an offhand way.

'No, I haven't. My old GP has retired.'

The doctor found a leaflet in her briefcase.

'That's a list of my surgery hours.' She put the leaflet down by the bed. 'The receptionist will fix you up. And here's a note for you to take to the X-ray department one day next week, we'd better check on that thick head of yours.'

No sooner had she gone than a large, red-faced, black-haired young man appeared and pulled a chair up beside the bed.

'Acting Detective Chief Inspector Smart,' he introduced himself.

'That sounds important,' said Chris, warily. 'What's been happening?'

Dave Smart smiled. 'I hope you can tell me. And I only sound important on very temporary promotion.'

'I can't remember a thing since yesterday.'

'Tell me about yesterday from the beginning.'

It sounded very trivial, as Chris recounted it.

'You bought some daffodils?' Dave Smart repeated after him, an incredulous note in his voice. He ought to be used to the human race by now but it gave him a surprise when a matricide talked about buying daffodils. 'And you gave some to the probation officer?'

It did sound rather odd, put like that.

'I bought the last bunches in the shop. It seemed to be a day for daffodils. And the probation office needed cheering up a bit. They weren't only for my probation officer, they were for all the staff. It was an impulse.'

'And the other bunches?'

'They were for Mrs Atkinson, my next-door neighbour. I was going to take them round to her after my bath and evening meal. My hands were scratched—there's a stray cat I've been feeding and he's fierce—and I was going to give the daffs a good soak while I was in the bath and putting disinfectant on the scratches. The last thing I remember is stepping into the bath.'

'It is a very good thing you didn't touch the taps after you stepped in.'

'I ran the water first.'

'You seem to have escaped with slight burns. Your bath's outlet pipe had been wired up to the electricity circuit, with a timed switch set to come on at seven o'clock. Is that when you usually take a bath?'

'Quite often.'

'So you were out of the house between...' Dave Smart flicked back the pages of his notebook and quoted the times. 'And during the time you were at home, you saw no one except your neighbours the Atkinsons, is that right?'

'No one.' Chris looked dumbfounded.

'Right. Thanks, Mr Simmers. I've been authorised to tell you that we found some fingerprints which are not yours, nor are they Mrs or Miss Atkinson's or the probation officer's. I gather the Atkinsons keep a key to your house.'

'Yes, and I have one to theirs—at least, I expect I still have it. We always used to. In case of emergencies.' Chris was floundering again. 'So you found the prints of whoever did it?' he asked.

Dave Smart nodded. 'It looks like it. Whoever did it wore gloves, but they must have been awkward when making the connections, so they'd taken them off,

189

then put them on again. The prints were in a corner of the cellar-head area, a hidden spot, also on the electric meter and fuse switchboard. Some had been wiped, but a few had been missed. We were lucky to find them.'

Chris found himself blowing out his breath, and a feeling of justification and relief flooded him.

'We might get to the bottom of it all, then,' he said. 'Not that they seem to have been serious attempts on my life. I mean,' there was bravado in his face and voice, 'tampering with bike brakes and ladder rungs, hardly James Bond stuff, is it? Now if a man came after me with a gun, that would be more like it. I don't see how I'd get out of that alive.'

'You don't rate near-electrocution a serious attempt?' asked Dave mildly. 'It's got to be guns to be serious, is that it?'

'Or knives, I suppose,' bragged Chris. 'Man-to-man stuff, that's what I mean. These Hidden Hand incidents, they aren't much.'

Fortunately Dave Smart had heard this sort of big-man talk before and knew how high to estimate it. Chris Simmers was terrified, and who could blame him? Perhaps it would be the knife or the gun next time. And would he be talking out-of-character nervous macho talk then?

'Now, Miss Atkinson and Mrs Atkinson, only a few questions,' Dave was saying a few minutes afterwards. 'About yesterday. What times did you see Mr Simmers, did you see anyone else go to the house, what times did you yourselves come and go?'

'Nobody went to the house,' Anne said positively.

'Except the electricity man,' amended her mother.

'Electricity man?'

'He came soon after Chris—Mr Simmers —had gone out. It isn't long since the meter was read, I told him, because it was done when they reconnected the supply. Then he said, oh, he hadn't come to do that, he'd come to repair a small fault, and what a pity Mr Simmers was out because he wouldn't be able to come this way again for a fortnight, so of course I let him in.'

'Did you stay with him, Mrs Atkinson?' Dave's voice was absolutely impassive. He might have been reading out the weather forecast for shipping.

'I had my own work to do. He was in uniform, all correct. I said he was to tell me when he was finished and I'd lock up again. It isn't as though there is anything valuable in that house. There's nothing to steal.'

'There's something to steal in every house, Mrs Atkinson. Can you describe this electricity man?'

She couldn't—or not very well. It was as if the uniform had disguised any other characteristics he might have had. Anne had been staring at her mother as though she had never seen her before. But when Dave Smart went, thanking them both, Anne said nothing about the episode, but finished preparing lunch and took a tray up to Chris, all without a word of reproach or explanation to her mother, who seemed serenely unconscious of having done anything untoward. 'You look as though you're enjoying yourself,' Anne said, gazing down at Chris lying in her bed. He looked embarrassed and sat up.

'It's not so bad.'

'Are you staying there all day?'

'The doctor said to stay until after lunch. I feel great, really rested. Thanks, Anne. Sorry I turned you out of your bed. It's a lot more comfortable than mine. I must get up soon, there are things to do.'

'Like what?' said Anne from the window, where she was looking into the street.

'I've been wondering if the cat was all right.'

'Dratted cat.'

'Sam, his name is,' Chris scolded her.

'*He*'s all right. You needn't worry about

192

him. I saw him hanging about this morning. You ought to put a notice on the gate, "Beware of the cat."'

'Did he attack the policeman?'

'Policeman? Plural. There've been masses of them. No. They were too big and tough for him. He picks on defenceless females.'

Chris was eating his lunch. He had made himself comfortable sitting up, and set the tray on his knee. 'You put your foot too near him. He thought he was going to be kicked. I did warn you.'

'Not soon enough.'

She had no intention of being soft with Chris. Not after the shock they'd had last night. It would be too easy to show him just how deeply she had been disturbed and upset by it all. Anne turned to face into the room. 'You look as though you might soon get used to that,' she went on.

'To being waited on? Spoiled, your mother would say? Not really. It's pleasant once in a way. I'd rather be independent, most of the time.'

'What are you doing when you've devoured that?'

'Having a cup of tea with any luck. Then I want to go home.'

'I thought you would. Your probation officer's been on the phone, even though it's Saturday. He wants to take you to the police station to talk to the Superintendent.'

'Steve rests not neither does he sleep, or something.'

'Toils not neither does he spin.'

'What time does he want me?'

'Two o'clock.'

Anne went away to have her own lunch, and Chris was able to shower in the very swish bathroom and dress in the clothes he had taken off the night before, which had been brought over from the floor of his own bathroom. As he went downstairs Anne appeared.

'Would you like to see in here before you go?' she asked, swinging open the sitting-room door.

To Chris's surprise the sitting-and dining-rooms had been knocked into one, and a classical pillar supported each end of the archway between. He couldn't help thinking the pillars looked incongruous in a small terrace house, but the through room was both light and elegant, if rather too feminine for him to feel quite comfortable in it.

'Lovely,' he said.

'You don't mean that. I wouldn't either.' Anne sighed. 'Too fussy. I feel more at home in your house.'

'Pull the other one. It must seem dead

grotty compared to this.'

'Could do with a bit of attention.'

Chris put out a friendly hand and squeezed hers quickly. 'Don't think I'm not grateful,' he said. 'But why should I drag you into all my troubles?'

'Because you've been my best friend all my life?'

'Aw, shucks...' He put on the kind of drawl heard only in the cinema.

'Go on. Mr Watson will be waiting for you.' Anne grinned at him suddenly, white teeth sparkling, red hair swinging loose and distractingly pretty on her shoulders.

Sure enough, Steve was waiting in the road outside.

'Sorry,' said Chris as he moved from the Atkinsons' front door to his own, which was locked. The policeman guarding the house handed him the key, which struck Chris as one of the odder events of the day.

'We haven't much time,' said Steve.

Chris took his black leather jacket from the hall-stand and checked that he had everything he might want. 'It's not fair to you to take up your weekend,' he said.

Steve shrugged. 'Happens.'

'Who are we going to see?'

'Acting DS Southwell. He's in charge of investigating your accident last night.'

'His weekend gone for a Burton as well.'

195

'It is only fair to tell you, Chris, that one of the things he is investigating is whether or not you have been staging these accidents yourself.'

Chris thought, You've gotta be joking, but didn't say anything. Lamblike, he climbed into Steve's car and waved to the policeman on guard duty as they moved off.

The Acting DS was a tall, thin, bespectacled, intelligent-looking man in his late thirties. Steve and Chris were asked to sit down. They sat quietly and waited. DS Southwell was behind his desk. He looked through his papers for a minute. Then he looked across at Chris with a friendly smile.

'I understand Mr Smart told you that we found fingerprints which we are trying to identify at the moment,' he said. 'We believe they belong to the man who fixed the trap for you. If he is a known criminal we will trace him.'

'You don't believe I've been doing these things myself, then, sir?'

'We had to check that out, I'm sure you understand.' Southwell paused, remembering he was talking to a murderer, and matricide at that. 'Do you realise how lucky you are to be alive, Mr Simmers? I asked Mr Watson here to bring you so that I could put you in the picture and ask you if you would leave the area for the time being. We haven't the manpower to protect you and you seem to have some pretty determined enemies. We would rather have you out of harm's way for a week or two, say.'

'I'm sorry, I can't do that.'

'Is money the problem? We might be able to arrange a loan from Social Services.'

'I'm not prepared to leave.'

'Your life appears to be in danger.'

'I'm sure you're right, sir. But there's a mystery behind all this and I believe the answer to it is in my house. Some odd things have turned up already. If I go on looking I'm bound to find the secret, the reason for these attacks. It's the only way.'

Bob Southwell settled back in his tubular steel chair and dug its back legs into the floor tiles, as he had done many and many a time in his old office downstairs. The Super's office was going to be just as bad if he was Acting Super for long. Already the round depressions in the floor were the despair of the cleaners. There was a square of carpet, but it didn't cover the whole office.

'What are the odd things that have turned up already?'

Haltingly—for the whole thing sounded

funny, to say the least—Chris told him about the newspaper advert for someone descended from Nournavaile, the book of cuttings he had found about a press photographer of that name, the last page which had been roughly torn out, his grandparents whom he had called Nourny. He didn't mention his obsession with the murder, his search for details of the trial. After all, there was nothing new so far on that one.

'There's more, sir. I know I will find more. I've barely started. The house repairs seemed more urgent, but I think these people want to scare me away more than anything, so that they can find whatever it is. Annie Atkinson tells me the house was ransacked after I was arrested, twelve years ago. Whatever they were after they can't have found. They are trying to scare me away so that they can look again.'

'This doesn't hang together,' was the opinion of Bob Southwell. 'Why wait until you come out of prison to search further?'

'I don't know. Perhaps my being here acted as a catalyst.'

'Oh yes? Big word. We can't be responsible for you if you stay.'

'That's all right. I'm not very bothered what happens to me.' He added, 'Although I'm sorry to be a nuisance.'

Bob turned to Steve Watson. 'We can't *make* him go away, Steve.'

'No, sir.' Steve sounded resigned. He was a stubborn devil, Chris Simmers.

'And you shouldn't waste a lot of probation service time on him either.'

'No, sir.'

'On your own head, young man,' was Bob's final word to Chris.

'Yes, sir.'

9

In the end Chris did not return home that day. When he was brought back from the police station by his probation officer, he was looking so white and exhausted that Steve steered him towards the Atkinsons' door. Anne came in answer to his knock, and after one look at Chris's face she swung the door wide open and said she hoped they both had time for a cup of tea. She showed them into the elegant through room which Chris had glimpsed briefly that morning. Mrs Atkinson was there, sitting in a blue silk-upholstered armchair elaborately fringed, and she was watching television.

'Time for afternoon tea, Mother. Shall I get it?' asked Anne.

'Yes, dear,' was the response, and Mrs Atkinson smiled at Chris and Steve politely before turning back to the TV programme. The two men sat down carefully on the long settee against the wall, which was upholstered to match the armchair, a blue marvel of fringing and tassels.

Anne served them with tea in white china cups decorated with harebells. When they were on their second cup and fourth biscuit, she remarked, 'We hope you'll agree to stay with us for another night, Chris. It would be a pleasure for Mother and me, we don't often have visitors.'

'There's the cat,' said Chris.

'How do you mean, there's the cat?'

'Sam.'

'I don't know which cat you mean,' said Anne, who was in a humour to tease, if only to stop herself from weeping.

'We were talking about him earlier today, while I was eating lunch. You *know*, Anne. The stray cat who turned up. You were there when I fed him for the first time, and you told me, Mrs Atkinson, about the noise he made that night, defending the house against attackers, and he went for you, Anne, you can't have forgotten that.'

'Oh, *that* cat,' said Anne. 'I don't imagine he realised he was defending anything except himself.'

'You know I've gone on feeding him. He will be disappointed if he comes and doesn't get fed. About six, usually.'

'I'll tell you what,' said Anne. 'I'll go round and put food out in your yard. If he attacks me—he would be defending your house, of course—I shall sue you for damages. How's that?'

'Thank you,' was all Chris said, but he

smiled, in the way she had remembered all these years.

'Tins of food in the cupboard?' she asked, and he nodded.

'So, cat provided for, you'll stay the night?'

'It would be better,' the probation officer advised him.

Chris realised how easy it would be to accept, to go to bed early—very early, say in about five minutes—snuggle down in that warm comfy bed and stay there until morning. It seemed that Anne read his thoughts.

'I'll bring an omelette up as soon as I've fed the cat,' she said.

On the Sunday morning about eleven, after a big breakfast, another shower, and several cups of coffee, Chris went home. It was simple enough; out of the front door of one small terrace house and in at the front door of the next. So why did he feel as though he was exchanging safety for danger? All right. So he had an unknown enemy who had tried to electrocute him in his bath. The house was still his refuge, his home. He was as determined as ever to discover the reason for the attacks, as careless as ever about his own safety. But something had happened to his nerves.

As soon as he put his hand on his own

gate Chris was reassured, by an event so surprising as to be almost unbelievable. Sitting outside the front door was the battered angry old tom-cat, basking in the sun. At the sight of Chris he rose, stretched, arched his back, reached out with his front legs and put out his claws before retracting them slowly and luxuriously, unfurled his pathetic string of a tail, and miaowed unmistakably in welcome. As Chris came through the gate and put the key in the lock, the cat rubbed, for a fleeting moment, against his legs.

Looking down in astonishment, Chris wondered if he dare offer to touch the wild creature, but at the approach of his hand the cat Sam backed off nervously and hissed. It seemed better to leave well alone. But when the door was opened, Sam followed Chris inside.

'Not time for tea yet, old fella,' said Chris, feeling that the cat had made a subtle difference to the way he had been feeling about the house. The cat stalked through the hall and into the dining-room, where he sat down on the hearth rug and made himself at home.

The Atkinsons had gone out to have Sunday lunch at a country pub. They had offered to take Chris with them, but he had refused, politely but firmly. Mrs Atkinson hadn't really changed her attitude, he knew, although she was being kind. And Anne—well, Anne needed keeping at arm's length, now more than ever. For her own sake as well as his. She was worth something better than the creature he had become.

Eating beans on toast at the dining-table, Chris was both pleased and astonished by the cat Sam. Not that he wanted a cat, or a dog, or any kind of pet whatever, but the fact that this savage and independent creature had accepted him as a friend in a hard world touched him. At the usual time he fed the cat, and at bedtime Sam went out willingly enough, and was nowhere to be seen next morning.

The previous day Anne had mentioned that she would have to work overtime for several evenings during the week. Mrs Atkinson had promised to look in on him from time to time, and offered to do his shopping. Chris had accepted this suggested help, because he knew recent events had sapped him and he needed time to recover. He wanted to stay quietly in the house.

Something was occupying his mind—the idea that the house held the answer to the puzzle of the attacks upon him. If only he could find—what? He didn't know what; something, which he would know when he found it, which would hold a clue...

Meanwhile it occurred to him that the house could do with a thorough clean from top to bottom, in addition to the start he had already made on windows and sundry clutter. If there were more booby traps, he would find them. If there truly was a clue, he would find it. A systematic search, that was it. Clean and search together. Obsessively.

Living for a short time in the house next door had made a difference to him, he realised that. It was so spotless. Too spotless, uncomfortable for ordinary mortals. But it had been transformed in the last twelve years while his own house had been left to rot. His house exemplified the fashions not even of his mother's day, except for her bedroom, but of the previous generation. His own room was the only part which was of his own devising, and displayed his enthusiasms of a time which, although it still touched his heart, had gone and must be replaced by new growth, new tastes, new ideals. He had welcomed the old things unquestioningly; but now he felt an itch for change.

He rang through to next door and asked Mrs Atkinson to bring him an extra supply of bin-liners when she went out shopping. There was going to be a throwing-out session, definitely. And it was to start in the attic, where he and Anne had made such startling discoveries before, and work down to the cellar. Every wall, every cupboard—and being an old house, there were a lot of cupboards—was to be cleansed, and in the case of cupboards and drawers, emptied.

Over the next three days, during which Anne worked overtime every evening and they didn't meet, he carried out this plan of campaign. He did a little at a time, finding that although he had become used to cleaning in prison, he now tired quickly. It was a strange feeling. He'd always had enough energy and to spare.

Most of the boxes in the attic he threw away after checking through them. Some things were too good to discard altogether. He thought of Lucy Grindal and put them on one side. He dusted down the attic walls and ceiling and scrubbed the floor. Then he cleaned down the attic stairs and the first-floor landing, and went on his busy way through the rest of the rooms.

By Thursday morning the house was almost as spotless as Chris could make it, and a good deal barer than before. He had enjoyed these last days, but now was beginning to feel ready for company again and hoped that Annie had finished her overtime for the week.

Since he had been at home, he had received a good deal of mail. Some of it was junk mail. Some was from various authorities, in plain brown envelopes. It wasn't very interesting. This morning there was junk and one plain brown envelope. He had had many similar plain brown envelopes. He didn't bother to open the post. There was a corner of the cellar he hadn't finished the previous day, a corner with a heavy box.

The box turned out to contain the best china, which had always been kept for special occasions. As Chris carried it up the cellar stairs and into the kitchen, he realised that some of his tiredness had worn off and he was feeling a little stronger. Standing the china on the draining board to wash later, he left it to prepare lunch and noticed the post on the table. He took it into the dining-room to read while he ate, together with a short-bladed knife to open envelopes. He looked at the junk mail, which intrigued him, because he hadn't seen anything like it in prison, and left the plain brown envelope, which didn't excite him. He ate a light lunch, then let in the cat.

Sam had become steadily more at home. He came in now for a late breakfast, with a squall of demand, looking up angrily with his great golden eyes. Once satisfied with a saucer of top of the milk Sam went to sit in front of the gas fire, like any old household cat. He even allowed Chris to stroke him very briefly, on his head. The grey fur was unbelievably soft to touch.

At last Chris got round to the plain brown envelope. He wondered why he had hesitated to open it. There was nothing strange, sinister, or off-putting about a brown envelope. No doubt it would prove to be rubbish, like the rest, and would soon join them in the kitchen waste bin. He picked up the vegetable knife and slipped its short blade along the top edge.

The single sheet of paper inside was the birth certificate he had sent for. Except that it was not a birth certificate. He opened the piece of paper out and stared at it, keeping it flat with his left hand while sipping from the cup of tea he held in his right.

The columns with parents' names drew his eyes first. Adoptive parents. Adoptive mother. Sheila Simmers. Adoptive father. Dennis Simmers. It was not a birth certificate at all. It was an adoption certificate.

Chris put down his tea with a shaking hand. They must have sent him the wrong one. This was nothing to do with him. But there was his name, Christopher Simmers. There was his address, the very house he was sitting in. There were the names of the father he had loved, and the mother to whom he was bound by countless ties, whom he had killed. Chris felt his whole world fall into grey shards of chaos about him. He was not himself, not Chris Simmers, not the child of his mother and father. The woman he had killed—if he *had* killed her, and he'd assumed that for most of the last twelve or so years—was not his real mother, whatever else she had been.

Adoptive mother. Not real mother.

I am no one. Not Chris Simmers. That is only the name given to me at adoption, according to this certificate. No one. Nobody. Nowhere.

The rest of the afternoon passed with Chris still staring at the certificate, trying to resolve his thoughts, to discover what, in a changing world, remained to him. At one point he must have let the cat out. At some other point he took his cup and saucer to the kitchen draining board, and, returning to the dining-room and feeling suddenly very cold, switched up the gas fire.

At last there was a tap at the back door, well after six in the evening. Stiffly Chris rose and moved from his position at the dining-table and went to open the door, reluctant, more inclined, once he saw her radiant face and hair, to bang it against Anne than to admit this unsullied girl. The old tom-cat, shrieking in protest at being excluded for so long, pawed at the panels of the door until Chris opened it enough for him to squeeze through.

'Me too?' asked Anne quizzically, and without a word Chris let her come in.

'What in the world has happened to you now?' she challenged him. 'You look awful. Has there been any more trouble? Has there been another attack? Are you hurt?'

'Come into the dining-room. I'll just feed the cat.'

He fed Sam in the kitchen. Meanwhile in the dining-room Anne had seen the certificate, which lay among the remaining ruins of his lunch, and picked it up. She was holding it in her hand when Chris came back into the room. The cat walked before him, tattered tail on high. Anne moved smartly out of Sam's way so that he could take possession of the old Art Deco fireside mat. Thereafter she avoided treading on the mat as though there were a time bomb on it.

She indicated the certificate to Chris. 'This?'

He nodded.

'A bit of a blow, was it?'

'You could say that.'

'When did you open it? This morning?'

'Lunch time.'

Realising that the table was still in a

mess, he cleared it hurriedly. On his return from the kitchen, she said, 'You've been sitting here brooding ever since?' His eyes, she could see, were full of pain and despair.

'I suppose so. I don't know how the afternoon has passed, really. It has been...' He swallowed the adjective. 'It's been awful.'

'Looks as if you were busy first thing,' said Anne, who had noticed in passing the bucket still full of dirty water, after being used to wash the corner of the cellar, in the kitchen with its companions the scrubbing brush and floorcloth. She had also noticed the bulging binliners in the hallway.

He nodded, thinking back and trying to remember the morning.

'So she wasn't your real mother,' said Anne.

'It doesn't make any difference, does it? To all intents and purposes she was. She brought me up.'

Anne had been examining the certificate with care.

'You've noticed the date on this? It was issued when you were six or seven.'

Chris hadn't noticed. Once he'd read 'Adoptive father' and 'Adoptive mother' that had been enough for him. He hadn't scrutinised the document as Anne was doing now.

'So you ought to remember the adoption,' she went on.

He stared at her.

'You don't, obviously, or you wouldn't have been taken by surprise like this. Didn't you tell me the other day that you have blanks in your memory apart from the one when Mrs Simmers was killed? Didn't you say you had a blank for when you were about six or seven?'

He answered slowly as if his voice was dragged out of him. 'That's right. The psychiatrists discovered it when they kept analysing me in prison. A blank for about a year, they said, as though it had dropped out of my life altogether.'

'Then the blank covers the time of the adoption, and whatever led up to it.'

'I can remember the first six years of my life, here with Grandpa and Grandma Nourny. Mother was here all the time at first, then she and Father used to go off together for long holidays. Then there is the blank before I start remembering again. Mother and Father were here all the time then, and Grandpa had become an invalid. I remember your parents coming to live next door, and you being born.'

'As you never let me forget.'

'Do I harp on about it? But I'm still getting used to the idea that you've grown up. Reminding you that you weren't always a competent and rather bossy woman, but were once my little schoolgirl friend next door, is my way of keeping you in your place.'

She pulled a face at him, restraining herself from saying out loud, 'You mean it's your way of keeping a barrier between us!'

Chris tried not to see that he had hurt her.

She conquered her emotion and went on, 'The experience of being adopted must have been traumatic. That's why you wiped it out of your mind.'

'I'm sure you're right. All I can say is that today everything changed for me. Now I'm nobody. I haven't a name, a family, nothing. Even my cherished memories of childhood must be all distorted, a sham, perhaps something I made up, a fairy story to comfort myself. Perhaps those first six years are only a chimera.'

'You do talk nonsense.'

Chris now noticed what she was wearing. A camel-coloured blouse and toning long-line cardigan over black trousers. She'd changed since arriving home from work, because her work outfit was a navy suit and white shirt, with hair drawn back. Now that sparkling red hair sprayed over her shoulders.

'You can find out more about this

and probably buy a copy of your real birth certificate,' went on Anne. 'I'm not sure, but a girl at work had the same problem and she saw a social worker first. They have a talk to you. It's quite a business, finding your real parents. Can be traumatic. They don't always want the contact.'

'That's putting the boot in, if you like.'

'I'm only giving you the worst scenario. It isn't likely that will happen, but you have to realise the possibility.'

'Presumably they never wanted me, so it will hardly be a new experience.'

Anne looked sternly at him, then went on, 'I'll ring the council first thing in the morning and find out definitely. Pull yourself together. Eat something. Go and buy yourself some fish and chips. Have a shave. Don't give way like this. The attacks on you never made you react as badly.'

'No, ma'am.'

'Tidy this room up.'

'Yes, ma'am.'

'I'm going now,' she said.

'Out with Graham again?' He felt the impulse to hurt her, and was appalled at himself.

'Not a bad idea. He's good company, not like some people I could mention who are feeling sorry for themselves. See you tomorrow.' And, carefully avoiding the cat, who hissed and aimed a blow at her as she went past, Anne went swinging out of the house, hiding in this show of impatience the sorrow and pity she was feeling. Pity would be the last thing he wanted, and the last thing which would be good for him.

Early next morning, Friday, after a sleepless night, Chris decided that he must ring the social services himself and not let Anne do it for him. If he was quick enough he'd get in first. It took a while to be connected with the right people, but at last he contacted a woman who knew all about such things. She suggested he went into the office in the first instance, bringing his adoption certificate, and made an appointment for that morning. He had decided that the unknown enemy was not going to make him afraid to go out of the house, he would carry on as normal regardless, so he kept the appointment.

'I see the adoption took place in our York magistrates' court,' said the friendly woman, he thought she was a social worker, who interviewed him.

'Yes,' agreed Chris.

'I take it you want to know your real parentage, and to get in touch with your real mother?' she went on.

He thought about what she had said; the assumption was that he might be an illegitimate child with father unknown, or

215

that a married woman had given birth to a child not her husband's, he supposed, or the woman would have said, 'You want to get in touch with your real mother and father.' So he answered, 'Real parents. I would like to know who I am and get in touch with my real parents.'

She took a copy of the certificate on the office machine and said, 'It can be traumatic, you know. I would like to suggest that you let me make preliminary enquiries, then we'll have another talk in the light of what I find.'

'How long will it take?' he asked.

'I'm not busy. No reason why I shouldn't go along and look at the records now.'

'Can I come with you?'

She hesitated. 'I would rather do things the usual way,' she said, 'but in this case I should find out very quickly. Would you like to come back this afternoon?'

Chris spent the middle part of the day restlessly. There was no reason to go home so he hung around town, watching the buskers who were playing and performing in the central streets, calling in at the library and looking at the newspaper adverts for jobs, finally eating a sandwich in one of the many cafés which put on a cheap menu for hard-up tourists. At last it was time to return to the office.

The woman, Mrs Smith, looked up as

though she was pleased to see him.

'Now then, sit down,' she said.

He took a seat guardedly, wondering what was to come.

'In your case,' she said, 'I can give you the information now because—and this may be a disappointment to you—as it happens both your parents were already dead when the adoption took place.'

Chris turned white and swayed on his chair. 'Now then!' said Mrs Smith. 'Hold on! I'll get you a cup of tea with sugar.'

He drank it automatically.

'So there is no question', she went on after a while, 'of your contacting them, which is the part which is traumatic. Often the contact is unwelcome. In your case it was because your parents were dead that the adoption took place at all. The persons adopting were your aunt and her husband, who were already taking care of you.'

'I see.'

She went on carefully, keeping an eye on him in case he fainted or something equally dreadful. 'I see no reason why you should not obtain your real birth certificate, because I can give you the details you need to apply for one. The only problem you will have, and I would like to help and advise you with it, is telling your adoptive parents that you have been looking into the details of your birth. They might be upset.'

'They are also dead,' he said, realising that she did not know about the murder of so long ago.

'Then your case is an unusually easy one. There might be other living relatives who you could contact, but if they are more remote, cousins, for instance, the whole thing is not so traumatic. You will be too late to obtain a copy of your birth certificate today, but you could go along first thing on Monday morning. You were told you were born in York, and the adoption certainly went through our magistrates' courts.'

'Can I see the record you saw?'

'I don't see why not, under these circumstances. I'll give you a note to the Clerk of the Court. The records are stored in the Assize Courts, that grand Georgian building, do you know it?'

'Built to designs by John Carr, altered and added to by the Atkinsons and their partners,' said Chris.

'I'm sure you're right. I'll give Mr Brown a ring and tell him you're on your way. There should be time this afternoon, although if they are like most people they will finish early on Fridays. The records have more details of the case than I have given you. I'm sure you would prefer to read it for yourself.'

With assurances that he would contact her if he needed counselling, or before seeking out other members of his family, Chris walked down the stairs and out of the offices gingerly, as though he was recovering from flu.

He walked to the castle, where the records he needed were held. It was a bright spring day. The Eye of York, that four acres or so of glowing green grass surrounded by the buildings of Clifford's Tower on its mound, the Debtors' Prison, now a famous museum, and the Assize Courts, still a working part of the judiciary, seemed as central to life as it had been for centuries. He remembered bringing Anne to visit the place and telling her its history. As usual there were groups of tourists all around, parking their cars in the spreading car-park, climbing the steps up Clifford's Tower's grassy mound, sitting on the central grass where once the castle deer had grazed, going into the museum, coming out of the museum, going to the café for refreshments.

He asked for the Clerk of the Court, showed Mrs Smith's note, and was soon in a quiet cool room waiting for the book which recorded the proceedings on that day twenty-five years or so before.

His adoptive mother had produced

documents proving that his parents were dead and that she and her husband were now resident in his grandparents' house, looking after the small Christopher, and wished to legally adopt him. The adoption had been agreed. It had all been so simple. But the import of those few words was so shattering that he responded to the Clerk of the Court as though he were a zombie.

On coming out of the stately Assize Courts, where records were stored in the basement, Chris went to the shop and bought a small notebook, then visited the café for another cup of sweet tea. He preferred it without sugar, but some instinct of self-protection warned him that he was in a dangerously shocked condition and needed to take care. As he sat with the tea in front of him, and a scone with butter, Chris wrote a note to Anne on a leaf of the notebook. Then he set off for home, still shocked, but the action of walking soothed him a little.

Passing the Atkinsons' house, he pushed through the letterbox the note he had written for Anne as he sat in the café. It was quite simple.

'Dear Anne, please do not come round. I need to be alone for a while. Will contact you. Chris.'

10

The weekend was a strange time. No Annie, no Mrs Atkinson. Chris went out to shop for food, cooked, cleaned up after himself, and thought about the change which had come to his life. He had some washing and ironing to do, he watched a little television on the small old black and white set which had somehow remained in working condition, listened to the tiny radio he had had in prison, and began to do a few exercises. It wouldn't do to let himself stay unfit. Seeing how many press-ups he could manage was a good way of forgetting his troubles.

When Monday morning came, he set off in good time to the Register Office in Bootham, the street which led north from Bootham Bar, hoping to obtain a copy of his birth certificate. He had all day to do this in.

The shady, pillared entrance and the cool interior were already familiar to him, and the same pleasant woman came to the hatch to answer his query. He remembered vividly how she had told him where to send his birth certificate application, how she had deleted one address and told him to write to another. He knew now that adoption certificates used to be obtained from the first address, and were now granted from the second. He asked if he could have a copy of his birth certificate and passed over a piece of paper on which he had written the necessary details.

'We are busy this morning but with any luck I should be able to fit it in for you before lunch time,' the assistant said.

'What time?' Chris asked, looking at his watch.

'You've given all the information we need. Shall we say that you call back at twelve o'clock?'

'I'll be here,' he said, remembering the little group of silver birches, set back from the pavement in a grassy area with seats, which he had passed on his walk.

Sitting in the gently moving shade of the birches' pointed leaves, at the foot of another, different section of the fortified city wall, he gazed at the traffic moving along Bootham, starting and stopping in accordance with the traffic lights, forming great immobile queues along the length of the road then slowly moving forward, stopping, starting, the drivers growing hotter and hotter and more and more bored. His eyes moved after them, as though they were images on the television screen, but he could not remember afterwards any thoughts which had moved through his head during the period of waiting. Then he went back to the Register Office.

'It's ready,' the assistant said brightly. She had been asking her colleagues during his absence, 'Wasn't that the young man who came in a while ago for an application form for an adoption certificate?' The one girl who had glimpsed Chris before, rather thought it was.

'Thank you.' Chris paid his five pounds fifty pence, took the envelope she offered him and left, all with a vague and zombie-like expression which troubled the woman a little. Certificates could be traumatic things. Birth, marriage, death, the three standard nodes in life, the points at which everything changed.

Chris did not open the envelope immediately. He walked along to Miller's Yard, bought a healthy wholemeal sandwich full of cheese and salad, and took it home to eat.

Opening his door, Chris now had no thoughts to spare for possible hazards and no fear of entering. The trauma of the present eclipsed everything else. His unknown enemies could attack him if they liked. They could kill him if they liked. He couldn't care less.

After his frugal lunch, Chris looked at the birth certificate. He already knew most of the information on it, but there were additional details, and these soaked into his brain. He felt that he was not the same person who had left his terrace that morning. There was so much to think about that he knew it would take him the rest of the day to do so.

Towards evening there was a howling at the door and he got up to let in the old tom-cat Sam. It was only Sam's insistence on being fed that prodded Chris into preparing for himself some slices of toast and peanut butter, which satisfied his hunger.

He had fallen into the old home habit of spending most of his time in the dining-room, but tonight the place was too full of recent memories. It was here he had been sitting all afternoon, gazing into space. Here, the last time he had seen her, Anne had come in quickly and shaken him up, insisting on him meeting her standards of regular meals and proper care of himself.

Tonight he wanted to be elsewhere, so he went into the sitting-room, or front room as his family used to call it. The cat Sam walked in after him and made a careful examination of this new environment before settling on a chair, giving his long matted grey fur a few ineffectual licks, curling up and going to sleep. The strange thing about Sam was that he was scrupulously clean in the house, as though he had never lived rough in his life. The rest of the evening Chris was once more gazing into space and trying to make sense of his life, or his memories of it. At least now he knew exactly what had happened. His glamorous, adventurous parents, Roger Nournavaile the brilliant photographer, and his wife Prudence, star journalist, their tragic death, his stay-at-home aunt and her husband taking over care of him and of the old couple, his grandparents, and in return sharing the home here. The decision to adopt him.

It was at nine o'clock that Chris roused himself to make a drink, and in walking through the hall to the kitchen noticed the hallstand as if for the first time. He thought of the Atkinsons' hallway, with its rather twee small curved table, and decided a table would be pleasant for his hall too. Why his mind should have latched on to such trivialities he didn't know, except that was how things happened, and sometimes trivialities were all one had to latch on to. He found himself planning to move the semicircular fold-over card table from the sitting-room, which was cluttered, into the hallway. He'd have to find somewhere else for the coats. What would he do with the hall-stand? Give it to Lucy Grindal for her good causes, he decided. On impulse he picked up the telephone and rang, there and then.

'Canon Grindal,' came a rich, deep, beautiful voice.

'May I speak to Miss Grindal?'

'I'm afraid she is out at present. Can I help?'

'I was only wondering if she would like a hall-stand for her good causes, jumble sales and that.'

'Who is speaking, please?'—very gently.

'My name is...' Chris hesitated. 'Miss Grindal knows me as Chris Simmers,' he went on. 'I live in Bishophill. I met Miss Grindal when she was collecting jumble. And her dog.'

'I expect she had Prince Rupert with her,' said Canon Grindal's friendly, calm voice. 'Of course she would be delighted to have the hall-stand.'

'I have some stuff in bags for her, but the hall-stand won't go in her car and I have no transport at present,' went on Chris. Not that the hall-stand would have gone on his bicycle either, even before it was smashed up.

'You must be the young man she mentioned. Did you give her a cup of tea?'

'I did, yes.'

'Am I right in thinking you aren't working at present?' Grindal had been doing some quick remembering. The slight break in Chris's voice had alerted him. The antennae were working overtime.

'That's correct.'

'If you are free, would you care to come for a coffee, tomorrow morning, about ten? You could tell me how much else you have for Lucy to collect,' said Canon Grindal.

'Yes.' Chris's voice sounded glad, relieved. 'I would like to come. Then I can tell you exactly how much stuff there will be for collection.'

'Tomorrow then. Ten o'clock. Or earlier if you like. Any time after nine thirty.'

'Thank you.'

What was I thanking him for? wondered Chris when he had put down the phone and walked into the kitchen. Sam, who had woken up and followed, announced he would like to go out, at once, please. Chris made his drink and decided on an early bedtime. Much to his surprise—he expected wakefulness—he slept.

In the morning, after giving Sam the cream from the new bottle of milk, Chris tried to examine the wounds the old warrior had acquired during the night. One side of his head was nearly covered with blood, but he resented Chris's interference and growled furiously, glaring with his

227

golden lamps of eyes, and demanded to be let out of the house again, though he had only recently come in. He then walked off, stiff-legged, in an offended manner.

'Have it your own way,' Chris called after him. The wounds must be badges of tom-cat pride, that was obvious. He himself still felt weak after the shocks of various kinds, but his strength was returning, he could feel that. The dustmen had called while he was out the day before and taken the absolute rubbish away. The house was looking very bare and scrubbed.

Towards nine o'clock in the morning Chris set off. He locked the front door casually, not caring who knew he was leaving the house empty, and walked away from it without a backward glance. The morning was fine and sunny and the journey through the city was a pleasant one, but he was too wrapped up in his own state of mind to notice. He walked slowly, stopping often, apparently to look down a vista or into a shop window, but in reality seeing nothing. It was half-past nine by the Minster chimes when he reached his destination.

Canon Grindal and his daughter Lucy lived in the house which went with the Canon's job, at the east end of the great cathedral. There was a small front garden, a narrow path, and an old panelled door with a knocker. Inside, though, the place was astonishing. It had been formed from two, possibly three smaller houses, for there were three staircases in various places. Immediately inside the door was a square panelled hall, Elizabethan in feeling, with the largest staircase rising out of it, the massive old oak banisters going up the side of the stair and continuing along the landing at the rear of the hall. Off on one side was a stately dining-room with a rich thick old Turkey carpet, which Chris glimpsed briefly through the open door.

'It's pleasant upstairs at this time of day,' said Canon Grindal, leading the way to their Georgian sitting-room which was on the upper floor. This was a long, low room, its white-painted panelling now faded to ivory colour, the carpet and the loose covers on the upholstered furniture in soft flowery shades. In honour of the calendar assertion that it was spring—confirmed by the delicate green of the trees in Dean's Park and the daffodils in a vase on a windowsill—the electric fire which the household used in the summer months had been installed on the hearth of the Adam fireplace, and Canon Grindal switched it on.

Chris sat down when invited, still in a daze. He had not quite got over the surprise of meeting Canon Grindal. How could that beautiful voice come from such an ugly face, with its broken boxer nose? This was people's usual first reaction to George Grindal, before they felt the full impact of his personality. Then they forgot the shape of his nose, and the bumpiness age had brought to his face.

In his turn the Canon had been assessing the younger man. Lucy had formed very strong ideas about him. She thought he might have recently come out of prison, and George thought she was probably right. Lucy also thought he needed help, and it looked as if she was right there too. All this had been decided in the Canon's mind before the kettle had boiled for the coffee, while little pleasantries were still being exchanged.

'I'm afraid Lucy's not here, you are out of luck,' George Grindal said. 'It's powdered coffee only when I'm in charge. You would have been given the proper thing if she hadn't had this meeting to go to. She is sorry to have missed you. Would you take a biscuit? They have little bits of chocolate in, we rather like them.'

Chris said he liked them too.

They sat in a comfortable silence for a while, busy with coffee and biscuits, before George Grindal decided it was time to get down to brass tacks. The young man himself obviously wouldn't.

'On the telephone last night you said that Lucy knew you as Chris Simmers,' he remarked kindly. 'What did you mean by that rather ambiguous statement?'

He had struck on the very cause of Chris's distress, and the tragic eyes which gazed at him told him so.

'Sometimes life changes,' Chris said, 'and you think you've never known anything about it at all. The things you were brought up to believe, you find aren't true. The things you thought you knew, even about yourself, are in fact totally different.'

'Tell me,' invited George Grindal.

'I shall have to begin at the beginning.'

'I have all morning,' George said expansively. He cleared his mind of everything else and prepared to concentrate on Chris and his concerns.

'I was born and brought up in a small terrace house in Bishophill,' began Chris. 'It belonged to my grandparents and when they died it was left to me. I am living there now. My childhood and youth were uneventful and unadventurous.'

'Happy?' asked George.

'Yes. Very happy, I think.'

'You aren't sure?'

'I'm no longer sure of the ground I walk on.'

'Fairly happy, then.'

'I had a good job in a bank, friends, a widowed mother, and that was it. Then to celebrate my twenty-first my friends and I went on a pub-crawl, though we spent most of the evening in one pub. I became very drunk. One friend took me home. In the morning I woke to find that my mother had been murdered with an axe and it seemed that I was the murderer. I have no memory of killing her.'

George met Chris's long searching look without flinching, though the crime was greater than he had expected. Was this man a matricide? There was a hardness about him.

'To cut a long story short, after twelve years in prison I came out on licence and returned home. Only, by degrees I have found out that the woman who was murdered was in fact my aunt, and she had adopted me when I was six, nearly seven, after my parents had been killed. My memory has a hiatus for that time. Yesterday I found out who I really am.'

'And that is?'

'My real name is Chris Nournavaile. My father was a brilliant press photographer who travelled all over the world to wars and revolutions. My mother was a journalist. Sometimes she travelled with him, and they were together in the East to record a revolution in words and pictures when fighting broke out near their hotel and in the course of it they were both killed by a shell fired by the government forces.'

George looked sympathetic. He knew there was more to come.

'The odd thing is that my solicitor told me, when I was first out of prison a few weeks ago, that a search was being made for a male descendant of someone called Nournavaile who lived back in the eighteenth century. Of course I didn't think it could be anything to do with me, but now it may be. "May learn something to his advantage," you know, the usual wording. And an odder thing still is that ever since my return home someone or some group of people has been trying to kill or injure me.'

That was when Chris paused. He had given a bald outline, with none of the nuances, the variety of experiences, which had been involved for him. But the old clergyman's expression was one of comprehension, and Chris felt he understood a great deal more than the words themselves had conveyed.

'I'll tell you what,' said George in that beautiful voice, 'we could do with a drop of brandy in our next cup of coffee. You could drink a second cup, I know.'

'Yes please.' And Chris smiled, in relief.

'But I won't have any brandy, thanks.'

'Lucy would say, "A trouble shared is a trouble halved,"' George quoted. 'You must go on and tell me all the details in a minute. Just let me fill this kettle. I brought a jug of water up with me. It won't take long to heat, while I find the brandy. If you don't want any, I certainly do.'

George was not operating on intuition alone. For the last forty years he had been devoting part of every year to helping young people in trouble, particularly young men at the age when they thought they were tough and strong, and events were liable to prove to them rather painfully that they were not as tough and strong as they thought themselves. George had encountered such young men in some strange settings, when they were in emotional extremis and could see no way forward. A simpler case, but the one most involved with publicity—or at least, notoriety—had been his encounter with the pop star, Poison Peters, in a sleazy London caff in the middle of the night—well, about three in the morning as far as George could recollect—when Poison had not been in any great trouble, but in a moral dilemma, if you could call it that. He had been invited to play the part of Christ in York's famous medieval Mystery Play Cycle and had been agonising over it. It was not a decision to be taken lightly.

'Read Luke,' George remembered saying to him. It wasn't going to be as easy knowing what to say to Chris Nournavaile.

'So you find that you have a much more vivid and interesting inheritance than you ever knew. Nature and nurture.'

'I was brought up—as my father must have been, now I come to think of it—in a part of the city which you could live in all your life and never leave, never cross the river to the main part, the historic core, or go outside the southern walls. There was plenty of employment, small workshops and factories, plenty of chapels and churches, pubs, little street-corner shops and larger shops on Micklegate, small terrace houses or larger ones, all life was there, if you like.'

'Do you feel the area has changed?'

'Oh, it has. I was a bit upset to find how much.'

'It is no longer as self-sufficient?'

'It's no longer as organically one, as united.'

'And from this environment, in which you were content, even unadventurous, your father had sprung into a way of life far more enterprising, a creative, dangerous, but exciting life.'

'I feel as though my own horizons had opened up, knowing about what he did and that he was my father.'

'You feel stirrings of the same possibilities in yourself?'

'Yes—possibilities—not necessarily the same ones.'

'Your aunt, who adopted you—she was not enterprising, or creative?'

'Not at all. Very much the opposite. She was my mother's sister. Looking back at her character and how she changed with age, and particularly at the fact that she left me in ignorance of my real parents, I wonder if she was jealous of their way of life, and their success in a different world to hers.'

'You have three problems, as I see it,' said George, who had drunk his second cup of coffee and wondered whether to make any more. 'First, adjusting to the knowledge of your real parentage. Second, the attacks on you, about which you must tell me more. Third, the fact that you do not remember murdering your mother—or aunt.'

'Yes.'

'The first you don't need help with. Time will adjust your ideas to these startling facts. The new knowledge will change you.'

'Yes.'

'You will probably want to talk out your emotions about your parents and the adoption, and if I can be a listening ear, you are welcome any time. You may decide, for instance, to revert to using your father's name. You may decide to make yourself known to the solicitors who are looking for male Nournavailes. But let us think about the other two points.'

Chris nodded in response.

'About the murder. You got drunk, you say?' George asked. 'Blind drunk?'

'I don't remember a thing.'

'And you had never been so drunk before?'

'Never.'

'But slightly drunk, I suppose?'

'Yes, tipsy. I remember those times.'

'Tell me,' went on George Grindal, 'how do you normally behave when you've drunk too much?' He was wondering about any underlying aggression in Chris's character.

'I've given up drinking alcohol. I haven't had any at all since that night, not that there was much chance in prison.' Chris sipped his brandy-less coffee, and thought for a minute. 'Well,' he went on, 'as far as I remember, when I was a bit drunk, I got silly—told long pointless funny stories which seemed humorous at the time, but when I sobered up I always felt I'd made a fool of myself. I felt guilty, too...'

'Guilty?' George raised his eyebrows.

'Yes... I'd do an imitation of Mother—I mean Aunt. It was quite funny, I thought

I was hilarious, but it seemed disloyal—she was a tiresome woman, but no need to wash family linen in public...'

'Have you ever got into a fight? In prison, perhaps?'

'Yes, I did. Got hauled up in front of the Governor. We were on a work party, and Mack, a bully of a man—some people called him Big Mack, but if he'd heard they would have regretted it—was having a go at Skinner, making out he should have been a Seggie—those are the segregated prisoners on Rule 43.'

'Yes, I know,' said George.

'No one liked Skinner, he went around grassing on people, and Mack said he was a child abuser, but he was a pathetic creature and to get a reputation as a Seggie is a terrifying thing. I saw red and lashed out. Mack might have slaughtered me, but the screws jumped in and separated us. Mostly, you know, I kept myself to myself in prison.'

'What did the Governor say?' asked George.

'Oh, he let me off lightly. I was very lucky.'

'Why do you think he was lenient?'

'We were on a work party demolishing an old shed. One of the screws spoke up for me, saying there was plenty of stuff lying around, lengths of wood and bits of old metal, I could have picked up to hit Mack with, but I never thought, just whacked him one on the jaw and then one into the solar plexus. That screw got me off the hook. He was tough but fair. He told me he spoke up for me because I was one of the few with common sense enough to finish a job off properly. He really tried to make good workmen out of us. Not all screws—officers, I should say—are bad, you know?'

'I've a great friend who's a prison chaplain and he says the same. Did you ever take drugs in prison?'

Chris looked across the rim of his cup at George, then answered, 'No.' He went on, 'I didn't want to become dependent. Life was boring but the drug barons were people I'd rather not tangle with. I never felt it was worth experimenting with drugs.'

'It's strange', George said, 'that you didn't take a weapon to that man you fought with. I say that because, after all, your mother—or aunt—was murdered with...did you say an axe?'

'Yes, I know. The odd thing is, I feel awful when I think of her dying like that—I feel less than the dust—and I must have done it—but I find it difficult, when I can't remember anything about it, to feel as guilty as I did when I'd made fun of her behind her back. I remember that all right. If only she had a grave, or a memorial for her ashes, I would go and tell her how sorry I am. It might not do any good but it would make me feel better.'

'You remember nothing at all?' asked George Grindal. 'Most people I've met who say they don't remember, in fact do remember, but not as though they had done it but as though they'd watched.'

'Not a thing,' said Chris.

To himself George thought that it didn't seem to be in Chris's character to commit violence. Drink made violent people more violent. They didn't start telling funny stories. Humour is a safety valve. Making fun of someone must release the tension.

If you can't remember you can't repent and be forgiven, he said to himself. 'Perhaps you didn't kill her,' he said aloud.

'I'm trying to find out more of what happened. That's why the whole thing of tracing back started. There are more secrets, I'm sure of that. Meanwhile the one I've found is hard enough to come to terms with. What would you advise me to do? Am I to announce to everyone that my name is Chris Nournavaile?'

George thought for some strange reason of the fairy stories he used to read to Lucy when she was little.

'You are like the prince in the fairy story,' he said now to Chris, with a whimsical smile, 'who was given a Cap of Invisibility. From your adoption you have been wearing it. Now you must decide yourself whether or not to take it off and reveal yourself as Chris Nournavaile, who may—or may not—be descended from the eighteenth-century Nournavaile, who is being sought.'

'The invisibility has not been total,' replied Chris. 'Someone has always known who I am.'

'The attacker—the unknown attacker?'

'Yes.'

'But although you may seem to be alone, you have friends.'

Chris looked surprised at the turn the conversation had taken. 'That's true. People have shown me more friendship than I expected. Mr Hale, my solicitor, was welcoming and kind. My neighbours— Anne, who was a schoolgirl when I went into prison, wrote to me constantly and is proving a staunch friend. I am only afraid she might grow to care too much—no way must she marry a murderer. Her mother, although she does not approve of me, has been a support. Miss Grindal I think of as a friend.'

'Myself, too, I hope,' said Canon Grindal.

Chris smiled, then went on, 'My probation officer has helped beyond the call of duty. I have acquired a kindly and helpful doctor. And then there is Sam.'

'Sam?'

'You might think me ridiculous. Sam is an old stray tom-cat. He is very *un*friendly, very aggressive, yet he has become my companion.'

'In the best fairy stories an animal companion is obligatory,' said Canon Grindal.

Chris could not help laughing. George poured them both a new cup of coffee, laced his own liberally with brandy, and handed Chris his plainer one.

'And now let's look at the facts,' he said. 'You do not seem to be basically an aggressive person. That's one point. Let's look at the old nature versus nurture thing. Your upbringing and life until twenty-one were uneventful—that's nurture. Your parents lived, in contrast, varied and exciting lives. One had artistic ability—you can't be a crack photographer without skill in composition and in getting the meaning out of the scene before you, as well as technical expertise. The other was a journalist—not my favourite form of life but enterprising and talented. What do you feel within yourself?'

'If you had asked me before yesterday,

I would have said all I want is a peaceful life. The last part of my sentence I was working in a tree nursery, growing trees from seed. It's one of the most exciting, meaningful things I've ever done. I would like to be like that Frenchman who quietly planted a forest and by that act improved the climate of the place he lived, bringing back the moisture, the rivers and streams, and created living beauty.'

'And how do you feel today?'

'Life seems to hold more possibilities. I'd still like to plant a forest. But maybe I could take up photography as well. Maybe I could photograph the animals who would come to live among the trees. Write about them. Travel—I've never thought of travel, and suddenly I'd like to do that, very much.'

'And look at trees and forests in other countries?' asked George Grindal, his eyes encouraging.

'Why not?'

'I am, after all, a clergyman,' said George, 'so you mustn't expect to get off without a word from the Bible. Take John's Gospel, for example. John the Baptist said, "A man cannot take anything at all, except what is granted to him by heaven." That is Peter Levi's translation.'

'I can only have what is right for me to have?'

'Ultimately.'

'I only plant a forest if it is right for me to do so.'

'Perhaps that is what it means.'

'On the other hand, if something *is* meant for me to take—or do—*not* to take it, or do it, would be equally against—heaven, if you like—as bad as burying a talent.'

'You might be right.'

For what seemed like a long time they looked at one another, weighing the implications, the possible further avenues along which this argument might take them. By mutual consent they left it to be thought over individually.

Chris went on, 'It is strange that since finding out all this that we've been talking about, I haven't cared about the attacks on me. I haven't cared if I was killed by them or not.'

'That must the effect of shock.'

'Or putting myself into other hands.'

'We are all in other hands, in one sense or another,' said Canon Grindal, glancing at his watch, 'whatever we choose to call them. Our talents, where do they come from? For whose glory should we use them? Our own? I think not. But you will have things to do, and so have I. Your cat Sam will be waiting for you. Don't forget. We haven't talked much about the attacks of which you've been the target, have we?

Are the police taking an interest? Not that you'd welcome their intervention after your experiences, but they can be a comfort as well as a threat. Let me know if anything else happens on that front. Come back or telephone whenever you want to talk, or just to be here for company. You are welcome.'

Chris walked home as unaware of everything around him as he had been on his way to see Canon George Grindal, but he felt much happier, more at ease with himself. He let himself into his house, followed by Sam, and stood sensing the atmosphere. It did not feel as though anyone had intruded, although on the mat was a postcard. He picked it up, wondering why it had not been delivered that morning. He went into the kitchen and opened a tin for Sam even though it was only lunch time and the cat was never fed until after six o'clock. Looking at the postcard, he realised that it was from his American friend of so long ago, Tom Bell.

'Tom!' Chris exclaimed. He stood turning the postcard over in his hands, noticing that it had been redirected from the Atkinsons' house. He expected that Mrs Atkinson had just got round to pushing it through the door. The postcard had a picture of Florida on one side and a good deal of close writing on the back in bright blue ink. Anne had written in minuscule letters on the corner, 'This came to us in mistake.' He could see why. The bold, curlicued handwriting was difficult to read unless you were used to it. It was a while before he understood the whole message and by that time the script had become crystal clear to him as it used to be. Tom wrote that he was sorry not to have been in touch, but he'd been travelling the world. Now he had the chance to return to England and visit his friends Chris and Chris's mother, and his old workmates at the electricity generating station. He hoped to arrive in two weeks. The date on the postmark was impossible to make out. Chris, wishing Anne was there so that he could tell her how pleased he was, looked round for some creature to confide in and saw the great golden eyes of the old tom-cat looking up at him.

'Tom's coming, after all these years!' he told the cat. 'Now we'll hear his version of that night, and what the surprise was, if he hasn't forgotten.' He propped the postcard on the mantelpiece and felt happy.

This uplifted mood lasted until late the following morning, when the gunman burst in through the front door.

11

The man with the gun barged through the front door, which for once Chris had forgotten to lock, kicked the door closed behind him, and opened fire straight away. He shot one bullet into the ceiling, and the noise filled the house with a sound that was unmistakable. There was no one in the road outside, but tourists on the walkway inside the city walls jumped, turned round, and wondered what it was. The explosion was followed by a minute tinkle of fragments of falling plaster from the elaborate moulding. The man seemed huge, menacing, terrible as he stood there gun in hand and at once let off another shot, this time at the floor where it ricocheted off the encaustic Edwardian tiles and buried itself in the wide skirting board.

Chris had heard the first shot and he came running, leaving the cat in the kitchen and himself darting into the hallway just as the third shot slammed into the sitting-room door. He confronted the gunman, careless of safety, saying, 'What the hell...'

The gunman pointed the weapon directly

at him and his finger was on the trigger.

Chris was certain his last moments had come. The bullet could hardly miss him. In a strange way he welcomed it, as a fractious child welcomes bedtime. Chris did not want to die, yet he yearned for peace, for an end to the attacks, the suspense and misery. If they wanted his life let them have it. He no longer cared. He had had enough.

The gunman's face was covered, all but his eyes, by a black ski-mask. His hands were gloved. His clothing was a fabric which would leave the minimum of fibres.

He didn't shoot.

He said, 'Shit, Chris, I didn't know it was you.'

Chris stood there. He said nothing.

The man lowered the gun, held it in one hand, and with the other ripped off his ski-mask.

'Damien!' said Chris in a sort of croak. His throat seemed to have dried up completely.

'They didn't tell me your right name,' Damien said in a shocked and rather aggrieved tone. His voice was much higher than its normal deep thickness. 'They told me it was a bloke called Chris Nournavaile.'

'You're telling me this is a contract

killing?' asked Chris.

'That's what it is, yes,' Damien said awkwardly.

'You said you were going straight when you got out.'

'It was the money, Chris. I was so effing short of dosh. You can't do much on what the government hands out.'

'So you agreed to kill someone you didn't know, for money?'

'Well, yeah,' said Damien, putting the gun down on the semicircular walnut table which Chris had moved into the hall from its previous home in the sitting-room. It was an elaborate card table which formed a circle when opened out. Chris had slid it along the floor with great care, and he was pleased with the new look of his hallway. The four legs of the table were joined together near the floor by a wooden centrepiece, turned and with finials top and bottom, which was a pest to dust but looked attractively decorative. He thought the table had belonged to the family for a long time. Now, seeing a gun resting on the glossy surface, he felt a sense of outrage growing in him and, all of a sudden, a longing to confront and defeat the enemy in his life. No longer a hidden enemy, but flesh and blood now, in the person of Damien, with whom he'd shared a cell for three of his prison years.

'Are you going to, then? Why not get on with it?' he shouted aggressively.

'Don't be daft, Chris. Of course I can't shoot you. I don't know what to do. If I go back and tell them, God knows what they'll do to me. They won't be able to send someone else because you'll know about it.'

'I'm so sorry to be causing inconvenience to the plans of you and your friends. Money, of course, comes before everything.'

'Oh, Chris,' said Damien, and looked thoroughly upset. 'I didn't know it was you, honest. What you using another name for? They only said there was a contract out for this bloke and if I was careful it would be an untraceable crime. I was only going to get half the money, anyway. They were keeping the rest.'

'Tough,' said Chris grimly. 'I'll take that.' He reached out to the table and took up the gun. 'There, I feel a bit safer now.'

'You were never at any risk from me. We're mates, aren't we? Say we're still mates, Chris.'

'I'll think about it. We might have *been* mates but I didn't know then that you went about shooting people.'

'I've never shot anyone in my life,' Damien said sulkily.

250

'You just came damn near it. Within a fraction of a second. Any of those three shots might have killed me, or your finger might have been already pressing the trigger when you recognised me and you might not have reacted quickly enough to stop yourself.'

'Oh, God, I'm shaking,' said Damien. He was, too. Chris could see that he was.

'You'd better come and sit down.' Chris led the way into the dining-room and used the gun to gesture with, indicating one of the fireside chairs. 'I'll make you a mug of sweet coffee for shock,' he said, amazed at himself. Then he realised he was shaking too and had better make it two mugs. He took the gun with him into the kitchen, where Sam, undisturbed by the drama, was finishing his food. Chris looked at the light lunch he had been preparing. He felt as though that time had been in a different world. He thought about Damien. Of course, it was obvious. Damien was always influenced by whoever was with him at the time, and after they were moved into separate cells he must have been with a real hard set. All Chris's efforts to reform him had been overlaid by the newer influence. Chris curled his lip. Fancy presuming to try to reform anyone, when he himself...

It was while Damien was drinking his

mug of hot, sweet coffee that he said, 'I daren't go back, Chris. No way. They'll kill me. Not only have I not killed you, but I've given the whole game away.'

Chris gave him a long, hard look. 'You'd better do it properly, then. Names, places. I'm going to tell the police and you're going to give them a statement.'

'They'll put me inside and throw away the key,' said Damien.

'They won't if you play it the way I'm telling you.'

'I can't grass them up.'

'You haven't much choice.'

Neither of them spoke for a while, then Chris said, 'I suppose I'd better give you some lunch. But I'm ringing the police station first.'

He took the gun out into the hall with him. They had had the wall phone fitted to save space, and the cable was long enough for him to stand near the open door into the dining-room and keep an eye on his uninvited guest.

'They're coming to fetch us, in quarter of an hour,' he told Damien when the conversation was over. Dave Smart had remembered immediately about the attacks on Chris and although he had sounded astonished at the way Chris was speaking of the gunman, he'd agreed they would try to go easy on him if they could and if he came up with genuine info.

Chris rearranged the light meal on to two plates, glad that he had put the leftover salad in the fridge for the next day. It was already prepared and made the single lunch into a double quite easily.

They sat on either side of the dining-table, where Chris had eaten so many meals throughout his life, and ate together, Damien very conscious of the gun, which lay by Chris's hand.

The police took charge of the weapon, which was a relief to Chris. He had asked if he could be present at the interview, and as Damien had no objection, he was. Acting DCI Dave Smart and another policeman did the questioning. Chris made notes, even though Dave said he'd see if a transcript could be supplied.

'It was nothing personal,' Damien said. 'Nothing personal against Chris, only there's this contract out, see, on his life. They've been trying to scare him away or organise an accident and it hasn't worked, like, they even got some French hoods over on false passports to run over him and that didn't work, you know, so the punter, the bloke who is paying, like, said he'd up the stakes and we were to go for it and make bloody sure this time. It was too good an opportunity to make some dosh to miss, like, you know.'

Dave Smart didn't see, neither did the other policeman, and neither did Chris. They all wanted to know who was behind the whole thing and why, but it became clear that Damien was only a pawn in the game—the fall-guy if things went wrong—and he hadn't been let into the secret of who, why, and what it was all about.

'I don't want releasing,' he said fervently. 'Please keep me inside... If you've a cell free,' he added politely.

'We haven't,' Dave Smart said curtly. 'You'll have to take your chance. We're releasing you on police bail. Mr Simmers here is refusing to press charges for attempted murder or conspiracy to murder so we can't keep you in on those grounds. The bail is for the gun, which you don't have a licence for, et cetera.'

'They'll kill me,' said Damien fearfully.

'They'll have to bloody well kill you, then.'

Chris had said nothing at this point, but when the interview was over he asked if it was all right if Damien stayed with him for a few days, while he was out on bail.

'You must be stark raving bonkers, in other words, potty,' said Dave Smart.

'We're in the same boat now, me and him,' Chris said. 'They'll be out to get both of us. We might as well protect one another.'

'You realise this character might try again?'

'Try again to kill me? He might but he won't.'

'Couldn't you charge me with attempted murder, Chris?' Damien was pleading as they walked back to the terrace, both of them watching the street scene round them intently and fearfully. 'Go on, be a sport. They'll have to find a cell for me then.'

'Shut up, Damien.'

Tired of not seeing Chris, Anne came round at six o'clock that evening. She shouted 'Coo-ee!' and walked in, as she usually did. Not finding Chris in the kitchen she went through into the dining-room, and stopped short when she saw a great, hulking figure lying back in the fireside chair nearest the window. When he heard her approach, Chris had jumped up from his own chair and was facing her as she entered the room. He saw the shock and revulsion on her face.

Turning to look at Damien, Chris saw on his face an expression of lust and frank appraisal. Damien's eyes were looking Annie over from head to foot, returning to her pert bosom and shapely legs and hips. She was wearing a long royal blue jumper and emerald green leggings, her face as usual was bright and cheerful, and her hair was its usual buoyant, bouncy sparkling red.

'I didn't know you'd got company,' Anne said stiffly.

'May I introduce Damien. We shared a cell for three years.'

'Pleased to meet you,' said Anne, not looking at all pleased.

'Charmed, I'm sure,' responded Damien, in his thick, heavy voice, his eyes hot.

'I'll come back later,' said Anne, turning to go.

'Annie!'

It was too late. She was already half-way through the kitchen. Chris raced after her and caught her up as she opened the door from the yard into the back alleyway.

'What is all this?' he cried, catching hold of her arm.

'It's one thing that you were in prison, Chris, but I'm not hobnobbing with people like that, not for you, not for anybody.'

'He's not a bad chap,' Chris said awkwardly.

'I don't like the look of him. And it was only too obvious that he liked the look of me. I wouldn't care to be in the same room alone with him.'

Something impelled Chris to be frank. He drew Anne further into the alley, away from his own yard, and spoke quietly.

'It's a queer story,' he said, 'but it has helped me and the police to get at a bit of the truth. There's a contract out on me, Anne. That is, someone has offered money to have me killed.'

'I know what a contract is, if it's "out on" someone.'

'They asked Damien to do the job. He burst in with a gun at the ready and fired three shots in the hall. Then I appeared and he recognised me and stopped shooting and took his mask off and apologised.'

Anne looked absolutely horrified. 'You're not serious?'

'Yes. We've been down at the police station this afternoon and he's made a full statement, names, places, everything. The police are going to follow it up. Meanwhile he's staying with me for a few days because when they find out what's happened they'll turn on him, probably kill him.'

Anne gave him a long, long look.

'You must be out of your mind,' she said with conviction.

'You share cells with all sorts of types in prison and, believe me, Damien was one of the best cell-mates I had.'

'I shudder to think of the others,' said Anne.

'In the end he must have done me a good turn. The police are taking it seriously. They are determined to catch these enemies who've been doing all these things. Though they obviously aren't my personal enemies. Damien didn't know who had put up the contract money, and they are the real enemy.'

'Well, I'll tell you one thing for nothing, Chris. It's him or me. While he is in your house I'm not crossing the threshold and that's that. I think you're an idiot for harbouring him.'

'It's possible. I'm going to risk it.'

'Goodbye then,' Anne said firmly. 'I'll see you again—if at all—when he's cleared out.'

She went, and Chris returned to his house.

'She's a smasher,' Damien remarked as soon as Chris appeared. 'Is she your bit of stuff?'

'No,' Chris said. 'She's an old friend.'

'Not old,' replied Damien. 'I wouldn't mind a bit of that.'

'You can keep your hands to yourself,' said Chris furiously.

'Sorry, mate. If it's like that...'

'It's not like anything. I'm not having her going round with either you or me. No ex-cons for her. She's too good for both of us.'

Damien thought he'd better change the subject.

'You know, since I got out I've done nothing but think about birds,' he said. 'I've been obsessed with sex. The porn I've watched on video you wouldn't believe. There's some good stuff about at present. Real hard core. The lads and I put in a lot of time watching it when we can't get the real thing.'

Chris detected a familiar note of boasting. 'You and that crew who wanted me killed?'

'Well...'

'Well yes, you mean.'

'When you first got out, didn't you think about it all the time? Any tart in a pub or on the street, you start thinking what she'd be like, you know, didn't you, now, Chris?'

'I had other things on my mind.'

'Well, most blokes do when they first get out. Think of nothing else, I mean.'

'You never leave prison, that's my conclusion for what it's worth, Damien, because it never leaves you. It is going to stay with me for the rest of my life. Prison number, prison clothes. Only a few personal possessions. No responsibility for your own conduct. You feel like an empty shell, not human any more. That's never going to leave me. I'm not saying I've had no sexual thoughts, it wouldn't be true. But they haven't been out of control or an obsession, like yours. No. I've been realising for the first time, now I'm away from it, exactly what prison has done to me, exactly what the experience is, the powerlessness, the denial of dignity...'

Looking at Damien, Chris realised that he was bored and didn't understand what Chris was on about.

'We'll watch telly if you like, it's in the other room. But I haven't any porn videos to show you, I'm afraid.'

'Can anyone see in off the street?'

'Not really. There are lace curtains.'

'Well, we won't turn the light on, eh?' suggested Damien.

'When it starts to get dark I can draw the thick curtains.'

'When it gets dark I'll go to bed.'

'You can sleep in the back bedroom.' Chris remembered that his own little room had a lock on the door, and he remembered with relief.

It was the following morning that the postman brought a packet to the house. He couldn't get it through the letterbox and knocked on the door. Chris, who was coming downstairs at that moment, opened the door and took the packet. He noticed that it was a padded envelope with something inside, and laid it down on the hall table. Damien was already up and in the kitchen, making toast.

They ate breakfast amicably, with only a few remarks from Damien such as 'This is better than in the nick', or 'Isn't toast good when it's hot?' and 'I like this marmalade.'

Chris cleared the table and prepared to wash up, and Damien wandered off restlessly into the hall.

'There's a packet on this table for you,' he called to Chris.

'Oh, yes, I'd forgotten it. I wasn't expecting anything. You can open it if you like, Damien.'

Damien thought this was a treat. He hardly got any post and loved opening parcels. He turned the packet over in his hands, then with strong overgrown fingernails he plucked at the end, pulling the sides apart. There were a few staples which he was concentrating on dislodging when the whole thing blew up in his hands.

Chris jumped a mile when he felt the blast and heard the explosion. The cup he was holding crashed into the sink. The first thought that flashed into his head was that Damien had somehow got hold of another gun and was going to shoot him for real this time. But it hadn't sounded the same as the gunshots. Perhaps it was gas exploding somewhere. He turned round gingerly, wondering if he dare move.

The door from the kitchen into the hallway had been blown open, and he could see right through to the front door, which seemed to be intact.

He saw the papers first. The table he had so carefully eased into the hall from the sitting-room was tipped over and broken, and from it had spilled a mass of papers. They had spread out over what lay on the floor, in a sort of heap.

What lay on the floor was Damien.

After standing rigid for several heartbeats Chris ran forward. Damien was lying with his eyes shut, head against the bottom step of the stairs. He lay awkwardly, and was bleeding. The blood gushed up through the papers.

Chris fell to his knees and picked up some of the papers so that he could see Damien better. Subconsciously he noticed they were mostly letters, both with and without envelopes. They were in the way, and becoming bloodstained. Quickly he moved them to one side, shoving them into a rough pile near the skirting board. The smashed table lay across Damien's legs. Chris grabbed it and stood it up. The base of it was all right, it was the top that was smashed. Damien groaned and opened his eyes.

'What happened?' he said thickly.

Chris didn't want to tell him. Didn't

want to tell him that his right arm ended in a mass of pulp. Didn't want to tell him that his face was streaming with blood.

'I don't know. Stay there. Keep still,' he ordered. 'I'm going to phone for the ambulance.'

Damien shut his eyes. 'They got me,' he said with conviction. 'I knew they would.'

He went quiet and Chris phoned 999. Then he opened the front door on a beautiful late spring morning, the trees still fresh green across the road, the birds singing, the city wall rising creamy white in the sun. The ambulance should arrive any minute.

He thought about the bathroom first-aid box and fetched a wide crepe bandage to try to stop Damien's bleeding. Some time he'd heard about tourniquets and as he watched the fountain of blood he wished he knew how to do one. He applied pressure higher than the gush of blood and succeeded in stopping most of it. He knew that you were supposed to put something firm over the blood vessel then twist a stick or similar in the bandage and tighten it, but he also remembered that that whole procedure could be more dangerous for the patient than leaving things alone.

So as things seemed to be a bit better under a tight bandage he left Damien and dashed round, getting the house ready to leave—water heating turned off, windows closed, back door locked, front door key ready in his pocket. He found his jacket and checked that he had some money in case it was needed. It only seemed like centuries from the phone call until the arrival of the ambulance. It had been seven minutes.

He rang the police from the hospital, while Damien was being examined and going through the first processes in Casualty, and asked for Dave Smart.

'Mr Smart,' he said, 'a letter bomb arrived at my house this morning. Damien's hurt, I'm ringing from the hospital.'

Dave, who had liked Damien about as much as Annie Atkinson had, asked, 'Are you all right?'

'A bit shaken.'

He explained that the house had been left as it was immediately after the accident, except that he'd stood the table up and pushed the papers to the edge of the floor.

'What papers were these?' asked Dave.

'I really don't know, Inspector. They looked like letters.'

'But you only had one packet, you say, from the postman?'

'Yes.'

'Where do you think they came from, then?'

'I don't know. Does it matter?'

'Everything matters. We'd better have the scene properly examined. Is the man likely to die?'

'I don't think so. It's mainly his hands and right arm, a bit of damage to the face. He's lost a lot of blood. They're transfusing now. His legs seemed all right to me, not broken, I mean. The table fell across them, at least I expect that's what happened, and they must be bruised, but I don't think they're broken.'

'Have you any idea who sent this bomb?'

'Damien thought it was the people he named to you yesterday, and that they'd got him.'

'And what did you think?'

'I thought it was for me.'

'We'll call at the hospital on the way and get the front door key,' said Dave Smart before ringing off.

12

Until that evening Annie Atkinson did not know what was happening. Her mother had heard the letter bomb go off, in the morning, but did not think to ring Anne at work and tell her of the strange noise, or the ambulance, or the police who arrived later that morning. Anne knew nothing of the events until she came home from work after five o'clock. As soon as she could, she went round to the house next door, where a policeman was on guard once more, and some of the scene of crime team were still busy inside.

'We've about finished,' one of the SOC men told Anne. He recognised her from the time when Chris had been nearly electrocuted.

She hardly dared ask the question.

'Who was hurt?' she said at last. 'And what was it?'

'That young man of yours is all right,' the officer said. If he hadn't been happily married he would have fancied Annie himself, and he had a soft spot for her. 'It's the other one that was hurt.'

Anne put up a prayer of thankfulness.

'What was it?' she asked again, and fixed appealing eyes on the policeman.

He looked round, sure that he shouldn't be telling her.

'You'd better ask the boss, miss,' he said, as Dave Smart came into view.

'Mr Smart,' said Anne persuasively, 'you know that I am a neighbour and friend of Chris Simmers. I'd like to know where he is and what happened.'

'As for where he is, he's at the hospital with his friend,' answered Dave, with an emphasis on the word 'friend' which Anne understood and Dave knew that she did. 'Letter bomb,' Dave went on, briefly. 'Keep it under your hat, will you?'

The police team were packing up, and Anne smiled, thanked Dave, and went.

She would not willingly live again through the hours which followed. The house next door was soon deserted and locked. She kept walking into the back alley and looking up at it, remembering the night when she had gazed up and seen the bathroom light, still on after goodness knows how much time. In the alley, the very spot where she was standing, she had quarrelled with Chris only hours before, and the words she had spoken came back to haunt her.

'Will you stop walking in and out of

the house, our Annie,' asked her mother at last.

'Sorry, Mum,' and Anne sat down on the elaborately fringed blue silk settee and tried to watch the television, but other scenes rose before her eyes, other dramas were unfolding inside her head. She was going over the whole course of her relationship with Chris. He had always been there, he was one of her first memories. When he went into prison her mother had not wanted her to write to him, but her father was alive then and he thought Chris was innocent, just as Anne did. He said she could write. 'But one thing you can't do, our Annie,' he'd said, 'is to visit him. I'm not allowing you to visit a prison.'

From twelve years old to sixteen she had written every week, letters full of riddles, little drawings, funny things that had happened, jokes.

Then when she was sixteen life had changed. Her interest in boys developed when after O-levels she went from an all-girls' school to the mixed-sex sixth form college to do her As. At the same time the first symptoms of her father's illness appeared, and Mrs Atkinson's attention became more and more fixed on her husband as the years went by. Anne had been a bit wild in those years, and it was surprising that she kept up the correspondence with Chris at all. His regular letters, which never mentioned prison but discussed the books she was reading or the gossip she told him, were sometimes not opened until her conscience jogged her into writing back.

After Anne's father died things changed again. She became the focus of her mother's attention, and there was for both of them a long trauma of grief. The parties and boyfriends dropped away. Chris's wise, comforting letters were a support to her and he regained his importance. She realised that none of the boys she had knocked around with had been as good a companion as the boy next door. The ones she still saw were old workmates, pals, not lovers. She had looked forward to Chris coming out, and now...

If she had ever pretended to herself that Chris was only a friend and neighbour, she could no longer sustain the illusion. He was all that mattered to her. She thought this was not a very politically correct attitude, for a self-possessed, independent young woman who always stood out for her rights and for full equality. She had tried to keep this particular emotion out of it, to feel only what she thought Chris wanted her to feel. She had intended to be a friend in his need. Not to fall in love with him. She didn't think she had fallen, exactly. He had changed; he was harder, more impervious, not at all the kind of man she intended, one day perhaps, to fall in love with and marry. So if she had not fallen in love—she scorned the very phrase—what had happened to her emotions? Why was the thought of his peril like a knife in her heart? Why did she long to be near him at the hospital, sharing his vigil by his unprepossessing friend?

After a short time she got up and went out again, and this time she heard the cat, miaowing plaintively by Chris's back door. She hated the cat, vicious, savage creature. But no way could she hear his cry and ignore it. Chris would have fed him long ago. She fetched the spare key to Chris's front door from where it lay in a box and went to let herself in. She walked past the scene in the hallway, still one of chaos, even more so after the efforts of the scene of crime team, through the kitchen and to the door into the back yard. That key was in the door lock. The cat came in with a cry that said, plainer than words, 'About time too.' She opened a tin of cat food and emptied it on to the enamel plate which was used for the cat, and filled his water dish. Until the creature had finished eating she did not feel she could leave the house, and she went out into the hallway again and looked at the muddle on the floor, shuddering at the blood. Picking up one piece of paper after another—letters or envelopes—she soon realised that the subject of this correspondence seemed to be the name Nournavaile. Putting everything down again more or less where it had been, she went back into the kitchen. Hadn't she told Chris to research his grandfather's family? Had he taken any notice? No, he hadn't. As soon as the cat was finished she opened the back door again and shooed him on his way, then made all secure and let herself out, locking the front door firmly.

During the rest of the evening she strongly resisted the desire to go outside and fidget about. She sat on the settee as if glued. So she missed seeing Chris return, at about half-past eleven, tired, grey-faced, dragging himself along the few feet of front path. He had taken a taxi from the hospital and left it at the corner, wishing to walk to his home, quietly, hoping to take it unawares, to sense before entering if any more schemes had been hatched, or further snares laid for his feet.

He had not thought of Annie the whole day. Even now, when he saw the cat's dish and full water bowl and knew that she must have fed Sam, the thought only flickered through his mind without arousing any emotion, even that of surprise. He felt totally exhausted. Any images going through his head were of Damien. Damien sulky, Damien aggressive, Damien sleepily making toast, Damien's look of pleasure as he went to open the packet, Damien on the floor, the blood spurting, Damien white and silent, lying in the ambulance, Damien with blood transfusing into his arm, Damien going into the operating theatre, Damien lying still unconscious, Damien's flicker of life, Damien under sedation, Damien at long last drifting into sleep.

There had been interruptions in this progression. Policemen asking for statements, nurses telling him to go and get something to eat, canteen staff serving something on to a plate—he could not even remember what he had eaten. Many, many cups of tea and coffee. Doctors telling him he could stay by the bedside, his own realisation that Damien must be almost despaired of for them to do this, his hand on that great paw, the left paw, which seemed to have escaped the main force of the blast which had taken off the right forearm, looking at the passive face, what he could see of it among the bandages.

Chris fell into bed.

The next morning he slept late, and

when he did rise, he ate a hasty breakfast, gave the cat the cream from the top of the new bottle of milk, and set off immediately for the hospital. He dare not telephone before going—it would be worse, if they told him bad news over the phone. He walked, not having his bicycle, although he could probably have caught a bus. It suited his mood far better to get the exercise and the fresh air. He spoke to no one on the journey, and did not want to speak to a soul.

From the outside, Anne had inspected his house carefully before setting off for work. She had seen that his bedroom curtains were closed, and guessed that he had been home late and was still asleep at that hour. The dining-room curtains were closed also. The cat was sitting on top of the wall, sunning himself in the early warmth. His long grey fur was tangled and there was a new wound on his chest. Gazing down at her with those great inimical golden lamps of eyes, he did nothing to encourage her to touch him.

She decided to spend her lunch hour on a bit of family history, on Chris's behalf, thinking it might lift her spirits to do something for him, even something in which he hadn't the slightest interest.

That evening she was hovering outside her front door, making dabs at the neat, tiny front garden with a hand-fork which was more decorative than useful, when Chris came home. Anne heard his step and stood up, not moving towards him, and looked in his direction. He stopped by his own front gate and spoke to her.

'You've heard what happened?'

'A bit,' she answered. He looked unutterably strained. His face was grey and she could tell that he could hardly stand, but the change in him was more than that. She had hardly seen him for days, since he sent that note round asking her to leave him alone for a while because he had things to think over. His discovery of who he really was, was unknown to her. Their only contact had been her brief visit when she encountered Damien, followed by the row between them in the alleyway. She did not know of his visit to Canon Grindal, or the sea-change which his discovery was slowly bringing about in his ideas and perceptions of himself and of life. But it was plain enough to her that there had been a change in him. It seemed that he was partly a stranger, as indeed he was. The man who had shared a cell for three years with Damien, and regarded that person as the best cell-mate he had had in twelve years, had always been a stranger. The Chris she knew had still been there. In fact *that* Chris, submerged for so long, was the one he, too, had returned to, anxious to recapture his previous life. There had been times when she glimpsed the harder Chris, but they had been fleeting. Now, as they stood silently and looked at one another, while the first rain for several days began to mist down into the road, the difference in him really came home to her. It was, she knew, not only the change twelve years had brought, but a new change superimposed on that one. How she could tell this so clearly she did not understand, only that it was an instinctive realisation, one of the many messages which had always passed between them without words.

'We must talk, Anne,' he said quietly, and she noticed his use of 'Anne' as opposed to 'Annie', and knew that the talk he intended was a very serious one.

She answered with a bright tone, that she had been digging up his family tree and had a lot to tell him about the Nournavailes.

'I look forward to hearing that,' he said, still more formally, 'but not now. I can't really think of anyone but Damien. He took the blast which was meant for me, and he isn't out of the wood yet, by a long way.'

'Would you like me to get you a meal?' she asked.

'No. I'm not hungry. There was plenty

to eat at the hospital. Have you fed the cat?'

'Not tonight. I would have done soon, if you hadn't come home.'

'Yes. Thanks for feeding him yesterday.'

She shrugged her shoulders and pecked at a stray weed with the hand-fork. 'It was nothing.'

He wanted to reach out a hand towards her and lay it on her shoulder, but felt as though he was not in the same world. He was too bound, as if in iron, by the changes which were working in him and which he didn't understand. If he had tried to put it into words, to explain it to her, he would have said that he felt as though something was happening which he had to go along with blindly, and where it might lead he had no way of knowing.

They parted without speaking further, but although an onlooker might have thought there was anger, or at least dislike, between them, they knew that was not the case. Their personalities were too close, through a lifetime's association, the feeling between them was too deep. They parted not in anger, nor in love, but in an interim, a no man's land. She went into her house with a serious expression and spent the rest of the evening like one who awaits momentous events which they cannot influence.

He, though, was to cope with a visitor before he could find dreamless sleep in bed.

It was after he had solaced old Sam, who felt it was far too late in the evening to be fed. He had acclimatised very quickly to being Chris's cat, although he still asserted his independence often and vigorously. Feet, if accidentally too near him, still suffered his ferocious attack. This night, after eating and drinking, he was more affectionate than usual and sat on Chris's knee. At this Chris thought he would have a go at untangling some of the beautiful long fur which was so sadly matted and ruined. He had lain a soft baby brush near his chair for just this chance to do something about it. Gently he touched the cat with it, almost stroking with the friendly bristles. To his pleasure Sam sat still and put up with the brushing.

'If you would let me do this every day, you would soon be a very beautiful cat,' Chris whispered to him. How that brutally aggressive male face and those angry claws could ever become beautiful Chris could not have said. It was not for Sam's potential beauty that he loved the cat, yet the length and silkiness of the grey fur was amazing when it was brushed out. Chris had to choose parts of the cat which were on show without moving him, and also bits which were not in too bad a state. He knew that he hadn't reached the point of being able to tackle the tangles and the places where blood and pus had matted the fine threads. How long he would have been able to continue this grooming if they had not been interrupted, Chris never knew.

There was a hammering on the front door, and Sam at once leapt down from Chris's knee and demanded to be let out. Chris opened the back door for him, before approaching the front. He did not waste thought on wondering who might be there.

On the short length of path stood a tall man in a long overcoat and wide-brimmed hat. By now the rain had intensified into a downpour, and the hat brim dripped water.

'Mr Nournavaile, I presume?' asked the tall man. His accent was Oxbridge.

'Yes?' responded Chris after a moment's hesitation, wondering what on earth?

'I bring news of something which may benefit you. May I come in?' The stranger's general air was remarkably like that of the three wise men.

Chris wondered if this was a new approach to selling double-glazing, and he was too exhausted to want to deal with anyone, but he opened the door and gestured the way into the sitting-room. The blood and papers were at the foot of the stairs, between the sitting-room and dining-room doors, and this way the visitor did not have to pass them, or even see them, for it was fairly dark and the hall light was not on.

'Now, if you can tell me what this is about...' Chris said. The tall man had taken off his hat and coat, and Chris had placed them on an upright chair which stood in the corner of the room.

'My card,' said the man, and taking the piece of pasteboard, Chris read, 'Mr Florian Poste, solicitor and genealogist. Specialist in wills and descents.'

'You will not have heard of me.' It was a statement.

Chris agreed.

'But I know a great deal about you. I have been tracing you for some time, Mr Nournavaile.'

'Really?'

'We specialise', the solicitor said portentously, 'in tracing beneficiaries of wills. Beneficiaries who may not realise that they *are* beneficiaries. We particularly co-operate with our partners in the United States. I have called to tell you that you can claim to be a beneficiary under the will of the late Arthur Z. Nournavaile, of Rideaux County, America.'

'Really?' said Chris again.

'And my firm would like to represent

you in making a claim to your inheritance.'

'You would?'

'That is what we specialise in. We have successfully claimed for literally hundreds of people who would not have known, but for our work, that they were beneficiaries.'

'That sounds a very worthwhile activity,' Chris said.

'In your case we have already invested months of work. You have been difficult to trace, Mr Nournavaile.'

'Go on.'

'I can tell you that your ancestry goes back to one Rebecca Nournavaile, who had twin sons in 1785.'

Chris thought to himself, Yes, I know, they were baptised on the first of November that year; he knew that from the newspaper cutting. 'That seems too long ago to be relevant to my life,' he said aloud.

'It is very relevant, Mr Nournavaile.'

'Do you work for Donne, Donne and Flight?' asked Chris.

'Certainly not.'

'I wonder how many different sets of genealogists are tracing me. It must be very important.'

Florian Poste quelled him with a glance. 'You are descended from one son who remained in England. Arthur Z. Nournavaile of the USA was descended from the other twin, who emigrated to

America in the early nineteenth century.'

'Rebecca I know about,' said Chris. 'Who was the father? I suppose she didn't manage it on her own?'

The visitor shook his head. 'It is a sad story,' he said. 'And as it has taken us so long—and much expense, may I say—to trace you, you will understand that I am not at liberty to disclose the full facts at present. It is doubtful if, without our expertise, you would be successful in any claim you might make. That is why I'm afraid we must have an agreement between us before divulging anything further.'

'Oh,' said Chris, feeling inclined to turn the man out into the rain, but sufficiently intrigued to want to hear the rest of it. 'Can I see this agreement?'

'You have nothing to lose,' said Florian Poste, taking a folded document from his inner pocket. 'And everything to gain. Without us you would not even know about your possible claim on the estate of Arthur Z. Nournavaile of the USA. All you have to do is sign at the bottom, Mr Nournavaile, both copies, and we will be able to proceed with a claim on your behalf.'

There was silence for some time as Chris read carefully through the document.

'You are asking me to sign this document,' he said at last, 'which gives your firm fifty-five per cent of anything I may successfully claim from this estate?'

'That is correct. You would not know of the possibility of a claim but for us, and if you tried to claim independently, then, I am afraid, we might decide to represent another claimant.'

There was silence again.

'I can let you think it over,' said Florian Poste, 'until tomorrow night. I would not like to rush you, Mr Nournavaile, but as it happens, in this case there is some urgency.'

'Really?'

'There is. That is why I came along this evening, as soon as we were able to confirm your present address. There is extreme urgency about the claim. If you were to endeavour to use another solicitor, delay would be caused which would be fatal to any chances of success.'

'I want to sleep on this,' Chris said. 'Thank you, Mr Poste, for taking the trouble to trace me and come here, and I appreciate that your firm has been involved in time, trouble, and expense. Because of that I intend to consider your proposition carefully. At the moment I am very tired, having had two stressful days, and I must ask you to leave me to think it over.'

The solicitor put on his dripping overcoat and hat, gave Chris the card

282

of the hotel where he was staying, said farewell courteously and left, trudging off into the rain.

Left alone, Chris noticed, as if for the first time, the state of the hallway. He was too tired to do anything about it, but he promised himself that it would be his first task in the morning. He looked at his watch. It was not too late to ring Annie. He quickly dialled her number. When he spoke his voice had much of its old casual intonation.

'You'll never guess what has happened, Annie,' he said as soon as she came on the line. 'No, I'm not telling you now. It would take too long. But come straight round after tea tomorrow night, and bring that family history you've been doing with you.'

'You've forgotten that it will be the weekend.'

'Yes,' he said after a moment's thought, 'of course. Well, I have a job to do first thing in the morning, and then I must go to the hospital, so can you come during the afternoon—about two?'

'I'll do that.'

'Right. See you then.'

She was left wondering. The tenseness of the scene between them earlier in the evening might never have been. Had it all been her imagination?

13

On the Saturday morning Chris was appalled when he stood and looked at the floor of his hallway. How could he have lived in the house for two whole days and done nothing about it? It was the sight of Damien's blood which smote him like a thunderclap. It was still there, crying out to heaven. It should have been cleaned away immediately, once Damien was in hospital. But was that the case? Was it not of importance, the fact that his friend had bled for him, too great an importance to be cleaned away as if it was nothing? He felt as though it should be honoured, that blood, not swilled down the drains as if it was of no account. But what had to be done must be done.

Chris fetched a bucket of warm water and cloths and set to work on the floor. The papers which had been scattered about were now in a pile by the skirting board, a neater pile than when he had shoved them roughly to one side. He lifted the pile and laid them on a newspaper on the dining-table to be seen to later. Then he had a clear run at the tiles. It was coffee time before he had the hall floor to his satisfaction. It gleamed brilliantly in the sunshine streaming in through the open front door. The pattern of tiles, first laid when the house was new, was now all visible—Chris had thrown away the shabby strip of carpet earlier that week. The late Victorian walnut card table which he had moved into the hall with such reverence was now a wreck; he pushed it unceremoniously back through the doorway of the sitting-room. The tiles were in shades of terracotta red, soft mustard yellow, white, grey and black, the red, yellow and white predominating. As they dried, he noticed that where the daily wear of a century had worn away the surface, they were drying dull and the brightness was dimming. Searching in the cupboard under the sink he found some polish which he had bought, not sure where to use it but feeling it might come in handy. Reading the instructions, he found that all he needed to do was to spread it on a damp cloth over the tiles, and it would dry to a shine. He did this, and sat, drinking a mug of coffee, on a stool in the kitchen doorway, watching the polish dry and marvelling at the pleasure such an ordinary thing gave him.

But there were still the papers, in that pile on the dining-table.

First he trod warily over the newly polished floor to have a proper look at the Victorian card table. This was a piece of furniture he had known all his life. His 'mother' had set great store by it, not liking him to put anything down on the gleaming surface. When he had accidentally knocked against it with his feet—and growing lads' feet are not always under their control—she had shouted at him in a way which made him avoid the table in the future. That was why he had moved it so carefully, feeling that by touching it at all he was breaking some taboo, and that by changing its position in the house he was exerting his new-found authority over the building and all its contents in a very bold and enterprising way.

He had always known that, being a card table, the fold-over leaf opened out to make a baize-covered circle. Once or twice he had seen his 'mother' lift the upper half to check the condition of the baize inside. But he had never been aware of what was now pitiably obvious. The whole top had been smashed, and under the folded-over top, now matchwood, was revealed a hidden compartment, a few inches deep and semicircular in shape. This too had been severely damaged, but the way it had been constructed was clear. He assumed it had been meant for the storage of packs of cards, dice, markers, or anything else that was needed for play. He could see that access to it had been by revolving the fold-over top, when half at a time of the storage compartment would have been accessible.

The compartment must have been crammed with the letters which had fallen out as a consequence of the explosion of the letter bomb.

If he wanted to discover the secret of the house, he had done so at last, for at a glance he had seen that some of the letters and envelopes were in his 'mother's' handwriting, others were in the bold, blue, curlicued hand of his friend Tom Bell. The strange friendship of these two people, the fact that neither of them would discuss with him whatever it was which gave them so much satisfaction to talk about to each other, had obviously resulted in this copious correspondence. The envelopes were all from Tom, he had noticed. The letters his aunt had written in reply were there in the form of copies, produced by carbon paper under the letter-paper. In some ways she was a cautious woman.

Chris wanted to go to the hospital to see Damien, and he wanted to go now, so that he could come back in good time for Anne's visit that afternoon. He stood and looked at the pile of papers and wondered what to do. It was clear from his careful cleaning and searching that nothing in the house could have been of the least interest to anyone apart from the family who lived there. Until these letters were exposed by the bomb. These, then, might have been the object of the search which had taken place after he was sent to prison. They might have some bearing on events since he came out. The last thing he felt like doing was reading them at that moment, but it was obviously not safe to leave them in full view through the dining-room window. At last he made his decision. He would take them with him. He found an old rucksack, made the letters into bundles and stuffed them inside, heaved it on to his shoulder, and left the house as quickly as he could to make his visit to the hospital. He'd have something to eat in the canteen there before going up to the ward.

Anne meanwhile was using her Saturday morning in researching further into Nournavaile family history at the York Central Library. She had done all she could from the International Genealogical Index, which was such a useful finding guide, long ago. Now she was searching for these references in the photocopies of York parish registers, of which the library had a small collection, and also the printed volumes of parish registers in the Yorkshire Archaeological Society's series, of which the library had a complete set of copies. Also the Freemen's Roll, and various other local sources. She found the work fascinating, if time-consuming. The morning flashed by. Much sooner than she expected, it was time to go home for lunch. It was no use going round to Chris's house until the time he had stated—two o'clock—so she sat for a while after eating, making sense of her notes, drawing out little family tree diagrams and trying to relate one item to another. The earliest mention of the name Nournavaile she had found was the most intriguing, although she thought it terribly sad. A little human story was there in the few words of the entry in St Olave's parish register for 1785. She was looking forward to telling Chris about it. He would be as fascinated as she was, that was certain. There was a little trepidation, too, mixed with these happy anticipations. Hadn't Chris said he wanted a serious talk? She hoped it wasn't going to be today. Some instinct was telling her that the omens were bad for serious talks. If it could be put off until a later date, that would be the best thing.

Damien was out of intensive care, that

was the good news. Chris found him in a small side ward, awake and conscious. He looked pleased when Chris appeared round the door. The side of his head was still bandaged, and of course what was left of his right arm was also wrapped in dressings. Chris nodded at him and fetched a chair to sit in.

'All right, then?' he asked. What a stupid thing to say, but what could anyone say?

'Not too bad,' said Damien, with an attempt at a smile. 'Considering.' He spoke with difficulty, the words seemed to force themselves out of his stiff lips.

'Look, Damien, do your folks know you're in here? I remember you were in touch with them when we were together in Wakefield.'

'The police told them. Me dad don't want nothing to do with me. Me mum's coming tonight, so she sez. She rang up to see how I was going on.'

'Well, that's good. Is there anything I can get you, fruit, choc, cigs, squash?' Chris wasn't sure if Damien would be able to smoke in the ward, and he didn't look fit enough to get out of bed and make the journey to the day room, where smoking was allowed. Fruit—would he manage to eat it? Squash—there was some already on his locker. Some chocolate might be the best bet. Damien had always been fond of Benn's Bars. They'd be sure to have some in the hospital shop.

'I could do with a beer but I don't think we're supposed to have anything like that in here.'

'There's one thing to be said for being in prison,' Chris said, 'it makes it easier to put up with being in hospital.'

'Better in here, in't it?' And Damien tried to grin with the bit of his face that showed. 'Warmer and the beds are more comfy.'

'The warders are prettier, too,' said Chris as a young jolly-looking nurse came into the ward. 'D'you know, I've been in and out of this place since I was released. At the moment they're putting me through a whole batch of tests because I was semi-conscious once for a long time.'

'She's a bit of all right,' said Damien, watching the nurse. 'You should see the one we get at night, she's a real cracker.'

'It's good to see you a bit better.'

'Oh, well,' said Damien self-consciously. 'No good moping, is it? I'm not dead, that's the thing.' Chris had to bend forward to make out the words, which came dimly and slow. 'I've still got me left hand,' Damien said.

'It could have been worse. No good moping, like you say.'

'I could have been dead.' And Damien's

eyes sought Chris's with the expression of a frightened child.

There wasn't much point in denying it.

In this kind of sparkling conversation they passed an hour, then Chris got up to go.

'See you later,' he said. 'I'll try to get back tonight. It would be nice to meet your mum.'

'See you,' whispered Damien.

'I'll bring you some choc tonight, mate.'

Chris walked out of the ward without looking back.

He reached home a little before two o'clock, made a pot of tea, and was just finishing his second cup when Anne reached the back door. She hesitated over walking straight in. In the end she knocked.

'Knocking like that, I thought you were company,' teased Chris. 'Come in, then, and tell me what you've been finding out. I bet I know some of it already.'

What a lot Anne didn't know! About Canon Grindal, and the man who had come last night. She didn't know about the way he'd been feeling, and she wasn't going to. She didn't even know about the real birth certificate.

Anne sat down at the other side of the table.

'Tea?' he asked her. 'It's still reasonably fresh.'

'No, thanks. I had plenty after my lunch. In an hour or so I wouldn't mind some.'

'Come on, then, let's have it. What are all these marvellous discoveries you've been making?'—and all the time, thought Chris, my knapsack is over there against the wall with those letters in it.

'It's an unusual name,' began Anne, with a pedantic air. 'But you always knew that.'

'Should be easier to trace, then?'

'Yes. That's true. Much easier than a more usual name like Smith, Clarke, or Wilson.'

'How far have you got back?'

'1785, actually.'

Chris could have guessed that, after the solicitor's visit on Friday night. He was glad he hadn't chipped in. It was going to be pleasant, listening to Anne telling him everything she'd found out, with that little air of self-consequence. He prepared to sit back and think of pleasant things for once, the magic of ancestors who were really his own, whose blood flowed in his veins, whose genes he might one day pass on to his own son. Or daughter. Or maybe he wouldn't have any children to pass anything on to. And would it matter, if he didn't? Would the world be any poorer? For missing a murderer's genetic inheritance?

He began listening again. Anne produced the little family trees she had drawn, and explained them. She traced step by step back in time and he followed her reasoning, nodding his head, asking questions, listening carefully to her answers. He pondered on the fact that his ancestry lay deep in this city. Some of his line had been Freemen of the City of York, an ancient institution probably started to protect trade, for only Freemen were allowed to carry on their businesses inside the city boundaries (apart from the area controlled by the cathedral church of St Peter). The Freedom was no longer of importance from a commercial point of view, but a source of pride all the same. Then, by the time she had explained back as far as the year 1800, he thought she must be thirsty with all that talking, and he got up to make a fresh pot of tea.

'Two hours have passed, Madam Annie,' he said, once more with that teasing tone in his voice. 'Time for elegant ladies to drink their afternoon tea.'

'I wouldn't say no,' she answered, and while he made it, she tidied the records of her work and put some of them away.

He found some cake he had bought the day before and set it on a pretty plate.

The best family china, which rarely saw the light of day, was one of the things he had discovered in his great cleaning session—it had been packed in a box in the cellar. It was now washed and in use, at least for times like this. He had piled it on the sideboard for the time being.

'I remember this china,' Anne exclaimed in a pleased tone. 'We used to see it every Christmas, am I right?'

'And birthdays.'

'True. Though only grown-up birthdays.'

They both welcomed the tea and the cake. It was a good way to spend time, to enjoy being together without commitment, all 'serious talks' put off to some unspecified future date, even the family history undiscussed.

'I haven't seen your horrible cat today,' Anne said at last.

'Oh, he's been around. This morning he was in as usual for his saucer of milk. I expect he'll put in an appearance about six. Sometimes he's more in evidence than that, but he's off today somewhere, hunting or fighting, I expect.'

'Typical male occupations,' said Anne in a playfully disgusted way.

Chris made no rejoinder. He was too happy in the moment to want to pick a quarrel with Anne, even in fun.

'And how is...Damien?'

'Oh. That isn't so good, really. He's conscious and realises that his right forearm has largely gone. But, as he remarked to me today, he still has his left hand.'

Anne shuddered. 'Gruesome.'

'And brave.'

'I suppose. At least he wasn't looking on the black side.'

'He was dominantly right-handed, in case you were wondering.'

'Any other damage?'

'I don't know what kind of state his face is in.'

'Terrific,' said Anne sympathetically. 'Can't you see it?'

'Not much of it.'

Neither of them spoke for a couple of minutes. That packet which was really a letter bomb had been addressed to Chris.

'Back to the family history, eh?' said Chris when the silence had gone on long enough.

'There were these two brothers,' Anne said, 'Joseph and Thomas. I was just going to tell you about their lives—we've been tracing your ancestry back to Thomas and you've been hearing about his descendants. Joseph and Thomas were twins. They grew up in York, and both were apprenticed by the parish. If I could explain that, they were born in the City Poor House, which was on Marygate in the parish of St Olave, where they were christened in St Olave's church.'

'Distinguished ancestors I've got,' Chris said.

'Various parishes contributed to the City Poor House and their paupers were sent there. Particularly poor women near childbirth. Then their parish had to make provision for the children when they grew older, and the usual thing was to put them out as apprentices. Of course, the possibility arose that if apprenticed to York Freemen, they would have the right to claim the Freedom themselves. The City authorities may not have considered this appropriate, so these two twin boys were apprenticed to tradespeople outside the city. That was all right, because they both finished their apprenticeship satisfactorily and Thomas made enough money to buy himself the Freedom later in his life. I was telling you about his later career, before you made the tea. Joseph married young, then he seems to have vanished from the scene. I don't know what happened to him.'

Chris nearly said, 'He went to America, and his descendant, Arthur Z. Nournavaile, left a lot of money by the sound of things...' but he decided not to say anything, only nodded his head wisely.

Then he asked, 'But why were they born in the City Poor House?'

'Aha, thereby hangs a tale,' said Anne. 'Their mother—'

'Rebecca,' said Chris as if prompting her.

'How did you know that?'

'Didn't you say?'

'I don't remember. Perhaps I did,' and she looked at him doubtfully.

He in his turn looked serene and unconcerned.

'Their mother Rebecca Nournavaile', she went on, 'had been married to a man named Joseph Burton. But unfortunately he had another wife, who claimed her husband. So poor Rebecca had to go into the City Poor House to have her twins, on the first of November 1785. She was from the parish of St Michael le Belfrey.'

'Well, I think that was pretty rotten of Joseph Burton,' said Chris indignantly.

'We don't know anything else about him. The record says, "of whose parentage and profession nothing can be collected".'

'I'm glad they decided to use her name for the twins. I wouldn't have liked to be called after that heartless man, Joseph Burton. So I'm descended from Thomas. I'm pleased about that. What happened to Rebecca afterwards?'

'I'm afraid I've no idea.'

'It wouldn't have been very comfortable or warm in the City Poor House, in that

November of 1785.'

'Probably not.'

'Thomas and Joseph must have been very close to one another. They would feel that they only had each other in the world, apart from their mother, of course. That story would set them apart from everyone else.'

'Yes, it must have done.' Anne put the rest of the papers in her briefcase. 'That's that, then. I can't take the tree any further back without doing a lot more work. The IGI always has to be checked, it is only an index, not by any means complete, and the original document usually tells you so much more. It would be more fun if you were doing the research with me. Think about it. But at the moment, I'm going. Mother will have cooked a meal.'

'Don't go for a minute,' he said suddenly.

She flinched. Was the 'serious talk' coming on?

'I want to tell you about the visitor I had last night. Perhaps you didn't notice but it came on to rain heavily. He was dripping wet. A tall man, with a posh accent. He was a solicitor. I have his card somewhere.' Chris got up and found the card on the mantelpiece, and passed it to Anne. She read it with surprise.

'He's coming back tonight. I've been

holding out on you, Anne. Most of what you told me today was completely new to me, but he had told me one thing—that in 1785 Rebecca Nournavaile had twin boys. He told me none of the other details you've found. He clammed up because he wants me to sign an agreement.'

'Agreement?'

'Apparently one of the twins went to America. As you've found my descent from Thomas, the one who went must have been Joseph, with his young wife. He settled over there and one of his descendants—I don't know any more than this about them—was Arthur Z. Nournavaile of Rideaux County, who died presumably not so long ago, and it seems I may be able to claim under his will. Mr Poste didn't tell me anything else, and he won't, until I sign this.' He produced the agreement and passed it to Anne.

She read it carefully. It took her some time. At last she cried out, 'But he wants you to sign fifty-five per cent of anything you might gain overto him!'

'As he points out, I would not have known I had a claim but for him and all the work he's put in.'

'It's monstrous!' cried Anne.

'As he remarked, if he hadn't put me in the picture, I wouldn't know that I had a

300

claim. As he also remarked, if I tried to claim without them they might drop me in favour of someone else with a similar claim.'

'That's even more monstrous!'

'So what do I do?'

'I don't know.' And the wind went out of Anne's sails.

'Exactly. And he's coming back tonight for a decision.'

'But you probably aren't a Nournavaile in the male line, if at all, even though that's what I'm researching,' said Anne. 'Have you got any further in tracing your identity?'

'Yes. I know all about it. I am a Nournavaile.' Then he told her of the events of the previous Tuesday.

'I knew that you'd been in contact with the social worker because I rang her, but you'd got in first.'

'I wanted to do it myself.'

'That's why you didn't want to see me.'

'Let's be accurate here. I wanted to do some of the work myself—yes. You have a tendency to wrap me in cotton wool. Although that's very pleasant I don't want it all the time. But that isn't why I didn't want to see you. When I found the truth about myself I was completely knocked for six.'

'Yes. I can see that.' Anne stared into space.

'There's a lot I haven't told you yet about that. Let's say briefly, my parents were dead when my aunt and uncle adopted me. Mother and Father had led adventurous lives. The photographer we found the scrapbook on, that was my father. I had to try to come to terms with what I had found out, which seemed to turn the whole world topsy-turvy. And I had to do that on my own.'

'And have you?' She looked at him solemnly.

'It's a continuing process. But it isn't the only thing going on. I've had a postcard from Tom Bell.'

Fetching the postcard from the mantelpiece, he handed it to her. 'It went to your house first, do you remember?'

'However do you make this handwriting out!'

'Well, that's practice.'

'He's coming!'

'Yes.'

'So you may be able to find out at last...'

'His evidence about what happened that night? Of course I'm hoping so. But let's be realists. He can add little or nothing to the evidence we already have, particularly since you've told me your little piece of the jigsaw. Everything points to his dumping me, blind drunk, on my bed as my aunt requested, saying goodnight as you overheard and going to catch the train, although, if you don't mind me saying so, Anne, the words you remember sounded more like Annie than either Mother or Tom.'

'But you're hoping for some little thing...'

'Yes.'

She looked at him and was surprised by the expression on his face. It brought home to her how much he cared about finding out, one way or the other, if he really was a murderer.

'There's something else, isn't there, Chris?'

'Yes.' Then he told her about the letters which had been hidden in the card table.

'How exciting!' Her eyes were bright, sparkling. 'When can I see them?'

'I want to look at them myself. Then I'll decide whether to show them to you or not.'

He has changed, she thought. I wasn't mistaken. Ten days ago he would have shared them with me right away, we would have sat next to each other and talked them over as we looked...

'I'm going.' She got up and put the rest of her research papers in her briefcase. 'Let me know how you get on. I like being in the picture.'

'Of course I will.'

'You're going back to the hospital?'

'Yes.'

'Then this solicitor's coming?'

'He is.'

'And you don't know what to say to him?'

'That's right!'

'Come for coffee in the morning,' he went on after a pause. 'I ought to ask your mother. I did ask her to have a cup of tea once and she wouldn't.'

Anne did not want to share Chris with her mother.

'She'll be busy cooking Sunday lunch. I'll come about ten.'

The phone rang. Chris went to answer it, Anne stood aimlessly, feeling that she ought to go but consumed by curiosity. She could hear his voice, animated, happy. He came back radiant.

'You'll never guess, Anne, but that was Tom. He arrived in York this morning. I invited him to stay here but he's already made arrangements. He's hoping to settle here for a while! He's talking about buying a flat! What do you think about that!'

Anne thought nothing to it at all. 'When are you seeing him?' she asked.

'Not till tomorrow, unfortunately. He

used to work at the electricity generating station, do you remember, the one on Foss Bank? He got a bit of a shock when he discovered it closed down after he left and now there isn't a trace of it. He's going round the estate agents today flat-hunting and then tonight he's meeting some of his old workmates. We're going to meet up tomorrow. He'll ring me later, or in the morning, to make arrangements.'

'By then you'll know what it was that he and your—aunt—were so thick with each other about, this surprise they had for you.'

'Yes. I didn't mention the letters to him. It seems like trespass in a way to read them at all.'

'Didn't you think', said Anne, 'that they might be what the break-in was about, that they might be the secret of the house?' She could see that this contact with Tom Bell—the sound of his voice on the phone—had changed his attitude to the letters.

'Yes. I did think that, but maybe I was over-reacting.'

'No,' said Anne firmly. 'Now you're being swayed by your pleasure at meeting your friend again. Read those letters before you see him. For some reason my judgement is that it is very important.' Why she spoke like that, she found it hard to say, and quarrelled with herself afterwards in case her feeling of intuition was based only on a reluctance to share her lifelong friend.

14

Chris finally settled down to read the letters over his meal at the hospital canteen.

Before leaving to go to visit Damien, he had sorted them into two piles, one of letters in their envelopes from Tom to his aunt, the other of her carbon copies of her letters to him. Now he sorted them again by date, so that the uppermost letters were the earliest and the latest were at the bottom. Both piles, in several bundles, were held securely by some enormous elastic bands which had been lying in a drawer.

As he ate Chris took one from the Tom pile, followed by one from the aunt pile. He had already become used to thinking of the woman he had known for so many years as 'mother', now as 'aunt'. It seemed absolutely right. That at least of his discoveries had fitted in so well with his emotions, his psyche, that it created no conflict or difficulty.

The shocks began immediately.

Even with the first letter.

Tom had made contact with his aunt long before he ever met Chris himself, yet when they two *had* met, Tom had given no hint of this. The first thing suggested to Chris's aunt by Tom was that Chris should not be told of the subject of their correspondence. 'Something which may be of benefit to him,' that was the phrase, now so well known to Chris, which was the reason given for writing in the first place. 'A pity to let him know if it is all to end in disappointment,' was another phrase which seemed to leap from the page. Tom, apparently, was interested in family history and engaged on a special quest which was to bring him to York to consult the records held in the city. This might result in the possible benefit. Chris's aunt had replied with enthusiasm. That was right in character, Chris knew only too well. She loved being in on anything which truly concerned other people and which they didn't know she knew about. Secrets, they were like honey to a bee to Mrs Simmers. At once Chris knew why the whole thing had been kept from him, why the letters were hidden in the one place he hadn't known about and so wouldn't be likely to look.

He hardly needed to go further before sitting staring at the canteen wall, his food forgotten, remembering the times he had returned home and found them sitting together talking, then suddenly falling quiet as he walked into the, room. He remembered the hushed voices he had sometimes heard on first opening the door, which had faded so quickly. And all because of some possible benefit to himself.

He only read a few more letters at that time. For one thing, he was anxious not to keep Damien waiting for visitors when everyone else would be having theirs. After putting the letters away again in the knapsack, the few he had read now at the bottom, he went upstairs to the ward. There was one visitor already by Damien's bed, a small, square woman with artificially blonded hair sticking out at all angles from her head. It was not until she turned and introduced herself as 'Damien's mum' that Chris realised, from the age obvious in her face, that she was in her fifties. She was one of those stalwart women who go through life meeting it day by day, never looking more than a week or two ahead and usually not that. Her clothes were out of date yet timeless, the short skirt and high heels, plunging neckline and gaudy artificial jewellery. Her hands showed that they were used to working. It was easy to imagine them scrubbing steps, in spite of the large rings. She was on friendly terms with Chris at once.

'It's so nice to meet one of Damien's

friends,' she said. 'I've brought him some spice. Liquorice Allsorts and humbugs. And some fags.'

'I've brought him some Benn's Bars.' Chris responded to her smile.

'Ooh, aye, I'd forgotten he likes them. Benn's Bars, Damien,' she said, turning back to the bed, nodding and smiling, as though Damien had not been able to hear for himself. Perhaps he couldn't, through all those bandages, though Chris thought it was more likely his mother's mannerism. He soon discovered he was right, because she repeated everything he himself said, to Damien, who didn't attempt to speak much and usually only indicated his response by the look in his eyes.

'You never know what's going to happen to people, do you?' Damien's mum said confidentially to Chris. 'Fancy him getting his hand blown off. He'll have to learn to manage with the left one now, as I was saying to his dad. His dad wouldn't come with me, you know. And I walked from the station. It's ever so far to walk. Because I didn't know about the buses. Dame will have to come home now, as soon as they let him out. I've told him, I'll look after him. It won't be any trouble. I'm only working part-time now his dad's back in work.'

Chris felt that this was a load off his

own shoulders. He had been going to offer Damien bed and board until he was fully fit, and hadn't been looking forward to the extra work and responsibility. His privacy and peace were very precious to him after twelve years in prison. Now he would be able to rest easy. There was no doubt Damien's mum would not only protect him and cosset him, she would also dragoon his dad into proper fatherly conduct, at least on the surface. And whoever had agreed to organise the contract killing on Chris was not likely to bother any longer about Damien, particularly when he was in another city and protected by his family.

It was the end of visiting time before Chris went. He had enjoyed talking and listening to Damien's mother. Her conversation was salty and full of jokes. Good humour and resilience seemed to shine out of her. When they had to go Chris offered her a ride in a taxi to the station, saying he would have hired one anyway, which was not strictly true, but he was glad to be home quickly and back to the task of reading the letters.

Anne had been right. No way should he meet Tom again without knowledge of the deception which had been practised upon him. Whatever else the letters contained he needed to know. As he worked his way through them, Chris became more

311

and more appalled at what had happened. Long before first coming to York, Tom had been using Chris's aunt to do research for him, and paying her an hourly rate.

Thirteen years before, family history had not yet been made easy. The family historians had been working away during those years, indexing, transcribing, and publishing various records. Members of the Mormon Church had worked like beavers. Nowadays there was reference material on microfilm which at one time would have taken special journeys and expertise to research.

Nowadays, Anne had had an easy time of it compared with Mrs Simmers and Tom. They had to wade through original registers or Bishop's Transcripts to many of the city's twenty-four or more parishes, as they had existed at various times during the previous two hundred years. Marriages which took place in the bride's parish were particularly difficult to find. They had discovered these by the traditional methods of looking for needles in haystacks.

When Tom had actually arrived in York, met Chris, and become his alleged friend, Mrs Simmers still kept a record on paper of their research, and of everything Tom told her about the possible riches which might come Chris's way. She had noted down their conversations. It was through these notes that Chris found out that they had decided to tell him of his prospects of wealth on his twenty-first birthday. His face twisted into a wry expression when he read that. So that was the great surprise which his 'mother' was to tell him the morning after the drunken binge. He had come to hate everything that reminded him of his twenty-first.

It was some little consolation, in the last notes he read, to realise that his aunt had been looking forward very much to telling him of his golden prospects. He remembered the words Annie had overheard, even though he had no doubt they would have sounded rougher, more uncouth, in the original. He had always believed that his 'mother' loved him, in spite of her difficult ways, and here was the proof of it. She wrote, 'How much I'm looking forward to seeing his face when he hears the news!'

It seemed that she and Tom had proved, beyond any possibility of doubt, that Chris was the sole surviving male descendant of Thomas Nournavaile, son of Rebecca, born on the first of November in 1785 in the York City Poor House, just as Arthur Z. Nournavaile of Rideaux County in the USA was the sole surviving descendant of Joseph, twin brother of Thomas, who had emigrated with his young bride so very long ago. *And Arthur had left the bulk of his fortune to be divided between genuine surviving male descendants of Thomas.*

Providing they were found before twenty years had passed from the date of Arthur's death.

It was then that Chris started shuffling through the papers he had already read, trying to discover at what date Arthur Z. had died. He was sure he had seen it somewhere. Yes, he found it. As he had already suspected, the twenty years were almost up. There was only a month left in which to claim. Then he remembered that in half an hour or so the solicitor who was so anxious to represent him was due to call back again, and that the following day he, Chris, was to meet Tom. Chris found he had a problem. Was he going to let the solicitor represent him, and lose fifty-five per cent of whatever wealth might conceivably come his way? Or was he going to approach—say—Humphrey Hale, who had cheered him so much by being welcoming when Chris had first come home? That reminded him that he had commissioned Hale to write in response to the advert in the *News of the World*, asking for more information about the search that was in progress for male descendants of the name Nournavaile. He hadn't heard a thing, but it was actually quite a short time since he had made the request. Solicitors probably took several days to get a letter out, then it had to go to London, then the solicitors the other end had to reply, and then Hale would have to get in touch with himself, Chris. It would all be long-winded, one could be sure of that. He should have checked up, asking what progress was being made. But he had not known it was important. He sat down and wrote a letter to Hale, explaining all the turns of events since they met, the urgency, and asking him to negotiate with Mr Poste on the matter.

The knock on the door came at exactly the time Florian Poste was expected. At least it wasn't raining tonight. He came in and Chris politely offered him a drink.

'I haven't anything alcoholic, I'm afraid,' he apologised, 'but there's tea, coffee or cocoa, if you would like any of those. Oh, and orange juice.'

'Nothing, thank you,' smiled Mr Poste.

'I understand', Chris stated, 'that I am the sole male descendant of Thomas Nournavaile, born on the first of November 1785 in the York City Poor House. So your suggestion of representing other claimants if I did not sign your agreement does not wash. Arthur Z. was the last descendant of Joseph, Thomas's twin, I believe.'

Poor Mr Poste looked staggered by this

calm announcement.

'How did you know?' he asked.

'It was not as difficult as you make out.'

'You started with the knowledge of your real name, and the date I gave you, 1785. And such a lot of work has been done on the records lately. When we began to search for descendants a few years ago it was not so easy. Then, we thought there might be masses of descendants, and spent a lot of time searching areas which were in fact fruitless. For example, we spent a fortnight searching through the whole of the 1851 census for Middlesex. A very good clue had led us to believe that there might be descendants there. Unfortunately there were not. Otherwise we might be offering to represent them, Mr Nournavaile.' He looked at Chris as if he would have preferred these other, legendary, more amenable claimants.

'Then, you see, I already have my own solicitor, and he has already made approaches to a London firm who were advertising for descendants,' was Chris's riposte.

Mr Poste's quite pleasant face began to look rather vicious. 'No one but ourselves could possibly claim in time,' he said angrily. 'We have our partners on the other side of the Atlantic and they have great experience in this field. They could move instantly.'

'It's because that's probably true that I am not rejecting your offer out of hand,' said Chris. 'First of all, can you explain to me why so many different people are involved in this search which has been going on?'

'There's the Nournavaile Institute,' Poste said. 'They are sure to be involved. After all, if you don't claim, what is to happen? There is a sealed envelope to be opened in that event, but everyone in the trade is convinced it will mean the fortune goes to the institute.'

Chris gazed at him with his mouth open. 'Who are the Nournavaile Institute when they're at home?' he asked at last.

'They combine a large care-home for the old with research laboratories. The home is profitable, very, as everyone believes their old people are getting the best care there is, which is probably true. So relatives are willing to pay top whack. The research side has been breaking new ground lately and may well have a money-spinning breakthrough on their hands. They will need an immense amount of money to develop it, though.'

'How come they are called "Nournavaile"?'

'Old Arthur Z. thought they were doing a

317

good job, as they no doubt are, and used his influence to get them some state funding. He helped them financially himself too. The name is in compliment to him. In his will—I have a copy if you wish to read it—he trusts them with the task of searching for the male heir or heirs of Thomas. If not found twenty years after his death, the sealed envelope is to be opened.'

'Surprising,' was Chris's comment.

'An open invitation to skulduggery,' said Florian Poste.

'Given today's accessibility of records, it shouldn't have taken more than twenty days to find that I was the sole descendant,' said Chris.

'Except that you were passing under the name of Simmers. Anyway, it really takes much longer. A few days might satisfy an amateur, but there would be too many errors or possible errors in their work. Evidence has to satisfy a judge and jury in America. They don't like large fortunes passing out of the country, either. So one has to do a lot of negative searching, as we call it. Searching not to find a person, but to prove that there is no other claimant than the one already found. Illegitimate children, for example, have always been regarded as proper heirs in America, although until recently that was not the case in Britain. It almost always means a simply colossal amount of work, though I don't deny it has become much easier with modern technology. There are a number of American firms who derive a large part of their income from tracing lost heirs. I am the English representative of one of them. Although in this case the will entrusts the institute with searching for the heir or heirs, it does not exclude other agencies from finding them. They are only enjoined to search. You follow?'

'It doesn't matter legally who finds the claimant?'

'Exactly so. The claimant is the person who must claim. Not the Nournavaile Institute or anyone else. Of course, the claimant has a lawyer acting on their behalf.'

'Thank you for your explanations, Mr Poste. But your "agreement"—no way am I signing that. You will have to settle for your expenses plus a much smaller fee or percentage. And even that only payable if indeed there is some result from all this, enough to be worthwhile.'

'Oh, it is worthwhile.' Poste's tone was heartfelt. 'I can assure you of that. We would hardly have been tracing you if there had not been a considerable amount involved.'

'Here is a letter to my solicitor.' Chris

gave him the letter. 'You can't do anything now until Monday morning, but I would like you to negotiate terms with him.'

'And what am I supposed to say to my principal?'

'Exactly what I have said.'

Mr Poste looked annoyed.

'Stay until Monday lunch time,' Chris suggested. 'By then you will have seen Mr Humphrey Hale, who can deal with you better than I can. I will also have seen an old friend of mine who may know something of the matter.'

When Florian Poste had taken himself off in something of a huff, Chris had time to think of Tom Bell, alleged friend. He thought bitterly of the joy with which he had received the postcard, the first word from Tom for over twelve years. Why had he gone away at that crucial time, catching a train around midnight, on the very day Chris was twenty-one, when the plan had been to tell him of the possible good fortune on that day? Why had he left it until now—with only a month to go before it would be too late to claim the legacy—to make contact again? Had he by any chance already made the claim? Had he pretended to be the last descendant of Thomas Nournavaile, himself? He would certainly have known enough about Chris to make an impersonation realistic. He had all the evidence required from the records. But surely if that was the case he would never have shown his face again? No. That idea did not stand up. A proven claimant would have brought an end to the entire search, which was obviously still going on.

One thing Chris had been longing to do for years was to make contact with Tom once more, yet since reading the letters and notes concealed in the card table, he almost wished he was not going to see him. He had to remind himself that Tom might have further information which might help to explain the murder.

The evening was graduating into night. There was nothing useful he could do, apart from making a hot drink and going to bed. Sam had not been around since shortly after being fed. He probably had a lady-love somewhere, Chris thought. He then thought of Anne, and the pleasure with which they had shared afternoon tea together. He would have liked to speak to her on the phone, but it was growing late, and they were meeting in the morning.

Chris gave up and went to bed.

Anne appeared looking delightful as usual, at ten o'clock precisely. She didn't knock on the door this time. She opened it in her old fashion and called, 'Cooee!' and then walked into the house. She was dressed for spring, in a swinging, swirling yellow skirt and white blouse. A blazer, casually slung over one shoulder, was being held by one finger hooked through the loop at the neck. Chris, hollow-eyed after a restless night, was cheered immediately by the sight of her. Faintly through the open door they could hear church and cathedral bells ringing over the city.

'Ready for coffee?' he asked her. Sam, who had come in through the open door, miaowed as if in answer.

'Oh, top of the milk for you,' Chris said to him. 'Caffeine isn't good for cats.' Then, opening the door to the cellar from the hallway, he said, 'Damn. No milk left.'

'Are you still storing it on the cellar-head?' asked Anne. 'What's wrong with the fridge?'

'Habit,' said Chris as if he was thinking of something else.

'You'll have to start a new bottle.'

'Yes. I'll buy some more later, if I run short, from the corner shop.' Chris fetched the new bottle from the doorstep. He found Sam's saucer. Then, pushing the point of his elbow into the centre of the milk bottle top, which neatly lifted the foil seal, he poured the creamy top of the milk into the saucer and put it on the floor for Sam.

'He gets treated better than I do,' said Anne. 'Do you always give that old tramp the cream?'

'He likes it.'

Chris poured more of the milk into a saucepan and put it on the gas stove to heat for coffee. He knew Anne preferred her coffee made with hot milk. He liked cold milk in it, himself.

'Are you going to tell me about the letters?' asked Anne eagerly.

Chris was watching the pan of milk. 'In a bit,' he said. At last, when the milk was about to rise and foam over the pan, Chris lifted it off and reached for the coffee.

'What's the matter with the cat?' asked Anne.

Chris put down the saucepan so quickly it splashed on to the stove.

Sam had lifted his chin from the cream and the fur under his mouth was stuck together with it. He had licked his lips and reached his long tongue down to clean his chin. Now he was trying to walk away from the empty saucer, but instead of his usual straight line across the floor, he seemed to be staggering about. As they watched, puzzled, he lost control of his back legs. They swung over sideways before he could make them obey him again. Then he stretched his head forward, retched several times, and began to vomit.

323

'Put him outside, quickly,' cried Anne.

Chris grabbed the roll of kitchen paper and tore off several pieces to clean the floor. He knelt down beside the cat. The creature's stomach heaved and heaved again, and he was sick once more. Chris mopped up. Anne said nothing.

For a few seconds the cat was still, and they both watched him and held their breath. Then the heaving and vomiting began again, seeming to last for ever, and this time he also lost control of his bowels and bladder. Anne reached for him to lift him and put him out into the yard, but even in his agony the cat would not allow such unauthorised behaviour. He howled faintly but angrily at her and lashed out with his claws and seemed altogether to be possessed by fury. She could do nothing with him and Chris reached out his own hands, crying to the animal, 'Sam, Sam, be calm now, Sam, Sam...'

Hearing him the cat swung round and Anne drew back. Sam tottered towards Chris, dragging his back legs uselessly. Chris touched the top of the grey head gently with the tips of the fingers of his right hand and spoke caressingly. 'What's the matter, boy, old boy...'

The cat began to sink to the floor and

its head drooped towards Chris's left hand, while with the other he continued to touch Sam soothingly. The cat collapsed. Chris's left wrist was under his neck like a pillow; Sam's body was dropping to the floor as if boneless, broken.

Anne could see Chris's face and could hardly endure watching the raw emotion showing on it. All he could say was, 'Sam, Sam...' repeating the cat's name in the last moments of its life as though he could not bear what was happening, the inevitable outcome of this pain. The cat's head felt heavy on his wrist as though it had relaxed completely, yielding itself to his sympathy. Chris continued to stroke with fingertip touches while he felt as though his heart would burst with the distress of the moment.

The whole thing had not taken more than eight minutes.

'He was fine,' whispered Chris as the cat's body stopped jerking. 'There was nothing wrong with him. He was fine.'

Heedless of the mess on the floor Anne was now kneeling beside him. She reached out gentle fingers and closed the lids of the cat's eyes over the deep gold of the large irises. The pupils seemed to have contracted completely. She moved the limbs of the dead creature so that he appeared to be lying in a natural position, as if asleep with his head so confidingly on Chris's wrist.

Then, while Chris sat on his heels stunned, one wrist supporting the cat, the other hand still gently caressing its head, Anne set about cleaning up the floor with the roll of kitchen paper.

It was some minutes before either of them remembered the pan of milk on the stove, but they seemed to think of it at the same instant, Chris lifting his head and looking up at the stove, Anne stepping over to it and turning off the gas.

'Lucky you didn't set it down on the flame,' she said, 'or there would have been a mess.'

'The milk,' Chris said in a kind of hoarse whisper. 'We'd better not drink that milk.'

She looked at him.

'It must have been the milk. We'd better have it tested. Don't touch it whatever you do.'

Their eyes met over the body of the cat in a long, direct gaze.

'If you hadn't given that cat the cream,' Anne put their thoughts into words, 'we might both be dead by now. Although it may not have acted so quickly in humans—we're so much bigger.'

'Equally lethal, though, I should think.'

Neither of them doubted that this was

another attempt on Chris's life.

'You'll have to report this to the police,' said Anne. 'Poor old Sam.'

Chris's face was wet with tears.

15

The phone call from Tom did not come until eleven. Anne had been restless for some time, saying that she had promised to go to see her old lady in Kyme Street who was giving her such marvellous memories of Old York to record on tape. She had left the tape recorder in the scullery—utility room—ready to pick up on her way out. Yet she could not make up her mind to part from Chris. The cat Sam was now lying in his little shelter on his dry sacks, waiting for Chris to decide what to do with his body.

Chris's voice sounded dead even to his own ears as he answered the phone. He could not infuse any enthusiasm into it.

'You all right, Chris?' asked Tom.

'Fine. How did the flat-hunting go?'

'I've got the key to see one today. Sounds as if it will be great. Thought you might like to go with me, give me the benefit of your advice.'

'That would be interesting.' But Chris didn't actually sound as though he thought so. He was dreading seeing Tom altogether.

'Would you like to come round here first?'

'Bit short of time,' was Tom's answer. 'I could meet you at the flats at twelve, how would that be?'

'Where are they?' asked Chris.

'Right near you at the end of Vincent Street. You know that old chapel, a big round red one, been empty as long as I've known York, used to be used to store furniture in, they've been converting it into seventeen flats. I'm looking at one on what you call first-floor level.'

'The Victoria Bar Primitive Methodist Chapel, you mean? Interesting curves to the main roof? Red brick walls with enrichments in white brick, and slate roof?'

'That's right. Only a stone's throw from your house.'

'Architect, William Peachey of York,' said Chris, who had taught Anne all she knew about the history of Bishophill, and a good deal that she had forgotten.

'You'll be interested to see the flat, then,' said Tom.

'Yes.'

When Chris had put the phone down, he said to Anne, 'I wonder why he didn't want to come here.'

'Bad conscience,' said Anne, who had by now been let into the secret of the

329

letters and notes. 'Conspiring with your mother, then pretending he knew nothing about you or her, after he'd managed to get to know you.'

'Looking back on the affair, it seems singularly pointless.'

'You don't know the point, that's all. That correspondence is so important that they burgled to try to find it.'

'I don't want to take it with me when I go to meet him.'

'Leave it in our house,' suggested Anne. 'Mother is staying in. Mind, she'll be asleep after dinner. But we don't eat till half one at the earliest. You'll probably be back before then. And the milk. If anyone breaks in they might take that. You want to give it to the police first thing in the morning. They'll get it examined and analysed to find out what's in it.'

Chris agreed, and Anne slipped round home and locked the knapsack full of letters away in a cupboard, together with a carrier bag containing the milk, now in a thermos flask, and the milk bottle and foil top.

'Do you want to see the flat?' he asked her on her return.

'Not particularly. But I do want to see Tom. My memories of him are vague.'

'When you've finished with your old lady come along. You're only going to be round the corner. We should still be at the flat, probably talking. We've a lot to catch up on.'

'I might just do that. Chris, can't you get it into your head that Tom might be a villain?'

He hesitated. 'Villain is too strong a word. He knew all about the inheritance and yet he never let on. He'd done all that research, with my aunt's help, and never told me a thing. I realise they were planning to tell me as a surprise, but you can hardly call it above board. If someone deceives you one way, all your trust is gone.'

'Of course the whole thing was underhand, traitorous. There must have been some plan to get all the money. He hasn't been in touch, has he?' Anne looked disgusted.

'Don't jump to conclusions, Annie! He's been going round the world, he said so on his postcard. He's been in all sorts of out-of-the-way places. However angry and disappointed I feel over his deceit, his friendship was once important to me, and he may know something about that night that has never come out in evidence yet. I must go with an open mind.'

'For heaven's sake!' cried Anne.

'He's my only chance of discovering new evidence. I can't pass up the chance. I've got to know, Anne.'

There was no possibility of Anne settling down to a nice cosy Sunday morning session of reminiscence with the old lady in Kyme Street. She went along with her tape recorder, set it out on the old lady's coffee table, and was about to begin, when she realised that it would be hopeless to try. She apologised, said she wasn't feeling well, accepted a cup of tea, and left. By her watch it was a few minutes before twelve. She mooched along Vincent Street keeping an eye on the chapel at the corner. Vincent Street was one of Bishophill's nicer streets of small terrace houses. They had tiny gardens in front, larger than either Chris's or her own. The shrubs and climbers were putting out spring leaves and growing their flower buds, and a number were in flower already in addition to the ubiquitous daffodils. Anne thought that in summer this was the prettiest street in the area. She walked along now trying to be unobtrusive, which was difficult in a swirly yellow skirt. A youngish man was lounging about at the far end of the road, and she thought he was probably Tom. He seemed to be about the same height as Chris, medium build, with designer stubble, and wearing casual clothes. His hair was fair, the sun glinted on it and made his chin bright.

At last, a minute before twelve o'clock,

Chris came walking along. Tom went a few yards to meet him, they clasped hands. Then they turned and walked towards the old chapel. Because Anne had come that way, she knew that there were no workmen there. Presumably the key Tom had to the flat was actually two keys, one for the outer and one for the inner door. The flats on the top floor were finished and sold, and so were most of those on the first floor. The work still going on was on the ground-floor flats and on the exterior, where the white decorative bricks had become very decayed and were being carefully replaced, which meant hacking them out one by one.

Once the two men had disappeared inside the building she dropped all subterfuge and walked openly along the pavement. Tom had left the outer door unlocked behind them, assuming it had been locked at all. She pushed it open very gently and stepped inside.

It was extremely weird. This level had been the main area for the congregation, but now it was only a dark space cluttered by steel columns, with an uneven, treacherous floor on two different levels, and a thick coating of dust. The voices of the two young men came to her faintly. They must have stood here for a minute as she was now, before climbing the staircase, or they would have been inside the flat and she would have been unlikely to hear them.

Anne moved quickly but quietly to the foot of the staircase. She might not have noticed it if she had not heard the voices. It was very unobtrusive, because it was a spiral one with a door at the bottom. She moved to and fro, in and out of the outside door, as silently as she could, grateful to be wearing soft-soled casual shoes. After a minute she understood the layout. The spiral staircase had its own special little section. It was self-contained, and must have been a side stair for limited use. Entering on it from the uneven floor, she climbed half-way up the flight and knew that only a few steps higher would take her head above the floor level of the flats.

She stood her tape recorder near her feet, not wanting to be cluttered up with it, and at once thought of recording—what, she didn't know, but something. She had the feeling the two men were going to have a row. Nearby was a temporary plug fixed up for the use of the builders. She plugged in the tape recorder, and slid up the steps as quietly as she could, then listened.

'It's a very nice flat,' she heard Chris say, 'but I want to talk to you about something different, Tom. The night you went away. I don't suppose you know what happened after you left me at home, dead drunk, but if you will I want you to go over the earlier part of that night, bit by bit.'

As soon as she heard the beginning of this, Anne went into action. She took the microphone from the tape recorder and wedged it on top of a new light fitting on the axis of the stair and waited with it, almost holding her breath. This was a conversation she wanted on tape, then she and Chris could always play it over again, if they wanted to discuss it. She was so familiar with her recorder, so rapid with it, that she caught the end of Chris's sentence at the beginning of the tape.

When, at midday at the end of Vincent Street, Chris walked towards Tom, he saw that the man had hardly changed at all since they last met more than twelve years before. The beard was shorter, a mere stubble, but it had never been long. The clear direct gaze out of piercing blue eyes was the same. Something in Chris shouted, Beware! Tom extended his hand and Chris felt very unwilling to shake hands with him, a physical revulsion, but it was possible he was doing the man an injustice. There might be some perfectly simple explanation. So he shook hands. The inner voice was even more insistent. This man is danger, it said. It was as if messages, clear even if unspoken, had passed between them with that touch.

'Long time no see,' said Tom.

'True.'

'You're looking well.'

'So are you.'

'The flats are just here.'

Chris followed Tom into the doorway.

'This was where the congregation sat.' Tom indicated the dark encumbered space.

'I do know. I have lived in this area all my life,' said Chris. Except for twelve years, he added to himself.

'The agent said I was to go up a spiral stair on the right.' And, turning and looking about, Tom found the door to the spiral stair, curled in its shell. He opened it and indicated that Chris go up first. With a courteous gesture, Chris gave him the precedence. Tom began to climb. Chris followed him. At the top they were on a landing with a small window, and ahead was the door to the flat. Tom unlocked it and they went in. Again there was a little pantomime at the door, with Tom gesturing Chris in first and Chris returning the compliment so that Tom went in first. No way was Chris going to turn his back on this man. The rooms were well planned and Chris felt he wouldn't have minded moving in himself. Freedom from the pressures of the past, freedom from the vulnerability of his own house, freedom from the deadly legacy of secrets which weighed on his spirits. He made admiring noises as they walked round, always making sure that he was facing Tom or behind him. Tom was making cheerful exclamations about this and that feature of the flat. It was only a few minutes before they were walking back to the landing and Tom was turning to lock the door behind them.

That was when Chris began to speak about what really mattered to him, the words Anne overheard from the bottom of the stair.

Tom did not answer at once. Then he asked why it was important.

'You wouldn't know, of course,' Chris said and his voice dragged as he approached the point of his question. 'You see, my Mother was murdered that night, after you left. You might have seen something. Someone walking towards the house, for instance. They put me in prison for the murder.'

'Not for long enough,' said Tom. 'You weren't supposed to be out so early, were you?'

'I got full remission,' said Chris, surprised. 'You mean you knew about Mother?'

'Your aunt, actually, wasn't she?' said Tom in a rather nasty way. 'Oh, I know all about it, Chris. I had other friends besides you in England. I kept in touch with what went on. It's unfortunate for you that they let you out early, isn't it?'

'What do you mean?'

'I would have thought it would be obvious by now. You've been digging around, haven't you, you and your girl-friend? Digging into the past. That's why we have to get rid of you. I thought it would be enough, doing away with your aunt. You should have been in prison for another six months at least, under your adopted name, then it wouldn't have mattered. You could have lived out your little unimportant life in peace. I don't like having to kill you, Chris. But it seems I have to do everything myself. You've had the devil's own luck, haven't you? Well it's just run out.'

Tom drew a small handgun out of his pants pocket and aimed it at Chris.

Below them, although she couldn't see this, Anne was transfixed, flattened to the wall. She couldn't have moved if anyone had paid her in golden doubloons. Her mouth was open, her fingers grasping at the plaster.

'You're going to kill me?' Chris sounded perfectly calm, as if looking into the barrel of a gun was what he did every day of the week. It had been, lately. 'Just let me get this straight. I was put in prison—framed, shall we say—to prevent me claiming the Nournavaile fortune?'

'Of course.' But there was something not quite at ease about Tom. Chris remembered that his aunt had been axed down from behind. This was a murderer who didn't like to look his victims in the eye.

'You're telling me you were responsible for my aunt's death? But you were seen getting on the train...'

'It's possible to get off trains. They have two sides, you know. I enjoyed killing your aunt. But I didn't want to kill you, Chris. Only to have you out of the way until later this year. Why couldn't you be content with that?'

'Was all this your own idea?'

'Of course not. I hadn't the money to finance such a scheme. There's a cabal in the governing body of the Nournavaile Institute—oh, you've heard about the institute?'

'Aren't they a philanthropic—?'

'Nuts to that,' said Tom.

'So I didn't kill her?' Chris wanted it put clearly in words. This was what he had been hoping for—vindication—proof of his innocence. But he hadn't expected it to come quite like this.

'You're too stupid. I'd have done her in

long before if she'd been cluttering up my life. It was a pleasure to axe her. I did you a favour. Put you in a safe place till the danger was over. That's friendship in my book. But did you stay there? Not you, Chris. And would you be frightened away, once you came out, like a good little girl? Oh, no. Not you. A real have-a-go-joe. Well, tough.'

'Let's get this straight,' said Chris. His voice was strong and firm, as though the gun did not exist. 'I want to know what happened. You got on the train then got off again in the centre of the track, made your way out of the station by a side entrance somewhere, and came back to the house? No one saw you.'

'You have an alleyway down the back,' Tom said. 'I didn't intend anyone to see me. The Nournavaile inheritance is too important to make slips like that. It is meant for better things than for you to do as you like with. The plan worked fine. There you were in prison until after the last date for claiming it. But you got...'

'Maximum remission,' said Chris.

'Quite. So my friends tried to frighten you off. If you had gone away for a bit this scene wouldn't have been necessary. I have too much to do to trail back to York to safeguard the money from your claiming it. Only four more weeks and you would have been too late, even if you found out about it.'

'And then you would have claimed it? How do you make that out?'

'The will laid down an alternative distribution if the fortune was not claimed by the given heir before the scheduled date. It's in a sealed envelope but that didn't prevent the stenographer who typed it leaking the information for a consideration. I don't know why I'm wasting time telling you all this. I still don't want to kill you but I'd better get on with it.'

Unlike his aunt, Chris was prepared. What was more, anger was rising in him to a pitch he had never before experienced. This man, his false friend, had ruined his life and killed a woman he had, in a way, loved. That would have been enough. But that wasn't what was making his blood boil yet his brain feel cool and clear as ice. It was the death in agony of the old tom-cat, Sam, which was turning Chris into a fighting, killing machine, which he had never been.

A subdued shot rang out, but by the sound of it Anne knew that the bullet had hit a hard surface, not buried itself in flesh. She heard sounds which told her a fight was going on upstairs.

Chris was not the naïve lad he had been at the age of twenty-one. He'd kept himself fit in prison and learned a few tricks. The gun had wavered downwards while they were talking and Tom was enjoying his bit of rhetoric, until it was pointing at Chris's legs. When Tom decided to shoot he spent a fraction of a second raising the barrel to point at Chris's chest. In that fraction Chris made a sort of lightning weaving pounce and jerked Tom's wrist in the air even as the trigger was pressed...then a fight began for possession of the gun. The two men were much the same height and weight. From being a laid-back situation with all the winning cards in Tom's hands, it was abruptly a matter of kill or be killed. Chris was putting out all his strength to get the gun. Tom twisted and turned in his grasp, but managed to keep the weapon away from those iron fingers. They hurled themselves to and fro, falling on the floor, then scrambling up, always together, Chris's fingers tight round Tom's wrist, dragging, pushing, twisting to get that gun, their other hands hitting, shoving, their feet struggling for a purchase on the floor, slipping, kicking. This was all-in fighting with every fibre working. Chris had learned some mean, underhand methods of attack and he used them—Tom screamed in pain but nothing would make him lose his hold. He retaliated as viciously as he could, trying to work the barrel round to aim it at Chris's head. The fingers round his wrist bit tight into his flesh and he felt his hand going numb under intolerable pressure. He couldn't twist the gun barrel to aim it at Chris. Chris's fingers were strong and relentless. They moved up, gradually taking more and more of Tom's hand beneath them until they were covering his trigger finger and moving the barrel of the gun up, up, away from Chris himself. At this point Chris had proved himself the stronger and had mastery in his grasp. He twisted the gun. He pressed the mouth of the barrel into Tom's cheekbone. The last words Tom would ever hear were, 'This is for Sam!' hissed in vicious revenge so intense that it became fierce joy as Chris pressed Tom's own finger down on the trigger.

As soon as she heard the second shot and the thump of a falling body, Anne was up and running. She dashed up the stair, desperate with worry as to what she would find at the top. As her head rose above the level of the landing she saw Chris and at once her worst fear was over—he was alive—only to be replaced by other fears. He was lying across the prone body of Tom and both their hands seemed to be on the gun. Chris turned his head and saw Anne. Slowly he raised himself, first to his knees, then, unsteadily, to his feet.

He stood there and at his feet lay the dead body of Tom Bell.

'Oh God, Anne,' he whispered, 'what have I done?'

'Don't move,' she said. 'Look, we must get the police. And your probation officer. Before you move. Look, Chris, I've got what he said on tape. All being well. Unless anything's gone wrong. You've got to let me get the police in now.'

He looked blankly at her as if stunned.

'You're right. Get them,' was all he said.

'I'll be back in two minutes,' she cried as she circled down the stairs.

She ran to her home, dashed inside and to the phone. Steve Watson first. She had learned his number by heart. God! Sunday dinner time!

'You must come, Steve, at once, please, I'm awfully sorry to disturb you, but Chris has just killed someone, it's all right, it was self-defence...'

Steve hadn't waited for her to say anything else after the word 'killed'. He was out of the house by the time she realised he had rung off. So she rang 999 and asked for Dave Smart. Luckily he was there and available. He had only looked in for half an hour, but took the call.

'Mr Smart, please can you come at

once, Chris has killed someone, it was self-defence.'

'Who is speaking?' Dave asked sharply.

'Anne Atkinson. At Bishophill. Please can you meet me at the old chapel at the corner of Vincent Street?'

'Your dinner's ready, Annie,' said her mother, coming out of the kitchen. '*Sunday dinner,*' she added with emphasis, reading the signs aright. 'Don't say you're dashing off out again.'

'Got to, Mum.' Anne slammed down the phone and gave her a repentant kiss. 'Don't worry. Just serve mine, then leave it in the microwave, I'll warm it up later. Forgive me, darling.'

She got outside her house, then realised Steve Watson wouldn't know where to go. Ten to one he'd come straight round to Chris's house. She dashed back into her house again. 'Mother! This is an emergency. Please—leave what you're doing— can you stand outside and tell Steve Watson, that probation officer who comes to see Chris, that we're at the chapel that's being converted into flats? There's a dear. He'll be here any minute and I've got to get back.'

Mrs Atkinson thought there had been nothing but emergencies lately. She did what Anne asked her. She usually did, when Anne put her foot down or when there was a real need, however dominating she might be the rest of the time. Her daughter and her house were all she had in the world.

Anne realised that she had left the recorder plugged in. Her hair seemed to rise on her body. She could feel it on the back of her neck and also on her arms, her whole skin seemed to be crawling. That tape! If anything had gone wrong with that tape! Without it Chris was lost, it would only be his word and hers as to what had happened. Suppose it hadn't recorded anything at all! How did she know the plug was live? She didn't. It might have been a complete waste of time! No use! She never knew how she managed to go on running, that Sunday lunch time, when everyone who lived in the street was inside eating their Sunday dinner, and the pavements were deserted. But she did somehow go on running, and she reached the chapel at the time Dave Smart and a uniformed policeman drew up in a screaming police car.

'Upstairs!' she called to Dave. 'The spiral one on the right as you go in!'

He nodded and rushed into the building. She ran in after him, but deflected to the tape recorder. She turned it off, collected the microphone, and shut down the lid, all in a couple of seconds before following

Dave and his driver to the top of the stair, still not knowing whether or not she had recorded anything.

Chris had done as she told him. He was still standing there with the dead body at his feet, but now he had picked up the gun. Acting DCI Dave Smart came into view, and Chris held the gun out towards him in a supplicating gesture, the barrel pointing safely at the floor.

'Hang on,' said Dave. 'Evidence bag,' he said to the constable who had driven him. This man produced a plastic evidence bag and Dave delicately edged it under the weapon, then told Chris to drop the gun in. Dave breathed normally once more when the weapon was safely stored away. Then, having taken only a cursory glance at the dead man, he used his mobile phone to ring for the police surgeon and the scene of crime team.

Anne had never seen a dead body like this before, its tissues torn open, the delicate structure of cheekbone and eye socket exposed, its brain partly distributed over the floor and walls. After one glance she had to look away. She moved over to Chris and took his arm and stood looking earnestly at the entrance door of the flat.

As soon as suitable reinforcements arrived, Dave suggested that he, Chris and Anne go down to the police station and take statements. One of the scene of crime officers had chalked round Chris's feet. They went in the police car which Dave Smart had arrived in. So far, since those first words, Chris had not spoken at all. He was obviously in deep shock.

It was twenty minutes before they were interviewed. In the interim they had drunk two cups of tea each, but refused anything to eat. Anne bought some Benn's Bars from the canteen and put them in her pocket in case of sudden hunger pangs.

At last they were taken separately to interview rooms. Chris had Steve Watson with him. They expected Dave Smart to arrive, but to Steve's surprise it was Acting DS Robert Southwell. Steve knew him, and Chris, of course, had met him before, although he gave no sign of recognition.

'Now then,' Bob Southwell said pleasantly enough, 'this is an odd sort of way to spend a pleasant Sunday afternoon.' He hadn't had his Sunday dinner either. His family were eating it without him at that moment. 'At least we don't have to start looking for the persons involved. Turn that tape recorder on, James. Right. Now, Mr Simmers, can we hear your story?'

'I...I...' stuttered Chris. He was very pale. Steve looked at him, concerned. It was the first time he had really considered how Chris was feeling. Until then he had only been able to think that his worst possible nightmare had come true, and one of his murder parolees had killed again.

Everyone waited, looking at Chris and willing him to speak. After what seemed like aeons of time Bob Southwell said, 'We'd better get the police doctor to look at Mr Simmers, Steve. Can you arrange that, James? Meanwhile take him somewhere—another interview room, or the sick bay. That might be best, then he can lie down. You come back here, Steve, and we'll have a statement from you.'

16

The interviews seemed to go on for ever.

First Steve Watson gave Chris's history since his release, as far as he knew it. Then he went to be with Chris, while Bob Southwell and Dave Smart put their heads together and sorted out what records the police were holding which were relevant to the case. Bob remembered well how he had strongly advised Chris to leave the district for a time, and how he had refused.

Next they saw Anne, who came in carrying her tape recorder. What she had to tell them they found absorbing. When at last she had their permission to try her tape recorder and see what it had picked up, they all waited tense as wires.

It had recorded, that was the first thing. One of the things it had recorded was Anne's breathing, which didn't help matters. The tape as a whole was of poor quality, though the fact that there was anything there at all was startling enough. Some patches were clear, others, where the two men had faced another direction, and during the fight itself, were blurred and difficult to make out. The thing they did pick up was that Tom Bell was the aggressor. That came through very well. It worried Anne considerably that the part where Tom said he had killed Chris's aunt was overlaid by her breathing. She thought she had been holding her breath when he said that, but that wasn't how it came out.

'He said he'd killed her,' Anne kept on repeating. 'It cleared Chris completely. And he served a twelve-year prison sentence for that.'

'He might well be finding himself serving another twelve,' Bob Southwell said caustically.

'We can get it enhanced,' Dave told her. He hated seeing her strained face. Damsels in distress always touched Dave's heart. 'We should be able to make out the whole of it by the time the technological wizards have finished with it.'

Anne smiled, acknowledging his intention to comfort her, but she didn't feel much happier. She remembered something.

'The cat died this morning,' she told them.

'What has that to do with this?' asked Bob.

'Well, the milk was poisoned.' And Anne explained what had happened. 'I have the letters I was telling you about locked up at home, and the milk and the milk bottle.

The cat is still in Chris's back yard. We hadn't decided what to do with him.'

'You'd better go and get them. Dave, send James Jester down with Miss Atkinson in a police car. She can stay at home and he can bring the exhibits back. Don't worry, Miss Atkinson, we'll give you proper receipts for everything.'

'I'd like to make a copy of that tape, if you want to keep it,' said Anne.

'Don't you trust us?' Bob looked amused.

'I like to be on the safe side. Accidents can happen.'

'Do it before you go if you have a spare tape. Or I daresay we can find one. Get James, Dave, he can help Miss Atkinson.'

Bob was pleased to have Anne out of the way. Pretty redheads complicate an investigation. They bring in human emotions, particularly among the male police staff. And this one was intelligent and capable as well, apart from being in love with the murderer.

They had Chris in. He was far from being fit to be interviewed, so much so that the police doctor insisted on being in the interview room.

'Don't worry,' Bob Southwell told him. 'If he isn't fit we can do the real questioning tomorrow. But we want a word with him, officially, right?'

Chris sat there, looking vacant.

'He's under sedation,' said the doctor.

'We've had some results back from the forensic scientists, Mr Simmers,' Bob told him. 'On your letter bomb. There wasn't much left of it, and I don't suppose you're interested in the type of explosive, but you might like to know that it was posted abroad.'

'Abroad?' said Chris.

'Yes. They managed to piece together part of it.'

He produced the remains of the padded envelope, in an evidence bag. Chris looked at it. There was a little left of his address. It was not in Tom's handwriting, or he would have recognised it at the time, and joyfully ripped it open. But it had something familiar about it, now he stared at it with his full attention. Few people can disguise their handwriting completely.

'I don't recognise the writing,' he said, but in an unsure kind of voice.

'We managed to extract some DNA from the saliva,' Bob said.

There didn't seem to be any answer to that.

'About the people your old cell-mate Damien fingered,' Bob went on. 'We brought most of them in for questioning, and some of them are still with us. One gentleman matched the fingerprints left near your electric meter. One or two we had to release on Friday night for lack of evidence. I understand you had another attack this morning?'

'Yes.'

'One of our detectives has gone with Miss Atkinson to collect the exhibits—milk bottles etc. I asked him to bring your dead cat back, is that all right?'

'Yes, if it will help.' Chris's face worked as though he was fighting back tears. It wouldn't hurt old Sam for his dead body to be used as evidence. If there was any justice he'd now be in some celestial heaven for cats. But Chris doubted if there was any such place, for either cats or people, though he had plenty of evidence for hell. That was right down here on earth. If he had ever thought of marriage between himself and Anne—and he'd had to fight to keep the idea of it from invading his mind—that was out of the question now, and that was hell enough, without adding the idea of prison when they'd thrown away the key.

'We're keeping you in custody tonight,' Bob said, 'and we'll go into everything more fully tomorrow, all right?'

Chris smiled and got up. A young policeman went with him and locked him in a cell.

'Speak to the forensic lab, Dave, and

tell them not to forget a DNA sample from the dead man, will you? I think we'll have those letters in, too, that the girl told us about. Send the tape off first thing, or better still, today, if there's any way of doing that.'

'Surely will, boss,' said Dave. 'There's one other thing.'

'Yes?'

'He should be checked every quarter of an hour for suicide.'

'You think...?'

'He thinks he's lost everything, girl, liberty, this legacy they were talking about. Wouldn't you feel suicidal, particularly if you hadn't done any of it?'

'He killed a man today.'

'Who'd framed him, by the look of it, years ago.'

'We'd better take precautions, you're right. He may have had a very rough deal. Do you believe he has?'

Dave hesitated. Then he came down off the fence. 'Privately, I believe he's had a hellishly bad deal. I believe that man tried to destroy him, not once but many times. Isn't his the name we were given by those toe-rags? The name of the man who was paying for the contract?'

The name the toe-rags had given the police was indeed Tom Bell. Now he was dead they were all competing to throw the blame on him. The odd thing was that when the police went to the dead man's hotel room they found that Tom's passport was in the name of Dwight Brisling, employed as an accountant at the Nournavaile Institute for the Study of Ageing and Dementia. They showed the passport to Chris, who stared at it in surprise.

'But he didn't need glasses,' Chris said. 'He had twenty-twenty vision. Could see like a hawk. And he hasn't a beard in this photograph. But it's him, no doubt about that.'

Anne contacted Humphrey Hale, Chris's solicitor, first thing on Monday morning. She told him about the solicitor who had arrived at Chris's house so unexpectedly on the Friday evening, and the legacy, and about Tom Bell alias Dwight Brisling.

'There's supposed to be only four weeks left in which Chris can claim this inheritance,' she said, 'and in my opinion he deserves it, after the way he was betrayed by someone he trusted. What ought we to do, Mr Hale?'

'Actually, there is someone waiting downstairs—a Mr Florian Poste—who sent a letter up from Chris. I was about to open it, Miss Atkinson.'

Humphrey looked at her over his fingertips, which were pressed together in a praying position. 'I'll see what he says, if you don't mind waiting.'

He passed the letter to Anne after reading it, and rang for his secretary.

'Bring Mr Poste upstairs, please,' he said, then added to Anne, 'He's probably right in saying that with his contacts he can do better for Chris than anyone else can. I will try to check that out, as they say nowadays. The agreement he wanted Chris to sign was ridiculous in my opinion. We must persuade him to take a sensible percentage instead. You are absolutely right. Time, as they say, is of the essence.'

Anne, who was taking a day off work, stayed in the office while they discussed events, and to her surprise the two men of law got on very well together. It did not take long for them to reach a decision. Florian Poste would proceed with a claim, and reduce his firm's percentage to ten per cent. The fact that (over the phone) he obtained his superiors' agreement to this showed Anne and Humphrey Hale how very inflated the previous percentage must have been, if the legacy was large enough to afford them a handsome return on ten per cent.

Chris was brought up before a magistrate that same morning and remanded in custody. No one thought he would vanish while on bail, but the police were concerned about his safety. Until they had the results of the forensic work on the exhibits they did not like to let him go. In fact he was held in the prison hospital, with various medical people in attendance, trying to bring him out of the strange stupor into which he had fallen.

Florian Poste reported back a day or two later that his firm had been checking the conditions of the will and the claimant had to apply in person at the American solicitors' office, New York. The police said they could not see their way clear to allowing this. Once out of the country Chris might vanish into the blue yonder. Even though he seemed to have killed Tom/Dwight in self-defence, and to have served twelve years for a murder he didn't commit, they couldn't let him go to America to stake his claim to a legacy.

If he didn't stake his claim, the sealed envelope would be opened which gave directions for the disposal of the legacy in default.

The forensic scientists had proved that Tom, alias Dwight, had sent the letter bomb. Also that the milk had been injected through the foil cap with a particularly virulent poison by one of the group of criminals who had been attempting to nobble Chris—one of the two who had been released on insufficient evidence. After treatment, Anne's tape was clear enough to prove Chris's innocence of his aunt's murder.

The whole thing was a legal nightmare. In English law, Chris was still down as a murderer. It might be months before that record could be set aside and his innocence of his aunt's murder affirmed to the world. Also, he had just killed Tom Bell (now known as Dwight Brisling) and would have to stand trial for that, putting forward self-defence and hoping to get off lightly. So in America he was being regarded as a criminal. On the other hand, the case exposed a ring of conspirators in the top management of the Nournavaile Institute. Fraud lawyers in America were already busy on the possibilities of their equivalent crime to 'conspiracy to murder in pursuit of gain'.

At the Nournavaile Institute in Rideaux County the Director had been told by the state police that Dwight Brisling was dead. He had been told the circumstances, and about Dwight's previous activities, now nearly thirteen years before, when he had only been a young clerk in the accounts department. The Director, that handsome, distinguished old man, seemed to age ten years as he heard the story. Characteristically, he did not waste time lamenting Dwight's deceit, but was concerned at once about Chris Nournavaile, now in prison in England, awaiting the lengthy processes of the law. The tragic story of an innocent young man's framing and undeserved punishment struck to his sense of justice. The fact that Chris would, it seemed, inevitably lose the legacy he should rightfully have, made it even worse. As the days went by, one by one, leaving less and less of the month before the legacy was lost to Chris, the Director seemed to be increasingly weighed down by events.

At last the month was up, and the envelope opened. All the Nournavaile fortune now went to the Nournavaile Institute for the Study of Ageing and Dementia.

Then the local authority, Rideaux County, put in a claim to the fortune.

In the American courts, battle was joined between three claimants, the heir who was not at liberty to appear, the institute who had tried to obtain the money by crime, and the local authority who thought if it fell between two stools they might as well pick it up.

The Director made preparations to go to England and see Chris Nournavaile.

Chris was told Dr Albrick was coming,

but it did nothing to lighten his darkness. The state of stupor had given way to sullen despair. Prison is prison, even if it is on remand. Anne came regularly to see him, and Mrs Atkinson had sent a message to say how sorry she was that he had spent all that time in prison for something he didn't do, and she didn't mind his friendship with Annie at all now she knew the truth.

Chris was fairly certain he would eventually be released. One thing at least was clear. Chris had no memory problem over the death of Tom/Dwight. He remembered every second of it. What he could not tell anyone was that he knew—however much his lawyer might plead self-defence—that he had meant to kill a man, and that he had done it, and enjoyed doing it, and would do it again in the same circumstances.

Strangely enough his old memory-loss from his childhood, covering the period of his parents' death and his adoption, was gradually clearing. As mists lift to reveal mountains on a summer morning the features of his memory landscape were emerging from the amnesia. The details of his aunt's death were still where they had always been, lost in an alcoholic stupor.

It was nearly Christmas by the time the Director was able to visit England and Chris was still languishing in jail.

Matters had reached the stage where the authorities were quite happy for him to have leave to visit Dr Albrick, rather than go through the humiliation of receiving him in prison. Even Chris's conscience was gradually letting him have peace.

They got on well from the first sight of each other. Chris was taken at once with the austere, intelligent face of the scientist, his silver hair moving in the slight breeze, his thin figure, delicate but strong hands, and kind intelligent eyes. Dr Albrick in his turn at once liked the look of the young couple who walked towards him. Anne, out with Chris for the first time for months, was radiant, and as usual, becomingly dressed. Chris had suggested gentle neutral and white colours, rather than her favourite emeralds and brilliant blues, so she had confined the vividness to a long floaty scarf. Her natural gaiety and cheerfulness, her bright hair, clear complexion, and shapely figure would have attracted a stone, let alone the soft heart of the old man. Chris, too, looked almost happy. How could he help it?

Looking at the young man's face, the Director saw in it sensitivity and good nature, and the strong, self-reliant character which had been developing within him. As a man he was of medium height and slender, moving lightly, with dark hair and eyes as grey as glass. He held out his hand frankly and in friendship to Dr Albrick, as though he had won and not lost a fortune.

The Director put out both his hands. His life too had been shattered, all he had ever worked for was in ruins. Patients were leaving the institute in droves. A group of his heads of department were awaiting trial. The new breakthrough discovery might never be carried to success.

'Goodness knows no one can condone what Dwight did,' he said later, when they were sitting in the hotel lounge. 'As if any cause could ever be good enough to excuse...' He couldn't go on.

'We've got each other,' said Anne. 'It might sound trite but that's what matters to us. All being well Chris will be out of prison soon and then I intend to have wedding bells.'

'Do I get invited?' teased Chris.

'You're hopeful of release, then?' asked the Director.

'Hopeful, yes, but one can never tell with trials, juries, and judges.'

'I'd like to suggest that we press our lawyers to make an out-of-court settlement about the Nournavaile inheritance,' said the old man. 'You have the moral right to the whole of the money, I know, but you will have to face years of wrangling. If we could all agree to split it three ways...'

Chris looked at Anne. Then he turned back and said, 'We agree.'

It took months, even so.

Chris and Anne had been warned that in view of Chris's strange reactions at various times to stressful experiences, it might be wise if he led a tranquil life in the future. Nothing could be identified as wrong with him, but it was worth taking precautions. Following his father's career, for example, would be most unwise.

It would be all right to plant trees.

So Chris and Anne, leaving his York home to the care of Mrs Atkinson (who was given a free hand and a fund of money), wandered for a while round the world in a leisurely way, supporting tree-planting projects where they thought these were on the right lines.

Then they returned to Britain where they bought land and planted small woods. From time to time they visited York, where the two terrace houses had been knocked into one, which made plenty of room for themselves, Mrs Atkinson, and the children.

The publishers hope that this book has given you enjoyable reading. Large Print Books are especially designed to be as easy to see and hold as possible. If you wish a complete list of our books, please ask at your local library or write directly to: Magna Large Print Books, Long Preston, North Yorkshire, BD24 9ND, England.

This Large Print Book for the Partially sighted, who cannot read normal print, is published under the auspices of

THE ULVERSCROFT FOUNDATION